tive of a generation of women who were children in the 1920's and girls in the 1930's, and who have known a special kind of joy and trouble. The scenes happen to be laid in Philadelphia, in the Middle West, and in New York, but might have been equally true in any large American cities.

The rarest thing in the world is truthful confession from a woman whose confessions are worth hearing. From Kitty Foyle, born of modest Irish-American stock in a manufacturing region of Philadelphia, we hear what it was like to be an American girl in the years just behind us, and her look toward the future. In school, in business, in love, in her struggle against a massive and frozen social tradition — and in her defeat which looks strangely like victory — we get to know and admire her. Not even our sympathy can help her solve the problem she faces at the end. It has never been solved and it never will be.

KITTY FOYLE

CHRISTOPHER MORLEY

Kitty Foyle

J. B. LIPPINCOTT COMPANY

PHILADELPHIA NEW YORK TORONTO

All the requirements of the novelist are subsidiary to this, that he shall in his pages show us the result of the workings of the heart and brain, of the body, soul, and spirit of actual or possible human beings.

—George Saintsbury, *The English Novel* (1892).

KITTY FOYLE

1

WHAT A GRAND GUY. SOMETIMES HE USED TO SNEAK A slug of whiskey in the forenoon, against doctor's orders. "What I like about this Daylight Saving, you don't have to wait so long for a drink." Once and a while, when I'm fixing in front of the glass I give myself a wink, I can catch just a shadow of that mischief look of his when he took the bottle from the cupboard. He said "Rum, Rheumatism and Rebellion" as he felt the stuff warm up his giblets. That wasn't a bad summary of his troubles.

"Pop's Rheumatism" was one of the sayings of my childhood. It made things different in lots of ways. Nowadays I guess they'd call it arthritis or sciatica or maybe allergy. Whatever it was I've a notion he earned it. That, and because he worked nights, gave me the feeling as a kid that our house wasn't quite like others. I was ashamed of this but naturally I wouldn't admit it and used it as an excuse for boasting. It was people who worked at night, Mother said, were really winning the War, and I passed this on at school. Pop was night foreman at the machine shop, they worked right round the clock in those days making some kind of timers for shells. Backing up Ed,

Pop called it, Ed was somewhere in France. After being on the job all night the old man slept until afternoon. To keep me quiet I was allowed to go in the Front Room where I counted the pleats in that fan-paper in the grate or played with the toy snowstorm inside a glass ball. Fine days I was sent out to sit on the front stoop. That's the way I first learned females have to be careful sitting on high steps. I guess I made a racket indoors and was shipped out in a hurry. The old mail carrier came along. It was big doings when he brought one of those Y.M.C.A. envelopes from Ed. "Here's a letter from General Perishing," he used to say. This time he found me sitting there. "Hullo, sister, you look kind of sorrowful."

"I forgot my Pop was asleep."

"I'll tell you something else you forgot," he said. "Your drawers."

I looked, it was true, and I ran inside howling with embarrassment. I never could face that nice old postman again without feeling ashamed.

Sitting on the steps ties up with something big that happened about the same time. That was the return of the Keystone Division, 1919 I guess. I was eight years old and Pop took Mother and me downtown to see the Parade. Brother Ed was in it and we must have had some kind of pass to let us through the police lines; anyhow we stood at the front of the pavement on South Broad Street and watched them go by. I remember the scuff-scuff-scuff of all those heavy boots on the smooth street, and the statue of William Penn high up above. I had that statue mixed up in my mind with God, he was looking the other way and not paying any attention. As a matter of fact he was looking towards Frankford. I didn't notice faces or flags or uniforms I was so thrilled by that rhythm of feet. Then it scared me, it was almost like being hypnotized, the whole street swayed and trembled and I felt sick. Mother was angry at me for crying, and Pop lifted me on his shoulder. Afterwards he took us to Dooner's for lunch. Ed joined us there when his company was dismissed and the most exciting thing I could think of was to tell him I had been in disgrace for leaving off my drawers.

"Don't you worry, kid," he said. "The girls in France don't wear 'em at all."

Mother was horrified and said she knew the men would be vulgar if they came to Dooner's.

They had quite a squawk about it. The old man said "Ed, you can lick the Boches but you can't lick German-town." Mother came from Germantown which is pretty much the top shelf compared to Frankford. Then we had trouble getting home because the town was full of parades —or maybe I'm thinking of Armistice Day in 1918? Any-how on account of the crowd the only way we could get down to the street-car was to join a procession that was marching along Chestnut Street to the State House. Poor Mother said she never expected to be found crying in the middle of Chestnut Street.

I did the same thing in a dream once; I mean, marching in a procession because I needed to get somewhere in a hurry. That means something special to me. Lots of times you have to pretend to join a parade in which you're not really interested, in order to get where you're going.

Dooner's famous old hotel for men, ladies admitted only in the dining room, was another big name. Pop had been

11

going there ever since he was a young fellow. When he had to give up the machine shop and got a job as night watchman in the Federal Building he used to go to Dooner's for breakfast before coming home. Mother resented Dooner's, partly on account of the Kelly Street Business Men's Association. That was a sort of club of the steady customers; not always so steady either. Kelly Street was the little alley alongside the hotel. They had dinners where Pop usually got into some kind of humorous brawl with the Papists, he being Londonderry Protestant. Just calling his heavy overcoat an Ulster was enough to start something when they were all in the mood. One time he came home with a black eye; that must have been before I was born but Mother was still talking about it. There was some family joke about it turning both green and orange so at least it was impartial. After Mother died Pop said it wasn't much fun to go to Dooner's any more because there wasn't anyone to ride him about it. Then the old place closed up. I remember that because it was a big year for me, 1924. In those talks Pop and I used to have in the back yard he said a funny phrase, the Grand Climateric. The idea was that 63, seven times nine, is a big turning point in your life. "Sure enough," he said, "I'm 63 and good old Dooner's shuts down on me." I had a Little Climateric of my own that year which fixed it in my mind.

It wasn't long after that, other things shut down on him too; his prostate. When anything goes wrong with a man he sure lets you hear about it. If they've been athletes, like Pop, I guess they just think of bodies as something to have fun with, until the works begin to gum up. They

don't realize, the way women have to, it's a damn complicated piece of doings. I don't know the physiology of it,
but there was one word that had poor old Pop scared
into fits. I used to hear it so often it got familiar without
my knowing what it was all about. Somebody gave me a
kitten for my birthday and I wanted to name it, so I chose
this unusual word which sounded appropriate. When Pop
heard me calling it *Kitty Catheter* he was good and sore.

It was queer something always happened just when we
thought the breaks were coming our way. Pop had worked
like a dog and he was crazy ambitious for Mac and me.
(Denny and Ed were so much older there was no use
worrying about them. Denny was a grown man earning
his living when I was born. Pop used to say, Denny moved
out to Cincinnati and married a sternwheeler.) Pop wanted
Mac to go to Haverford and then that very year 1917 came
the War. Ten years later he set his heart on me getting
a chance. I was out in Manitou then, living with Uncle
Elmer and Aunt Hattie. I was all set to stay in Illinois and
go through Prairie College, but I just got started when
Pop had his trouble and I went back to Philly to take
care of him.

The old man and I were mighty close to each other. I
guess it was me tagging along so far behind the rest, and
then Mother dying when I was ten, and the old man being
home daytimes. He was good company, I guess it was the
Irish in him. Then he'd get what he called his black
streak, you could see the darkness come out on his face
like he'd swallowed something. "Kitty, get the hell out of
here, I got to be by myself."

Myrtle would say "What's wrong honey, has he Gone

13

Irish? You run out on the street and play." Usually I took my jacks out on the front stoop until someone came along and we'd jump hopscotch by the Methodist church.

I know more about it now. I'm never quite sure what I think about things when I'm with someone. Either I'm likely to be putting on an act, or else I'm thinking how much smarter they are than me and I better agree with them. You've got to get back into yourself to chew things over.

When Pop was feeling good he'd sing. He had a nice voice, I can drive myself crazy half remembering The Low-Backed Car, or that fool piece The Irish Jubilee. I never saw it written down but I can still hum some of the words the way he used to rattle them off—

Oh a short time ago boys, an Irishman named Dorrity
Was elected to the Senate by a very large majority,
He felt so elated that he went to Dennis Cassidy
The owner of a bar-room of a very large capacity.

With the words I can smell a whiff of whiskey and tobacco as I climbed in his lap. I didn't like it and often told him so, but anything was worth while to get that song—

Two by three they marched in the dining hall,
Young men and old men, and girls that were not men at all,
Blind men and deaf men, and men who had their teeth in pawn
Soda crackers, fire crackers, limburg cheese with tresses on,

and then something about

In came Piper Heidseck and handed him a glass of wine.

I hadn't the faintest idea who or what Piper Heidseck was. Years after, I found the name on a bottle the first time Wyn and I drank champagne together. It made me cry.

Even now, when the old man's been dead so long, I often think of him. There were things he said that I almost didn't notice at the time. Mother wasn't dead very long when one day Myrtle was hanging out wash on the line. In among his and Mac's big things were some of my pantywaists and nightgowns. He noticed them and said "I'll be glad when those clothes of yours grow up. It's lonesome washing that don't have a woman's shift among it." Lonesome washing—I think of that sometimes, the other way round. I guess there's a lot of women good and sick of nothing but feminine flimsies coming home in the bundle.

I think of Pop most for the help he might have given me when I needed it. By the time I was ready to ask his advice it was too late. The nearest he ever got to giving me a hint was a queer saying he got from grandfather who came fresh from the old country. It hurts—

> In house to keep household
> When folks wish to wed
> Needs something more than
> Four legs in a bed.

I wonder what happened to grandfather made that stick in his crop? He was in the Civil War and died long before I was born and thought of.

It used to make Wyn laugh when he found we lived just round the corner from Orthodox Street. That's in Frankford, and a long way from the Main Line, if you

15

know what that means in Philly. It's freight trains and coal yards and factories and the smell of the tanneries down by Frankford Creek. The fact they were building an L out our way was comic to Wyn; it was a New York kind of thing to do, not in the Philadelphia picture.

But I'm not thinking about Wyn just now; really I'm not. I'm trying to get ready to think about him by getting the B.U. clear in my mind. B.U. was what he called Before *Us*. He was wonderful at making up a language of our own. I guess all lucky people have one, but they're not likely to tell about it.

I've pretty much gotten over the idea I had once that I was queer, different from other people. But it was a funny way to be a small girl, alone with men so much older than me and then pushed out into a different world a thousand miles away. After Mother died various people, for instance Aunt Hattie, dinned it into the old man that I should lead "a normal life." That made him obstinate. He liked having me around, he gave me free run and then suddenly he'd turn cranky. One time Lena McTaggart and I hiked all the way over to where the Barnum and Bailey circus train was parked on a siding, in North Philly. Of course we were late getting back, he and Mr McTaggart each blamed the other, it was the beginning of a regular feud. "Listen, Mac," said Pop, "there's lots of leather belting made in Frankford, why don't you use some of it on that kid of yours."

After three boys, Pop was awfully tickled at begetting a female; I don't know just why. He enjoyed going to stores with me to buy girls' clothes. It was comical to hear him consulting old black Myrtle about what I ought to wear. I overheard her: "Dat chile gwine be handsome, you should doll her up a bit. Get her some froufrou." This did me good till I heard the old man say "She aint female at all. She looks just like me from the waist up, she's got no more shape than a cricket bat."

Out of the steam of the washtubs Myrtle said: "Shape'll come. Dey bulges here and dey bulges dere, all of a sudden dey's real pleasurable."

This didn't mean anything to me but it sounded hopeful. One day I found Pop waiting outside when school let out. Kids dislike their parents to step out of routine and also I was sensitive about the old man being so crippled up and walking on a stick. I wondered what the devil he was staring at us for. He explained, he was looking to see what kind of clothes the other girls wore so he could pick something special for me. Bless his old heart! It must have been then he got the plaid dress I was so proud of. I think that was Myrtle's suggestion, she heard Lena McTaggart and me cutting out paper dolls and discussing their costumes. Myrtle was proud of the fact we were "Scotch-Irish." She figured that Irish, like colored people, were sort of on their own, secretly at odds with the rest of the world.

When you're a kid it's a big help to have someone really proud of you and show it. That was Myrtle. Things I wouldn't have thought much about come back now because that old colored woman made a fuss about them. After Mother died Myrtle came more often and she certainly kept us up to the mark. There was Pop's walking stick with the silver handle and an inscription from the Frankford Cricket Club, she always kept it polished. "Let be that cane," she shouted at Lena and me when we wanted to use it in some game we were playing. "That's your Pop's gentility cane." After I got over the shock of Mother being dead in the Front Room I used to want to go in there sometimes, but Myrtle was always driving me out of it.

Colored people don't have to stop and think in order to be wise; they just know about things naturally, it oozes out of them.

2

THE BACK YARD WAS FUN. PEOPLE SOMETIMES SMILE AT
Philadelphia, but almost every house in Philly has a yard
of its own, no matter how small. The back yard and the
front stoop are what I remember best. It was more than
a stoop, a regular porch, with a thick blanket of white
rambler. On the posts were two rusty screw-eyes, ever
since the days they had a gate there to keep me from falling off the steps. "Good old Kitty," Pop said. "Whenever
she sees a place to fall off of she runs right at it."

In the yard, below the kitchen windows, was a wisteria
vine on a trellis. Sunday mornings when Mother went
to church and Mac slept late, the old man used to sit in a
wicker chair under the arbor and read the *Public Ledger*.
I was given the gray shawl to spread on the grass and study
the comics. When Mother got away Pop winked at me and
said "See if you can get the Pope's telephone number."
I knew where he kept it; it was his bottle of Vat 69.

He was pretty well crippled with arthritis. Every time
I'd hear the old wicker chair creak as he shifted he'd mut-
ter Oh Jesusgod. Mac learned from the doctor how to
ease him the way a trained nurse does. Mac would stand

19

with his feet braced against Pop's and hold out both hands. The old man would grab them and Mac would swing him up; they'd sway together like they were wrestling, poor old Pop growling with pain. There was never any need to worry about my learning bad words at school, I picked them all up listening to the old man in his rheumatism spells. Then Mac would ease him down into the chair again and Pop would take another shot of hootch which was probably the worst thing for him, and go on hunting for some cricket news in the *Ledger*. Maybe it's a good thing he died when he did, he'd be pretty sore at the old town now. There's no steam engines at Broad Street Station, and no morning *Ledger*, and I guess they've almost forgotten how to play cricket.

But I'm lying on the gray shawl, which the old man liked to see around, grandfather wore it for an overcoat when he came from Derry in a sailing ship because the Irish couldn't get enough potatoes. Maybe Pop feels better sitting in the sun, or he's easy in his mind with a naggin of whiskey and Mother at church. "It's wonderful," he said, "how people love each other when they're separated a bit." One of their wedding anniversaries fell on a Sunday and while Mother was at church Pop remembered it and had Mac put up the flag over the porch. When Mother came back along Griscom Street and saw it she was sore, because flags are only put up for wars and battles.

Under the arbor, specially if he could smell dinner getting ready, he'd sing some of those old Scotch-Irish songs. I never knew what they were all about, but when I had oatmeal he'd hum:

What's the rhyme to porringer?
Do ye ken the rhyme to porringer?
King Jamie had a daughter dear
And gave her to an Oranger.

I wasn't sure what was an Oranger except it was something that annoyed the Church of Rome and gave Pop
an extra celebration in July. The Twelfth, he said, was
three times as good as the Fourth. He celebrated the
Fourth for his sons, but the Twelfth for his father. When
he put on the orange sash we knew he'd come home stupefied. The worst fuss I remember was the time Mother got
angry and threw the sash in the garbage. Pop came out
about noon, after a long snore, and saw one end of it
trailing out of the can. He was wild, the vein in his temple
swelled up and he let off some Londonderry language.
"In the garbage, of all places!" he shouts. "Well," says
Mother, "that's the place for old oranges."

Mother's habit of throwing away things she was tired of
always gave him fits. There was an old sofa cushion, all
tattered and faded but he used it for years to put in his
lap when he was reading. His rheumatism made it hard
to hold up a book or newspaper so he laid it on the pillow
in his lap. I guess this particular cushion just suited him,
or he'd got fond of it. Come to think about it, maybe the
real difference between him and Mother was, he was the
kind of person who likes things when they're old. That
dirty pillow was a great comfort to him but Mother suddenly decided it wasn't worth mending again and threw
it out. She never learned you could do anything with the
old man if you prepared him for it beforehand; he hated
to be taken by surprise. He hunted for his cushion every-

21

where. When he learned it was gone I expected another explosion. He was so mad he forgot all about rheumatism and stood right up out of his chair without even a curse. I waited for the row, but after opening his mouth he sat down again and all he said was "Maybe you're right." Mother was so surprised she cried and went over to kiss him. I guess we knew then he was getting old. When you're old I suppose you just let things happen and think what the hell. She bought him a new cushion at Snellenburg's and he tried hard to like it.

That was pretty good for anyone that was half Irish. Him, I mean. He said I was lucky because my Irish was only a quarter; what he called the mixture of a good highball. Half and half is too strong, he said.

I like that twenty five percent. It gives me a private alibi for all sorts of grief and comedy. Molly said once that I was the kind of person to whom things happen. I guess that's true and it means various kinds of hell; but they happen mostly in the Irish Twenty Five. There's another part of me that keeps cool, ticks along calculating and steady, like the meter in a cab.

By the time you grow up you try to toughen yourself to quarrels and absurdities. When you're a kid they shake you up badly. But in spite of the general goofiness of our home doings I like to think of the little back yard for its feeling of security. Hot days there was a green shadow under the wisteria vine, and the damp drying off the brick paving where Mother sloshed it with the hose. She'd lift Pop's feet up on a stool and the cat would jump in his lap while Mother streamed the hose under his chair. There was a smell of roses along the board fence. Pop wouldn't paint it because he said the roses looked prettier against the weathered wood. He was home so much, either on account of working at night or his rheumatism, he kept the little garden in good shape. He used to say the smell of cut grass was the best perfume in the world, except maybe peat whiskey. Nobody knew the smell of grass better than he did because while his health was good he was groundkeeper and coach at one of the swell cricket clubs; he used to go there afternoons and teach the members batting practise. Once and a while he took me over to Germantown to watch. There was a big mower pulled by a horse that had slippers on his feet and made a sleepy sound. I mean the mower did. Then I got the idea of that grass perfume. It's a Philadelphia kind of smell, you don't get it quite the same anywhere else. There were men in white trousers in alleys between fish-nets, and Pop telling them what to do. I wandered round watching the horse and I heard a yell. A red ball came sizzling across the lawn and caught me right on the shin. They all quit playing to come and fix me up, took me to the clubhouse and fed me ice cream. I remember I rubbed ice cream on the bruise on my leg.

Pop used to tell us how ice cream was invented for the Centennial and Philly still makes the best anywhere.

There was another smell in the back yard, the chlorides Mother was always throwing into the little outdoor backhouse. It was intended for the servant, but we didn't have any except fat Myrtle the colored laundress who came Mondays and hung the lines with wet clothes. If you'd be walking through the yard they'd blow out and stick to your face. The john was under one end of the trellis and of course Pop used it because it was hard for him to go indoors and climb stairs. Mother thought it was terrible for him to use the same john as Myrtle but he said "Black meat's as clean as white." I would be playing in the yard and hear the old man grunting and cursing to himself as he cramped his joints in the privy. Little girls are more realistic than what people think, anyone brought up like me isn't ashamed of decent facts. That shabby little clapboard house and back yard, the street where the gas lamps had tops like hats, was homey and funny and felt secure. It was my own, no place I've ever lived since felt quite certain. It was a Philadelphia kind of feeling, sure of itself. Philly hasn't much idea what's going on nowadays, all she wants is not to be bothered or embarrassed, and coupons to cut. But she did give us a sense of solidity. Wyn said one time, she had her spell of modernism and revolution back in the 18th century and got through with it once and for always.

There must have been plenty to worry about if they had wits enough, but if I ever want to indulge private homesickness I think back to the sunbaked yard in Frankford, and the squeak of the old man's wicker chair and him jesusgodding himself as I lie reading the comics. If he remembers I'm listening sometimes he says *Conshohocken!* which Mother suggested as a substitute swear instead of *Jesusgod!* "Why don't Mac come down and give me a hand. Kitty, run tell him the old man's all twisted up like a cruller."

"The boy needs his sleep," Mother says. "You've done plenty good sleeping yourself."

That would start an argument, which I didn't under-

24

stand at the time but I can see it now. Mother was sore, I don't blame her, the old man always had a job at night and got his rest in the daytime. I used to wonder how a night foreman ever had a chance to beget. This was put into my head by coarse remarks of other children. There was an ornery little kid called Nellie Simmons in my grade. I suppose she overheard some vulgar talk at her home dinner table; anyhow one day walking back from school she sneered to me "Your father and mother do it in the daytime." I can still see the trees along the pavement and maple seeds lying there like little dress-hangers. The whole world turned black with shame and disgust and I ran home blind with tears and tripped over a root. The bash on my knee gave me something real to cry about. I guess that's a good thing: when you get all hopped up about some imaginary horror life smacks you something that actually hurts and you quit moaning over phony troubles.

Nellie was a mean little scut, she poisoned a lot of my ideas as a kid. I sometimes figure, if I had a child of my own could I work it so she wouldn't get tainted with all that trivial dirt? I guess it can't be helped. So many females are dirty-minded by nature, and they dirty each other. They get clean if they have the good luck to meet a man who's really sensible and sweet and can take the body as it comes. The funny thing is, Wyn said it was the other way round.

I think of Nellie sometimes, her thin pale face full of slyness and tattletale. She had greeny eyes and hair all stringy and sticky with jam hooked from the pantry. I haven't seen her for years but I bet things have been tough for her, and I can't say I care.

So Mother and Pop would get squawking, and it seemed to do the old man good; warmed up his blood maybe and softened those crusty joints. He'd forget about Conshohocken and come out with a real Jesusgod and heave himself up out of the chair before he knew it.

"We didn't do so bad, did we?" he shouts. "Three fine boys and this little naggin for a chaser? I guess she just got in before stumps were drawn."

I don't think Mother understood all his technical terms from cricket. But I don't know; mothers usually understand more than they let on.

He hobbles to the end of the yard and squats down to weed the flower-bed. After a while I join him there, thinking maybe I'll hear something more that's interesting. After a fight I always hung round first one and then the other, because they'd come out with surprising remarks. That's a delight to kids, who are smart enough to see that parents are most of the time putting on an act and only come through with the real dope when they're sore.

"It all comes under the head of amusement," he would say. "Get laughs, Kitty, get laughs. You'll need all you can collect."

He never got tired telling me how he gave the boys their first cricket lessons on the grass patch in the yard. Even when he was half crippled he still mowed and weeded the old batting crease where the wicket stood. "That's where I taught Denny to step out to it," he said. Dennis, he seems more like an uncle than a brother, he's 21 years older than me, was raised in the last great age of Philadelphia cricket. Pop never forgot that Denny once played for the

26

Gentlemen of Philadelphia against some English club that was touring. I think he was really a ringer. Pop said one of the Gentlemen came down with clap, and Denny took his place. But as the son of a pro I should think he was really disqualified? All that cricket stuff is very dim in my mind now, but it was important.

I suppose Philly is the last place in America where it still matters to be a gentleman. Of course the old man wasn't, but he was on intimate terms with gentlemen on account of cricket. At the clubs, and at the big private school where he was coach, he knew all the Rittenhouse Square crowd when they were just boys. He was invited to cricket club dinners and used to sing Irish songs for them. There's nobody so snobby about keeping up social hedges as somebody who isn't himself quite the real McKay. For Pop, men who didn't know about cricket hardly existed. Even foxhunting or harriers or polo were pretty middle class.

It was on account of cricket that Wyn first came to the house; he was getting some old scorebooks for that Hundred Years of Philadelphia Cricket they printed. It makes me smile now when I think it had to be me who stood up for the old Main Line social tradition when Wyn was all set to chuck it overboard. And that baby, if it had been born, would have been almost a gentleman because Wyn came from a cricket club family.

3

"YOU'VE GOT TO MARRY OR DIE TO GET INTO IT" WAS OUR saying about the Front Room. I had quite a vivid picture in my mind of myself getting married in there. Marriage, I thought, was wearing a whole lot of white satin and lace and having a cake with doves in frosting all round it like what I saw in Hanscom's window on Frankford Avenue, while the men got plastered in the kitchen.

Even after Mother died Pop made pathetic attempts to keep the Front Room special. He went in there sometimes to sit in the red velvet easy chair but I don't think he was ever quite easy. It didn't seem right to sit there in shirtsleeves. On the mantel was a wonderful gilt and glass clock under a glass bell; Grandpa got it at the Centennial Exposition in 1876. Philadelphia hasn't forgotten the Centennial even yet, the old man used to talk about it sometimes. If he was alive now he would pretend that this New York World's Fair was just an upstart, though I daresay he'd like its general Tammany flavor. That clock was made an imitation of Horticultural Hall, you could see all the works, which were usually slow. "It has Philadelphia blood," Pop said. The kitchen clock, a much more homely thing, was fast. Once we had an argument, how long would it be, with the two clocks getting farther apart from each other at a definite rate, before they would both again tell the same time. Mac said that was easy and went upstairs to figure it by algebra. Mother said they never would because two wrongs never make a right. Pop went in the back yard to think it over. Mac came downstairs once to ask, did we mean till both the clocks told the same time or till they both told the correct time?

The correct time, Pop said. "Gee," Mac said, "I bet that'll be about a thousand years." He went upstairs again to calculate, and didn't come back at all. Meanwhile they forgot to wind the clock and it stopped.

Pop and I were like those two clocks, so different but gradually coming closer together again. I'd go crazy if I tried to figure out the problem, but it gave me a notion there are a lot of lovely things just out of reach. That's how I felt, years after, when the old man died. So much comedy and hard sense and shyness in him and I could never get at it again.

I had to take care of breaking up housekeeping when Pop died in 1930. (Mac was the only one of the family left in Philly.) The Front Room was hardest, somehow, because it had never really been lived in. The stuff hadn't suffered the way everything else had. Some of it we shipped off to the other boys. Denny got the Centennial clock because he was the oldest, but I hope he don't keep his appointments by it. Most of the things went out as junk. No one but me was interested in the toy snowstorm. That was the glass ball that stood on a bracket ever since I remember. It was full of clear water and a figure inside, a little girl on a sled coasting down a hillside with a red scarf flying round her neck and a castle in the background. When you shook the ball she was surrounded by a whirling blizzard, then gradually it would settle down and was clear and peaceful. I took that with me and have it yet. The castle came to mean Wyn and the Main Line, and I say "Hello, little girl on a sleighride." So in a dumb way it reminds me of myself—not that I need much reminding.

It reminds me of something else too, if I let it. The day of Mother's funeral it was snowing. The Front Room never quite got over the funeral. I sneaked in there by myself when she was in the coffin. Everything smelled terribly sweet and dead. I had to give the glass ball a shake to reassure myself. But if anybody in the family has to be dead I was at the right age to take it, I was going on ten. With all my sorrow and surprise I was in a way proud too, I was figuring out the solemn way I would return to school and impress the other children. Then a dreadful thing happened. I was standing in the corner holding the snowstorm, in behind the lace curtains, and I guess the undertaker didn't see me. He tiptoed in to see that everything was all right. A speck of soot had settled on poor Mother's nose and of course that disturbed him. He took out a big white handkerchief beautifully folded; then I suppose it seemed a pity to spoil its creases. A property handkerchief most likely, used again and again. He bent solemnly over the coffin, gave a quick puff of breath and blew the smut away. There was something pretty grim about that, the idea of this stranger blowing in Mother's face and her not being able to resent it; not even caring. I burst into hysterical tears of anger and fright and he was very much shocked that I had seen him.

Aunt Hattie and Uncle Elmer arrived just then from Manitou and found me in a spasm of weeping, which I dare say they thought quite proper. I couldn't possibly have told anyone why I was crying. I could see the undertaker looking kind of worried for fear I would, and embarrass him.

Life's a lot different from what people pretend. That's why pretending is fun. I used to think it was some special wickedness of my own that made such queer things happen. Now I'm beginning to guess that everybody's like that. Wyn told me some of the weird things that happened in his family, which you would certainly never suspect from reading the respectful items about them in the *Public Ledger*. You see a lot in the papers about the Man's point of view and the Woman's etc., as if they were never the same. That's just a gag to keep women from being a nuisance, or getting too many of the good jobs. They're not really so different.

Maybe they are too, yes maybe they are. Oh, I like them to be different, thank God for it. I guess I was just trying to sell myself an idea because I'm so thoroughly licked.

Wyn and I were talking about it once; the difference I mean. I said Men and Women are the same at bottom. He razzed me about that. He said "You mean fundamentally. Sure. If you take a house and put new wiring and plumbing in it—"

"Especially plumbing," I interrupted.

"You don't call it a different house."

"But maybe it's a better house," I said.

One of the things that was so grand about Wyn, he

31

often made me think of things to say that were better than what he had said, and he loved it as much as I did.

But about the Front Room. It had long lace curtains at the windows. Aunt Hattie said she and Mother would as soon live in sin as in a house without lace curtains in front. Pop said "It's a good thing old Sundayschool John Wanamaker don't know where all his lace curtains goes, that's the first thing the madams buy to furnish up a house of call."

"How did you get to know that?" says Aunt Hattie.

Over in the far corner, near the snowstorm, was a hot air register with a fine warm blast from it, very soothing when it blew up your skirts. Women's legs have been cold so long nowadays, they don't know how good those old registers felt. You'd stand over it and catch the heat inside your clothes, then try to sit down quick enough to keep it warm on your bottom. I remember Pop, rheumatism and all, shining up the register with stove polish when Mother was laid out there. It was the last thing he could do for her.

Over the mantel was a big engraving of Signing the Declaration of Independence. Mac jeered at me once when I asked innocently, Did all the Signers live on the Main Line? In the fireplace, which we never used, the grate was filled with a big fan of white shelf-paper, folded in pleats like something by Schiaparelli. The marble-top table, between the windows, had a pile of Pop's albums and scrapbooks about cricket, and any number of photos of famous Elevens. The old man used to say that when he got rich he was going to get a lot of those photos framed; thank goodness he never did. Also there was a set of hanging

32

bamboo shelves filled with silver cups. Each cup stood on a doily and had in it an old red cricket ball, trophy of some big match or some time when Pop had done the Hat Trick, which I think was to bowl out three batsmen in one over? Anyhow he had the hat, a high silk stovepipe. He'd like to keep that in the Front Room too, but Mother wouldn't stand for it. She had it upstairs in camphor, he wore it at her funeral for gravity.

The chandelier had three crystals gone, probably from the boys taking them off to look at the light through them. Right underneath was a love-seat, one of those spindly little settees with two seats facing opposite, gilt legs and lavender silk cushions. Mother was so keen about that piece I think there must have been some story connected with it. I wouldn't be surprised it came from the old Upsal home in Germantown, I can't imagine Pop buying anything so nifty. Two people sitting there found their faces quite close and convenient, like Pop's fool riddle he used to tease us with. There's two sheep in a field, he says, one facing east and the other facing west. What'll they have to do to look at each other? Lots of people answer right away, they'll have to turn round. But of course they're actually facing each other already; just like in the love-seat. But that piece of furniture was too flimsy for any very spirited courting.

In spite of all these fascinating things the Front Room was sterile. Even the cat didn't go in there much. I respected it and knew it was important, but it never came to life for me until the day Wyn first called. Some committee was getting up that History of Cricket and Wyn was sent round to talk to the old man. It's funny how little

33

one remembers. All I can see is an attractive tweed suit in a kind of tobacco brown, and the loveliest deep maroon woollen socks. Nothing about Wyn ever pleased me more than his socks. He has a particularly attractive way of putting one leg over the other. Of course they're pretty long legs, but his foot always seems to hang down more gracefully than most men's. I don't know why but that's usually the mark of a gentleman; their legs fold over more neatly, don't bulge and stick out. Wyn thought I was kidding when I told him how much I liked this and I had to be careful not to make him self-conscious. If I told him too plainly I liked a thing he'd get shy about doing it, for fear I'd think he was doing it just because he knew I liked it.

About the knee-folding, Wyn said maybe it's a touch of English blood. But he added he didn't see why Englishmen's knees should be so flexible because after all they haven't used them much.

What made that first meeting a success was the fire in the waste-basket. Pop and Wyn were going through a whole mass of old scorebooks and clippings, chucking away what they didn't want. Pop shouted to me to bring the big peach-basket from the kitchen. I was introduced, of course, but it didn't mean anything, just some more nonsense about cricket. I'd been away in the Middle West for years and forgotten that cricket existed. Also I'd just nursed Pop all winter and got him through that first stroke and I didn't want him to get too lively and run up his blood pressure.

"Don't you get my Father excited," I warned him.

"I'm the quietest fellow in the world," he says, "I never

get anyone excited."

I was in the back yard sewing, it was a hot spring afternoon, and I don't believe there was a thing on my mind but hoping the visitor would clear out in time for me to rattle round in the kitchen and fix Pop's supper. I could hear them talking and I was pleased because the old man was happy. Then in their conversation Pop started throwing dead matches into the waste basket. To make sure they weren't burning he leaned over to look and without his noticing it some of his pipe ashes fell in. A few minutes later the basket blazed up. I heard the old man let out one of his profane yells, I ran in and met Wyn in the passage looking embarrassed and asking for a cloth.

"I'm afraid we've made a mess," he said. There's no one ever lived who can apologize more charmingly. It's really worth while for Wyn to do something wrong just to watch him ask pardon for it. Sometimes I've wondered if he knew that.

He had put out the blaze by pouring on it the whole jug of iced tea. So I made more tea, and they asked me to come and help them drink it.

That was Saturday the 25th of May, 1929, and the first day I ever took cricket seriously.

4

WHAT AN ADVENTURE, GOING OUT TO ILLINOIS AT THE AGE of thirteen. I'd never been anywhere outside Philly, except a few trips down to the Jersey shore. The old man and Mac took me over to North Philadelphia station to get aboard the Limited; I always think of it whenever I see that high windy platform. It was a scorching hot evening in late summer and a thunderstorm in the air. We had supper in the station restaurant, a big adventure for me, and they let me order whatever I wanted, mostly ice cream and Coca Cola. I was too excited to eat and I was feeling queer anyhow. I remember I wanted to ask them if tuberculosis begins with a pain in the chest, because I felt a sort of discomfort in what I used to think were my lungs; but of course I didn't ask; if they thought I was sick they wouldn't let me go. The old man had given me the most complete instructions about everything, how to get undressed in a Pullman berth, how to find the Ladies, what to tip the porter, and Uncle Elmer and Aunt Hattie would meet me at the depot in Chicago. What I really needed to know about of course they never told me.

The thunderstorm broke just as the train was coming

in, and the last I saw of Pop and Mac they were scooting for shelter in one of those little glass waiting rooms. Dear old Pop, when he most wanted to show his feelings he always looked fierce and he seemed to be glaring at me through the window as though he was sore as a goat about something.

The porter on the car was wonderful. As I once told Wyn, Pullman porters are the finest gentlemen I know; they ought to be honorary members of the Merion Cricket Club. He made up my berth before anybody and I got into bed, taking care not to bulge out against the green curtains which would have seemed immodest. Rather than run the risk of attracting any attention I kept my suitcase in the berth with me. But I felt awfully upset, which I supposed was just my excitement at going away. Then of course it proved to be the Curse, for the first time. I thought I was dying of tuberculosis, which in a vague way I knew caused hemorrhages. It must be a serious case because the hemorrhage had gone the wrong way. I wondered if they'd find me dead in the car in the morning.

I guess they must have told the porter to take special care of me, because though I would rather die than call for help, presently he asked through the curtain if I was all right.

I said, "I guess I'm sick."

"What seems to be the trouble, lady?"

To that I made no answer at all. I couldn't. With the intuition of a great gentleman he must have guessed, for soon after a large black hand came through the curtains and handed me a package.

I wish I could know how much of what I think now was really what I thought then, and how much is what I now think I should have thought? It's hard to carry thoughts along with you, like food in the icebox they don't keep, you kid yourself without knowing it. Pop had been telling me how exciting it would be to get my first sight of Ohio and Indiana and Illinois. "When you wake up," he said, "you'll be in Ohio." Goodness knows what I expected to see, I raised the blind ready for anything. As far as I remember it looked like nothing at all, just flat fields burned brown by the heat. As for the outskirts of Chicago, when we got there at last, I always think of Wyn's description of them: "civilization with its pants down." Though there's something encouraging in the long lines of stock and refrigerator cars you see outside Chicago. It seems as though there's a lot of food in the world and it keeps your mind on sensible things.

I guess I should have been noticing the bigness of America and all that sort of thing; actually I was thinking of the importance of myself. I had earned the peculiarly female privilege of feeling lousy. I was too scared about everything to know what to do about breakfast, but again that grand porter came to my rescue. As I didn't show any sign of life he came at last and asked through the curtain if I'd like something to eat. I suppose I mumbled something, the next I remember was he brought me a tureen of hot milk toast—on the hottest morning of summer.

I got off the train at last, I must have looked terrible, I know Aunt Hattie exclaimed; there's nobody who gets such wonderful dark rings under their eyes like the Irish; it was always her technique to speak of me as Poor Motherless Child, which just made me mad, and my retort was "I'm grown up!" They hustled me into the lunch room before we took the train to Manitou. The importance of having two railroad station meals in succession made me forget my troubles.

I get a little bored when I think about Aunt Hattie and Uncle Elmer, which is certainly ungrateful. They always knew all the unimportant things that were going on and very few of the important.

Now I'm thinking what I think now, not what I thought then. All I thought then, for a while, was terrible homesickness. I guess Uncle and Auntie found me difficult at first. They'd never had any children of their own; if they were ever young themselves they'd forgotten all about it. That fearful hot journey, I can feel the soot on my damp forehead, lay like a nightmare between me and Philly. It was too much, all at once. What a jolt it is when you first realize that you are *you,* locked into yourself and nothing to be done about it. But you wouldn't dare admit this to anyone. I don't know what I'd have done if it hadn't been for the dog, Pattyshells. He was called that because when he was a puppy he ate up a whole batch of pastry Aunt Hattie had ready for a lunch party. He was a big brown mutt with wonderful yellow eyes, and took to me at once. I used to tell him all sorts of crazy stuff when I couldn't talk to anyone else. I said to Wyn once, if I ever meet a man with eyes like Pattyshells' I'll tell him everything. And Wyn used to say, in the dark, Now pretend I've got yellow eyes.

That sweltering afternoon when we got down to Manitou. Brick-paved streets you could fry an egg on, and soft

39

coal smoke drifting across town, and those awful whistles from the railroad yard, and the gloomy bell every hour from the college. The college bell was Time, the engine screams were Distance. I wouldn't have said that then, but don't suppose kids don't feel these things. We drove up shady old Thanksgiving Avenue with its brown and yellow houses and scrollwork porches, and I realized to my amazement that Uncle Elmer Taswell must be rich. The front door had long church-shape windows of colored glass; everything was shut up tight to keep out the heat; and as we went in down the hall came a blast of fried chicken and thick gravy and crackling ham with sugar and cloves. There never was a town like Manitou for big eats, but I guess all the Middle West is the same. The way I was just then it made me gag; it smelled so damn wholesome, and I wasn't feeling like that.

When the first few terrible days were over, and I was registered for high school and got back my appetite, I was curious about myself, wanted to know if these strange experiences made me look different. By tilting the bureau mirror a bit and standing on the bed I could get a fairly good view of myself in the glass. I had a feeling I was doing something fearfully wicked, and there wasn't any way to lock my door, but Pat was lying on the floor like a door-stop, he noticed in hot weather that was the best place for a cool draught. I took off all my clothes and was looking myself over at various angles to see if I was anywhere near the same shape as some of the girls I admired in the movies. "The human form divine" was a phrase I must have seen somewhere and I said it to myself with satisfaction but honestly I don't think there was much divinity in that scrawny little nakedness. I've never been able to put on an act of any kind to my own satisfaction without something breaking it up, and sure enough Aunt Hattie started to come in. But it took long enough for her to shove old Pat out of the way so I could jump down from the bed and pretend to be getting something out of the bureau drawers. Aunt Hattie was annoyed finding me like that; the way she ordered Pat out gave me the idea she didn't think it was quite decent for me to be undressing with a male dog in the room.

I tried sometimes to give Wyn an idea about the years I spent in Manitou, except summers when I'd go back to visit Pop. Wyn was curious about it, because he had the Philadelphia idea that people west of Paoli are yokels and peasantry. The most significant thing that ever happened in Philly, though they don't know it yet, was when it quit being the terminus of the Pennsy Railroad and grand old Broad Street Station became just a turn-around for the suburban trains. When people are happy, like Wyn's crowd, you don't tell them things. In Philly they thought they were the End of the Line. But Manitou was a Way Station. The trains yelled all night because they were on their way somewhere else; to Chicago one direction, or Denver and Los Angeles the other. We kids used to go down to the Santa Fe depot to watch the flyer go through and get a kick to know that Doug Fairbanks and Mary Pickford were aboard. It was a regular social item in the local paper: "Miss Dorothy Gish passed through town Thursday evening on The Chief." Maybe it's good for a town to hear about things that go by without stopping. "In Philly," Wyn would say, "we're not interested in any-

41

thing until it stays here several generations. Even the *Saturday Evening Post* is still a bit of an outsider; that's why they always insist it was founded by Ben Franklin."

It was wonderful how Wyn and I could talk about things without getting angry. At least, without him getting angry.

5

ONE TIME WHEN WYN THOUGHT HE WAS DRINKING TOO much he tried what he called the Water Cure. Whenever he felt like a snort he'd take a long drink of cold water instead; or anyhow he'd take it first.

I'm trying to use memory as a water cure. I thought maybe getting into bed early and just thinking about things, getting them in order in my mind, remembering what came after what, and so much beauty, I thought that would be like dipping your hands in mountain water. It doesn't always work. I got so nervous I've been pacing round this damned apartment until I'm glad it's not a penthouse, I might have taken a dive.

Jesusgod, when I think I was 28 this year and what I've gone through in ten years, what everybody has gone through, it's almost funny. I wonder why they had to throw everything in the melting pot at once? First morals, and then economics, and now the whole international world. I tried an experiment, to see if I could find out what was the matter with me. I made a list of the various things that get me jittered. Business, radio, liquor, news-papers, cigarettes, sex. Maybe that's not the right order, it's just the way they come to mind. I thought I'd do without one of them each day in turn and see if it made any difference? I started out on a Monday, and I omitted each of them in turn for one day. As a matter of fact I'd been off sex so long I didn't even notice that part of it. I think I can say I'm affectionate but I'm not promiscuous. Cigarettes were the hardest. Then Sunday came along and just by chance all six elements happened to crowd into one day. That upset my reckoning and I didn't figure out which it was that was making trouble for me. I'll say one thing, that night I really slept. That's something.—Monday wasn't so good.

What gripes me is not having anyone to tell things to, I mean really tell, the way Wyn and I used to. It's funny, you can't really talk unless there's desire behind it. Maybe it's the different sound of the two voices, one female and one male, mixing into a chord like notes in music. Two female voices talking together is just chirping.

Some day, even if it makes a fool of me, I'm going to go into the Cathedral and find out about confession. I don't know how it's done, or if they take confessions from pagans, or if I'd have to sign up for a lot of things I don't believe? If I could just unload some of the things that burn me up, even if it short-circuited the priest, it might help. There must be some answer? I have a horrid guess that maybe the priests put on duty for confession are just young fellows fresh from seminary, put there to give them vicarious experience and wise them up to the troubles of the world. If his voice sounded young I think I'd beat it. No greenhorn could take confession out of me.

I don't like the word confession. It sounds as though one

44

was guilty of something. I'm not, I'm proud as hell. But I'd like somehow to be cross-examined, sort of put on trial to give testimony under oath, so I could get things straightened out. I'm always fascinated by those Question and Answer transcripts that get printed now and then. They're so phony and yet so much true human stuff comes through. I've even tried to do it to myself:—

Q. You realize that whatever you say will be used against you?
A. O.K. with me. It always has been.
Q. Do you plead guilty or innocent?
A. Guilty of being human, of having human desires and needs and hopes.
Q. You are accused of having been coarse or vulgar.
A. Not more than others, I think, only I was rash enough to express my thoughts.
Q. This made you happy?
A. No one has ever been happier. Oh please be sure the jury realizes that!
Q. Why are you not happy now?
A. Because I'm not making anyone else happy.

I suppose there would be disorder in court at this point, or some lawyer would offer an "objection"? What a cock-eyed word *happy* is, too; if you say it over three or four times to yourself it sounds positively insane. But anyhow I'm taking testimony from myself now and there aren't any rules; I'll appeal the case right up to the Supreme Court if necessary. God knows I'm paying costs.

Q. Did you make Wyn happy?
A. I think so. Yes, I know so.
Q. Then why did you leave him?

45

A. If I had done what he wanted, other people would have made him unhappier than I could have made him happy.

Q. What do you mean?

A. He was the product of a system. He was at the mercy of that system.

Q. Is it not your conviction that there are now no systems? That the whole of society is in flux?

A. Not in—I mean, not where Wyn lives.

Q. Was not the way you left him rather cruel?

A. Damn you, I was afraid you'd ask that. Yes, it was. But I *had* to be tough with him, otherwise he'd always have felt he had been unfair to *me,* and it would have made him wretched.

Q. You think, then, he is not unhappy now?

A. Yes. No. Ask that again, please.

Q. You think Wyn is happy now?

A. I think his life is full of delightful routine. He has what the government calls Social Security. Oh, and how. Read the *Public Ledger* on Sundays, or whatever papers they have now.

Q. You think you could have made something more important of him?

A. I could have taught him to do the Wrong Thing sometimes.

Q. What, in Philadelphia?

A. We could have lived somewhere else.

Q. Are you quite fair to Philadelphia?

A. I am thinking of it only as a symbol. Actually I love it dearly.

Q. But are they not the most charming people in the world?

A. Of course. But the enemies of the Future are always the very nicest people.

Q. You think the Future should be encouraged?

A. That's a goofy question, my darling; it's on our necks

46

already. And Oh God, Wyn was so much interested in it when he had a chance. What a man he might have been if everything hadn't been laid in his lap.

Q. Is your mind going to go round and round like this indefinitely?

A. How's about going to bed and try for some sleep.

I can't help laughing. I found myself continuing my cross-examination in the bathtub, which is a grand place to think. A sort of spiritual wash-behind-the-ears. It would be comical if the Defendant was carried into Court in a steaming tub. But it wouldn't be a bad way to get at the truth; if that's what they really want.

A word comes into your mind, and what a lot it starts. The word was Pocono. I dare say it doesn't mean much except to Philadelphia people. It's mountain country up beyond Stroudsburg, where the absolutely right people go for their particular kind of well-bred whoopee. That was the first place I ever saw mountains. Wyn said of the Pocono crowd, They can make even mountains behave. Sometimes we thought we fooled 'em. I hope there'll never be an earthquake up that way; I'm thinking of that big rock near Buck Hill Falls where Wyn and I buried our letters. Moonlight up there gets bright enough to read by.

Easy now, easy now. Pop used to say when I got too much steamed up, Take it easy, Kitty. I ought to learn not to try to tell anybody about anything. I used to get a laugh when people in Chicago talked about their local scenery, which they like to think is pretty swell; such as Lake Geneva up in Wisconsin, or the Mississippi at Nauvoo. Once I got peevish and said, You poor souls ought to see the Water Gap. They all thought it was just an em-

47

barrassing wisecrack.—Scenery in the Midwest is like rouge on a colored girl; it means well but it's kind of pathetic.

Q. Let's pull ourselves together. What was it about Pocono?

A. That was where I got some idea how simple and sweet things can be. The first time Wyn and I went away together I was so utterly miserable I didn't suppose we'd ever be happy again. He took me to a hotel in Harrisburg, where we got a lot of foul bootleg booze to keep up our spirits. Imagine trying to drink yourself into happiness on that speakeasy liquor. But lots of people were doing it those days. We didn't know any better.

Q. Harrisburg sounds like a queer place for an elopement.

A. Wyn said there were always so many freaks in Harrisburg, people for the legislature I guess, we wouldn't be noticed. It was pretty simple of him, because Wyn stood out as a gentleman anywhere. I can't imagine any place where he would have looked more unique. Poor boy, maybe it was nervousness or whatever, he drank so much he simply went to sleep and I lay and cried all night. Don't make me think of it, it was horrible. Oh my God, I remember when I packed up my bag again to come back, thinking how happy I thought I was going to be when I packed it before. Don't let women think about things like that; they know too much about 'em.

Q. Let's get back to Pocono.

A. Wyn took me there because he wanted me to go somewhere he loved. His family had a big camp up there, but we went to a little cabin on a lonely pond. It was off season, in autumn, but we went swimming and we built a big fire and lay on blankets in front of it. I was so stupid I hadn't ever known that Wyn was beautiful till I saw him stand on the beach. Wonderful to be

48

straight and clean like that, all the way up from your feet to your shoulders. And the firelight on the rafters of the cabin. What was nice, he thought I was beautiful too. Maybe I was; I felt so.

Q. What did Wyn say about firelight?

A. It was the first kind of light men and women ever made love in. Damn it, he ruined open fires for me; I can't ever see one and be happy. He dragged a mattress in from the bedroom and we slept there in front of the fire. Do you remember how we invented games?

Q. The one about the tunes?

A. Yes! He would tap off a tune on my back with his fingertips and I'd have to guess what it was. He never fooled me once, all the tunes he could think of were so familiar. But I caught him with Irish songs.

Q. And you had a language of your own?

A. But that grew up gradually. Oh I hope everybody in the world has had that, little silly phrases of your own that are so important. They get murmured under your chin or in the bend of your arm or between your breasts, you don't ever hear them with your ears, they just sink in through your body. As the Bible says, we knew one another. Oh, we did, and we argued about everything, and partly I thought he was God and partly I was just taking care of him. I knew I could never be ashamed or humiliated or unhappy again, I knew what life was for.

I get tired of cross-examining, I don't always think of the right questions to ask myself.

We brought grub with us and cooked it ourselves. Then Wyn piled the fire high with birch logs and we had coffee and cigarettes sitting on the floor and I watched the light on his shoulders and chest. It seemed perfectly natural. I don't know that anything else has ever seemed quite nat-

49

ural since.

I think it was then we had our grand discussion about the Social Revolution. Wyn said no woman really knows how to live until some man teaches her, and that in our time men were teaching women to lay aside taboos and formalities and makebelieves. From Wyn, that makes me smile! There never was anybody whose whole existence was so settled upon a whole lot of people doing a comfortable makebelieve. I couldn't argue about it then the way I maybe could now. I was in the absolute joy and glory of the big surrender. There was no past, no future, just firelight and the happiness of his strong hands. It's a good instinct for lovers to start those he-she arguments, it keeps emphasizing the difference, which is what they are really thinking about. The more he would tell me solemnly it was Man's job to teach Woman about Beauty the more he was really asking me to help him learn. What a baby he was under all his nice manners. I hope that Main Line crowd is good to him. I hate to think of his growing up, just a gentleman and nothing else.

It was a Social Revolution for me all right. In spite of the fact that Wyn himself knew almost nothing of life, all its small anxieties and makeshifts, problems of grocery bills and insurance and clean clothes, all the things you see written on people's faces in the subway, in spite of his comfortable ignorance of all that, it was his love that taught me everything. Maybe not so much his love of me, but the love I gave him. It was all very well for Wyn to sound off about woman giving up taboos and conventions. When a woman gives up her conventions she's really handing you something, because she only has two or three and they're all tied up with her actual physical existence. Men have any number of conventions and they can spare as many as they happen to feel like doing without.

Anyhow the kind of women Wyn was talking about live in a different world. I know because I remember the names he used to mention just casually when we talked. Most of them were women who'd had everything, and didn't know what to do with it when they had it; and how they resented anyone else grabbing a crust here and there. I think I learned a good deal when I came to New York and took to riding the subway. There's a lot to be seen in the faces in those trains, if you can read. In Philly, Wyn and his crowd hardly even knew there *was* a subway. They rode the snobway instead; the suburban trains. If Wyn and I were still having our arguments I can just imagine how sore he'd be, by this time, about the New Deal. Yes, a lot of it I dare say is cockeyed, just the same I'm definitely on the side of the under bitch.

In that little cabin up in the Poconos we noticed an amusing thing. There was an electric light bulb high up in the bedroom, with a string hanging down to switch it by. A spider wove his web at the end of the string, in such a way that it caught the string up in a loop which was filled with his fuzzy silk, and thick with small flies. He must have noticed there was always business right under the bulb, and made use of it for his own purposes.

I guess Nature builds her web right under the big bright light of sex, and she catches plenty. When you're in the web you think you're arguing about this and that. What you really mean is, Dearest, I want you.

6

THE FIRST THING THAT HAPPENED WHEN I GOT TO THANKS-
giving Avenue, Manitou, Illinois, was finding we had two
bathrooms. That made me realize I had made a big step
upward. Perspiration and soot aren't often mentioned but
they are important. Uncle and Auntie had a bathroom of
their own, and I was told that the guest bathroom was for
me to use. There was a great big wonderful tub and I was
about to get into it when Aunt Hattie came rushing up to
say that under no circumstances could I take a bath just
then. That added to my feeling of humiliation and discomfort.

What Aunt Hattie did first, I suppose, was to go to the
telephone; probably to call up Mrs Weissenkorn. Unless
I had heard Auntie and Mrs Weissenkorn on the phone
for four years I wouldn't know to what depths human conversation can sink. They had it all worked out in their
minds before I ever got there: Trudy Weissenkorn and I
were to be Best Friends. But Trudy, a little fattish pale
thing with eyes the color of oysters, was several months
younger than me, and she hadn't Matured yet. So that put
a crimp in the projected intimacy, because Mamma Weis-

senkorn was still wondering how to get round to telling Trudy about this Terrible Thing; and they didn't want her to get it first from me. That was a break for me; while they were still keeping Trudy and me at arm's length—as though I would ever have discussed anything intimate with the stupid little creature—I had palled up with Molly Scharf.

Another thing hit me at first was there being a phone in the house. Back on Griscom Street Pop never would have one. He pretended he couldn't afford it, but actually it was not to be waked up in his daytime sleep. Besides we didn't need one. The shops were just round the corner on Frankford Avenue, and most of our friends within a few blocks. But of course, since children are always sensitive about any kind of differences, I had an inferiority because we had no phone and our house was only two stories. To move into a big dwelling with three stories, two bathrooms, and a phone, was a thrill.

I don't know how I'd have got through the first bad days in Manitou if it hadn't been for the Paper Doll House. When I packed up to travel I intended to leave such childishness behind, but in a last desperate moment I included it. I suppose all small girls play the same game. You cut out, from the advertising pages of magazines, furniture and rugs and trimmings for each room in a luxurious imaginary home. These are carefully pasted in a scrapbook, and you take paper dolls on visits through these marvels of perfect equipment. The splendors of the Dream House are limited only by your industry with scissors and your access to the right kind of magazines. It is true that mine had perhaps too much of a Curtis Publishing Company touch, since the *Saturday Evening Post* and the *Ladies' Home Journal* were the papers most often seen in our house, but once and a while I'd get my hands on an architecture or interior decorating magazine and Mrs J. Lusby Lewisohn's Spanish Breakfast Grotto at Grosse Pointe would go at once into my mansion. It was grand fun to get together with another small girl on a rainy afternoon and go leisurely through the details of one another's Dream Houses, putting appropriate dresses on the paper dolls for entertainments of splendor. I had supposed that my new Maturity would do away with all this, but having brought the scrapbook with me, and the old Fanny Farmer candy-box with the family of dolls, I fell back on them in those lonely first days at Manitou. The dog Pattyshells was a big help, because I could explain all this to him without fear of being laughed at. The leading lady of my troupe of dolls was called Nancy Wynne, a name I had picked up from the society columns of the *Public Ledger*.

It was those paper dolls—all named for leaders of Philadelphia society I saw mentioned week after week in the newspaper—that started my friendship with Molly Scharf. It was a hot afternoon and I took my things down on the front porch. Uncle Elmer gave me a Sears Roebuck catalogue, which offered grand cut-out material. I was absorbed in the discovery of all sorts of additions for the Dream House, and wondering how to fit them into my already crowded scrapbook. A gust of wind broke the sultry stillness and dolls and cuttings blew out over the lawn. I ran to retrieve them, ashamed of such publicity, and a girl who was walking by helped me pick them up.

I was greatly embarrassed, but to my astonishment she said "I like to cut out too."

She came up on the porch to see my collection, and by the time Aunt Hattie discovered us there, and brought some root beer, we were great friends. Molly also had a Dream House, and I was much impressed by her ingenuity, she kept it loose in a letter-file instead of pasting in a book. That made rearrangements and additions much easier. She was much taken with the aristocratic Philadelphia names of my dolls which sounded very swanky to her. She insisted on "some good Philadelphia names" for her own paper family, and Mrs Rosemont Rittenhouse or Mrs B. Cynwyd Lloyd would have been surprised to know themselves leading a phantom life in Illinois.

I can see now, when I think about it, that my respect for Philadelphia society must have started in those long mornings keeping quiet with the Sunday paper while Pop was asleep. But it was funny, considering things that happened later, the way those names occupied my imagination in childhood. They fascinated Molly too, she swapped a plaid hair-ribbon for the privilege of calling one of her dolls Cadwalader Shippen.

Molly and I were secretly ashamed of this paper doll business, but we needn't of been, it developed later into a real interest in dress and furniture and it isn't just accident that she now has a fine job in the interior decorating at Palmer's in Chicago. Her father had the big stationery and magazine shop down on Main Street so she was able to get hold of all sorts of recherché magazines for us to cut up. We were both rather on the defensive, we were entering high school and that happens when a kid is most on

55

guard against betraying its feelings in any way, terribly anxious to do the right thing. Just when all sorts of queerness is churning around inside they begin to throw schoolwork at you in big chunks. The Manitou High School always had a fine reputation for studies, and that year was the opening of the new building, for which the taxpayers had gone down deep in their jeans. It was a fine plant with all the latest improvements, green blackboards and cafeteria and theatrical lighting equipment and bubbling-head drinking fountains at which I never could get a drink without soaking the front of my blouse. I think one reason the school board went so far into luxury was to put old Prairie College on its mettle, that being a private foundation which had been going on without much excitement since the Lincoln-Douglas debates. The new high school adjoined the Prairie campus and dwarfed any of the college buildings. In spite of which we kids looked with some jealousy or secret admiration at the college boys and girls, imitated their mannerisms, and wondered what it must feel like to know so much. It was a shock to this hero worship when the high school football team played the varsity and won.

In the big jubilation of the opening of the new building that year's high school freshmen slipped in almost unnoticed. I was in an acute state of sensitiveness, for mixed with a comical feeling of superiority because I came from the sacred East was the natural shyness of the stranger. I soon got the nickname Philly or Filly because the history teacher always called on me to answer any questions about the American Revolution. "Kitty," he would say, "tell us what happened at Independence Hall in 1787." It was no

56

good for me to insist, as I had been taught at home, that real Philadelphians never spoke of Independence Hall but always of the State House.

There was an opening celebration, when the whole school and parents assembled in the beautiful auditorium and the board of education made speeches and the high school band wore its new uniforms. A brilliant silk Stars and Stripes with gold fringes was unfurled, we recited the Salute to the Flag and the band played My Country Tis of Thee. My heart with rapture thrilled, sure enough, I think it was my first real sense of what they call Patriotism. You have to get away from the big cities of the East to feel it. Back East we are so concerned with being a Philadelphian or a New Yorker or a Bostonian or whatnot that the general idea of being an American doesn't occur. The big towns, Wyn used to say, have outgrown being patriotic. As for Philly, it invented the United States, then turned the idea over to other people to manage and went back to its own affairs—by which he really meant the Assembly, the Symphony, Cricket, and Fish House Punch. When I think back about it I can't be grateful enough for the chance I had of that Middlewest period. Those wide wide spaces all around, full of food by day and of stars at night. There didn't seem to be anything to worry about; in fact I don't think people were worrying much those days, what Wyn calls the Little Golden Age, 1924 to 1929. If you didn't know what to do with yourself you could always turn on the radio.

That was another thing we didn't used to have on Griscom Street. Pop said he liked to read his paper in peace without people talking at him out of the air. But Uncle

57

Elmer had just fallen for it when I came to Manitou; he said that if Sears Roebuck took it up it must be all right, though Aunt Hattie still had the idea it was dangerous in thunderstorms. I was one of the first generation that learned to do its homework with the radio turned on. Older people have kidded us a lot about that, but I think somehow it taught us to get the general drift of what's going on, all the miscellaneous chatter of life, without paying too much attention to details. Did you ever know a woman who really believes the things the newspapers make a fuss about? I never did. Women are a lot smarter than they let on to be. They know about fashions, which men haven't got the idea of. There are fashions in saying things just as there are fashions in clothes. You wear what other people are wearing not so much because it's attractive but so as not to be conspicuous; so you can go on being yourself underneath, without being noticed too much. Except by the people you want to be noticed by.

I'm mixing myself up. I'm thinking of those long prairie afternoons when Molly and I would sit in the living room with the radio going and getting our lessons for next day. Until Uncle Elmer came home from the cornplanter factory and turned on some program that told him what the Chicago grain markets had been doing. Uncle Elmer welcomed the radio specially because I think he believed it would keep Aunt Hattie from talking so much tripe over the phone. He nearly went crazy whenever she was on the phone with someone; whatever she said he would yell out suggestions or corrections; of course she got rattled, and whatever call she ever made she had to do it over again a few minutes later to straighten it out. Poor soul it came her turn to be corresponding secretary of the Women's Club and what a time they had. They'd been trying for years to get Vachel Lindsay to come and recite. When he did come Aunt Hattie somehow got him promised to have lunch at three different houses simultaneously. As a matter of fact he had such a good time with the kids at high school that he forgot all about his dates and stayed with us in the cafeteria. That was the first time any of us had seen a real live poet; he looked just like anybody you saw along Main Street. When he said the most romantic thing in Manitou was the C.B. and Q. yards and The Hump where they shunt freight cars, we didn't know what he meant, and the literature department, which was working hard on *The Lady of the Lake,* was upset.

If I could go to school all over again maybe I'd get more out of it. I wonder. Probably not if I had another little devil like Lydia Mason sitting at the next desk and turning everything into comedy. I admit, the reading they give you to study in the College Preparatory course does sound a bit haywire to the kids. To a bunch of youngsters in a prairie town The Ancient Mariner and Midsummer Night's Dream and The Lady of the Lake seem pretty weird, and they're loaded with dynamite in the way of unexpected laughs. I got along better than most with The Lady of the Lake, because in the glass case in the living room Uncle Elmer had a fine old illustrated copy. The pictures really gave me some idea of what it was all about. I felt it was *my* poem in a way on account of the lake being called Loch Katrine, Scotch for Kitty. What the rest of the class visualized I can't imagine. Certainly I don't think any of us had ever seen a mountain in our lives, nor a castle, nor a Highland Chief wearing kilts. Good old Miss Elliman, our literature teacher, loved all that stuff and tried hard to explain, but I remember best the crazy notes Lydia used to scribble in the margin and push the book under my eye. Roderick Dhu was quite a hero of Miss Elliman's but we preferred H. B. Warner. When the poem said that Roderick "surveyed the skirts of Benvenue," Lydia would write *He was probably some picker*. In The Ancient Mariner, which seemed to us pretty grand and goofy, was a line about some dame whose lips were red, her looks were free, and her locks were yellow as gold. Alongside that we would write *Jess Cornish!!!* The Cornish, then a senior, was supposed to be the wild woman of the school. It was a thrill for us freshmen just to pass her in the corridors; the whole school seemed more important and sophisticated to us because Jess was said to be so wicked. Mysterious rumors ran, she had gone down to Quincy with some boys and smoked reefers and stayed out all night. We doubted if even any of the students at Prairie College knew as much about Life as Jess Cornish. Very likely not, for we heard later that she was heaved out of there in her sophomore year.

I don't remember just when it came, but one tough spot was when we studied Midsummer Night's Dream. Miss Elliman had played a part in it in some open-air performance and she gave us the misty-eyed angle on the King and Queen of the fairies and the "kindly comedy" of Bottom. It was terrible what a lot of tough cracks we used to find in that dialogue; we'd all be gargling away in fits of laughter and poor Miss Elliman puzzled and distressed. I never had much idea what the play was all about, but in the strangest way kids guess some meaning underneath these things even if they're still too dumb to express it or too brazen to admit. I know now, my God do I know, some of the things those writers were trying to say.

All this fooling, I guess, was a crude way of trying to make these queer things real to ourselves, in terms we could understand? I've so often promised myself to read some of those old books over again and see what's in them. When Lydia would let me alone I got a thrill out of them and found they put pictures in my mind. Lydia got appendicitis and dropped into another section, which was good for literature. I could see Sir Launfal riding out in his bright array and chucking a coin to the beggar, and getting his come-uppance for it later. Another thing Miss Elliman sold us pretty well was the Eulogy in a Country Churchyard, because she explained the same kind of thing had been done in our own region, down at Spoon River, though not exactly a eulogy. Her poetry class always had to commit a picnic down there to get the idea well in mind. They cut up terribly on these literary picnics, and Miss Elliman would come back discouraged by their irreverence; but by the next year she had forgotten and was still hoping. Anyhow we got a sentimental load of Anne Rutledge, and thought in secret about the beauty of unhappy love and things blooming forever from the dust of our small bosoms.

7

I USED TO WAKE UP PRETTY EARLY IN THE MORNING. My room was on the south and east corner of the house—anyhow so Uncle Elmer said; the geography of the compass is something I never feel sure about. Uptown and downtown are the only directions most women figure on. After the dark little house on Griscom Street I was astonished by the flood of light that pours on a prairie town. The first thing you hear mornings in Manitou is the early Q train to Chicago. It's too early to get up and too late to go to sleep again. They have a legend out there that the morning yells of that rattler do a good deal to keep up the birth-rate.

After you get used to it, it's fun to be waked up every morning by a train. It makes you think about going places. I could hear the old thing rumble over the culvert on the north side of town and set off across the prairie. At Princeton the news company butcher comes through with box lunches. When Aunt Hattie and I would go on a Saturday excursion to Chicago, one of those elastic sandwiches would keep me champing all the way to the Cicero yard.

As soon as he heard the Q whistles Pattyshells would have to go out, pronto. To help me through my first homesickness he was allowed to sleep in my room, which astonished him. I used to recite the next day's lessons to him before going to bed. He was much better than Molly Scharf to study with, except that if you read him a certain kind of poetry he'd get excited and start to bark. That was one way of finding out if it was really good poetry. The Ancient Mariner and some of Vachel Lindsay would send him into fits, but Walt Whitman and Shakespeare never raised a hair on his spine.

I look out the window, down Thanksgiving Avenue, where the big elm trees have rumpled up the brick pavement. In winter time I can just see the window of Molly's bedroom, a little way down the street on the other side. If her shade is still down I know I better get back to bed a while. If it's spring, and the weather's warm, there are all sorts of interesting noises from outside. Down by the Santa Fe tracks I can hear the rattle of hoofs from the mule market where a big string of animals has come into town for sale. In the back yard maybe the splash of the hose where Bernie Janssen is washing the dust off Uncle Elmer's Studebaker. Bernie was working his way through college by doing odd jobs, one of those slow persistent Swedish boys. He's worried about his lessons too, I can see him repeating things to himself as he washes the car and sometimes he goes back to the door of the garage where he has a book propped up on top of a ladder. He eats breakfast with us and then goes to college. I had to give up walking down with him because he always wanted to recite his homework to me and I wanted to do the same to him. Certain days a week he turns up in military uniform because he has drill in the Officers' Training Corps. Those

63

days I really admired him, though I never got used to the idea of a boy having such pale hair. But at that age a kid has to have someone to admire, and he was the first boy I ever saw in Manitou. What was furthermore I thought it romantic that his name was Bernadotte, he said he was named for some famous Swedish general.

The old Manitou Opera House was still working occasionally, road companies would play there once and a while. My first winter a ridiculous melodrama called A Little Girl in a Big City came to town. All of us kids went, of course, and yelled and whistled and stamped, but we took it pretty seriously too. There was a scene where the Little Girl accosts the villain with the reproach "My Betrayer!" Molly and I didn't know exactly what she meant, but we got hold of the phrase, and one day I asked Bernie whether he would be My Betrayer. He was very much shocked, and after that our relations became more formal.

It was better to stay in bed until Aunt Hattie tapped on the door at seven o'clock. She felt more easy in her mind if she found me seemingly asleep. I had plenty of time to pretend because at seven o'clock Uncle Elmer's alarm clock would go off, and he would turn on the radio for his setting up exercises. Nowadays I regard the radio like liquor, you should never take it before lunchtime, so I don't know if people still use it for morning gymnastics. But the Little Golden Age was the time for that sort of thing; Uncle Elmer and everyone else was full of the notion that every day in every way, etc., the world was going to be more prosperous and more folksy and cut down its waistline and all the Socialists are crazy. I guess he was just at the dangerous age; I wonder why men's dangerous

64

age comes about thirty years later than woman's? Does it take them that much longer to see how hopeless things are? Or is it that all women's ages are dangerous? Anyhow, poor soul, he managed to stupefy himself with radio and routine. I could hear him grunting and his knees cracking as he did his exercises; then he'd come to breakfast shaved right down to the beef and we'd have the Jolly Bill and Jane program with our oatmeal. Though I believe Uncle Elmer thought it was dishonest to enjoy a Cream of Wheat program while we were actually eating Quaker Oats. But Quaker Oats made me think of Philadelphia, I could see the statue of William Penn on the Public Buildings looking off toward Frankford. It usually reminded me that I ought to write to poor old Pop.

It's awfully important for kids to feel some sort of routine and security behind them, and certainly I had that with Uncle and Auntie. There wasn't any of the uncomfortable feeling that the household was different, the way I had in Frankford. There never were people more regular than Uncle and Auntie; the fact they never had any children made them specially fixed in habits of all sorts, though Uncle Elmer enjoyed thinking of himself as very unconventional. He really had a notion that it was just some original kink of his own that made him want to do things exactly the way everybody else did them. I think about that a good deal, because I make my living now by trading on women's herd instincts, and I can see how useful it is for them to think they're exercising their own choices when actually they're simply falling in line with what some smart person has doped out for them. There are a lot more clever people in the world than you might suppose; particularly working on women; and merchandisers have learned to put ideas in people's heads without their having the slightest guess where those ideas come from. I've taught myself a lesson, or I hope I have: when I find myself thinking something I stop a minute and ask myself, Now who had it all figured out beforehand that was the way they wanted me to think?

I could see all this working out beautifully with good old Aunt Hattie, who was a pushover for any kind of thought-germ that was floating around. Some handsome Frenchman in a tailcoat would turn up to give a course of lectures at the college on Intellectual Women of the 18th Century, and Aunt Hattie and Mrs Weissenkorn would round up the culture-bearing mammals to go and numb their earnest bottoms on the college chairs. Aunt Hattie always supposed it was just God's Infinite Mercy toward Manitou that such lovely things should happen; she would be horrified if she knew it had likely been doped out by some propagandist in Paris who wanted to soften the shock of the French welshing on their war-debt.

Sure, you can figure it one way or the other; you may be wrong either way, but I do like my mind to have two-way stretch. As Wyn used to say, everybody has a Public Relations counsel—except the Public.

But I'm back at breakfast time, and good old Lena (another Swede; Bernie was some kin of hers) has packed us full of sausage and spoonbread. It's quite a hike down to school. I call for Molly who's probably waiting on her porch. We try to make an early start if we can so as to duck Trudy Weissenkorn, poor kid, who lies in wait for us a little further down, but usually she spots us. The dog Pat

66

sometimes walks with us as far as the Santa Fe grade-crossing, but he knows he's not supposed to cross the railroad. He pretends not to care, and turns back, but I always get a last look from his yellow eyes, it says quite seriously My responsibility is over, now watch out for yourself. Without it getting into words I hope everything will have been all right for us both when I see him again.

Aunt Hattie doesn't know it, but sometimes on the pretext of looking up something in our books we loiter on the Scharfs' porch, behind the creepers, until we see Trudy picked up by *her* pal, Ida Meagher; then we feel safe, and take the back way down Harvest Street, which runs parallel. The parental determination that Molly and I should include Trudy Weissenkorn in all our doings was very trying. Mrs Weissenkorn was painfully ambitious for her unfortunate shrimp, and had an idea that because I came from Philadelphia I would be a good influence for Trudy. I used to be invited to Weissenkorns' for supper and put through a catechism on Philadelphia, about which I knew nothing. Then I got desperate and in reply to questions about my "family" I finally blurted out that my old man was a night watchman, which caused woe when it got back to Aunt Hattie. I think Aunt Hattie had spread a little innocent hooey about her Philadelphia relatives.

As a matter of fact I don't think the Weissenkorns were any less kind even after they learned that I wasn't one of the Signers. Maybe they were secretly relieved; I know Mrs Weissenkorn was a bit in awe of Aunt Hattie the way large stout women often are of little skinny ones. Molly and I used to be invited to go with the Weissenkorns out

67

to their farm near Plautus, which is a suburb of Manitou about ten miles away. A barbecue out there was one of my earliest adventures, in the long hot spell my first autumn. The Weissenkorns thought it was high time for Trudy to learn to swim, and they were pleased when they discovered I didn't know how to swim either. The only bathing I'd ever had was down at the Jersey shore, and you don't learn much about swimming in the surf. Out at the farm there was a pond where Plautus Creek was dammed up, a muddy sort of hole with willows and cottonwood trees and a leaky homemade boat put together by the Debaugh boys, the sons of Mr Weissenkorn's farmer. The real bathing spot for Manitou was Clubfoot Lake, rather pretty with picnic groves and canoes and a diving float and a Log Cabin Tavern that sold bootleg corn whiskey and had a dance floor and a nickelodeon piano. But we were not allowed to go there until we learned to swim, and this muddy cow-pond back of Debaugh's Farm was where we had to learn. Trudy didn't have much gumption, she made a terrible fuss; she complained that the Debaugh boys were pinching her when they were supposed to be teaching her the strokes. Very likely they were; they were pinching me too, but I realized that the less yammering I did the quicker I'd learn. I set my teeth, mostly on mouthfuls of mud, but at least once on the Debaughs, and got the idea fairly soon. Then I could swim out to the middle of the pond where Molly was laughing at us and paddling on an old floating log. Poor Trudy was sloshing around with those freckled gaptoothed Debaugh yokels for many a visit. Molly and I got even with them by calling them Gurth and Wamba, the swineherds, as we had been read-

68

ing Ivanhoe. This made them sore. Then we all went up to the pasture, where they were roasting a pig in a trench. It looked pretty carnal and primitive to me, but I'll admit it was slick eating. Uncle Elmer and Mr Weissenkorn and Mr Debaugh would have a grand time checking over the farm machinery, and the rest of us would play I-spy round the barn. Molly and I pretended this was all rather vulgar, because we were in the Lady of the Lake stage and anyone less attractive than Roderick Dhu was beneath our level. As a matter of fact it was good fun if you took care the Debaugh boys didn't get you off in a corner by yourself. There were embarrassing moments, however, for instance when Molly went to the backhouse in the barn, which was built up high over the cow-shed. The boys had been laying for just such an opportunity, and reached up and tickled her with a fishpole.

There were plenty of times too when Molly and I were on the mischief end of a practical joke. Snooping around in the back of her father's magazine and novelty store Molly came on a lot of trick goods, things like sneeze powder and stink bombs and lapel-gadgets that squirt water in your eye, imitation ink stains to lay on the parlor rug, April Fool chewing gum with red pepper in it, all that sort of roughneck comedy props. The Scharfs lived in one side of a two-family house. Molly's room was up on the third floor, and behind it was a crowded storeroom where all the miscellaneous junk of the Scharf household accumulated, old trunks, and a baby carriage full of Christmas Tree ornaments, piles of old magazines and even a broken skeleton hanging on a stand which someone in the family had used studying medicine. The important thing was that a kind of air-shaft ran up to the roof between this room and the other side of the house, for ventilation in summer, and there was a little window onto this shaft on each side. It didn't take us long to discover that the similar inside room in the adjoining house was used by the colored girl who worked for the Nordstroms next door. We had been amused by her for a long time on account of her habit of talking to herself. We spied on her quite a lot, and found that at a certain angle we could see across the shaft into her room. She used to come upstairs to change her clothes before she served supper. That was our chance with the sneeze powder. My contribution to the stunt was a hollow curtain rod I brought from Auntie's concealed inside my dress and running down my stocking. We balanced the rod carefully, loaded with a big dose of powder, and when Tillie came near the little window we let her have it.

The effects were wonderful. You could hear her sneezing and coughing and mygodding all down the block, Mr and Mrs Nordstrom came running upstairs, and the Nordstrom baby woke and started to scream. Tillie made so much noise that Molly and I could laugh at our ease, but in laughing Molly got a backdraft of the powder and she also sneezed and strangled just as hard as the maid. In the excitement I dropped the box of powder down the shaft and it gradually spread into the dining rooms of both houses. We managed to get out the back way before the cause of the uproar was located. I took Molly up to Auntie's, where we explained her condition as a bad attack of hay fever. But it wasn't long before a telephone call put the fat in the fire. I had to go down to Mrs Scharf's to apologize. They were having their supper on the porch, because the inside of the house was still too full of sneeze. Tillie didn't bear malice; in fact she was rather proud of having been kidded by white folks. She had a roller towel round her neck to wipe her flat nose, and kept saying "Blessed Savior, de inside of my nozzles is burned to cinder."

Tillie unconsciously did much to encourage a scientific spirit in Molly and me. Someone had told Molly, one of those rumors that run through a school, that colored girls had blue nipples, and we spied on poor Tillie through the air shaft until we were convinced it wasn't so.

8

DOWNTOWN, NEAR THE HIGH SCHOOL, WAS THE BIG Square, with fine elm trees and still some of the old iron horsehead hitching posts. One side of the Square, I soon learned, was definitely good and the other was wicked. The east side was set up for religion, education, and culture. There were two big churches on that side, and the high school, the college and the Public Library were all in that direction. But on the west we got a feeling of devilishness. The town's oldtime hotel, the Manitou House, pretty well run down, was said to do speakeasy business somewhere at the back. I guess that accounted for the loud laughter we heard from the travelling men in rocking chairs along the verandah. Across from it was the opera house, and then a whole string of closed saloons. Behind these the street sloped down toward the mule market and the Santa Fe tracks; there was always a sort of glamor and wickedness about the Santa Fe. It made me think of Indians in blankets and moving picture stars in beautiful underwear. The solid old Q road, on the virtuous side of town, seemed much more respectable.

It was exciting to walk past the Manitou House, in twos

and threes. Its vague reputation for mischief gave its shabby porch and colored bellhops a look of mystery, and when a theatrical troupe came to town we would see their trunks going in there from an express wagon; perhaps even a harassed-looking ham in a fur-collared coat. Rumor was that behind the dingy lace curtains at the tall windows private parties were held, and champagne had been served. Jess Cornish had been to one. Molly Scharf was forbidden to enter the place, which made it irresistible; so one day after school, first we did a tour of the Square to be sure no one was watching, and then went brazenly in on the pretext of leaving a note for an imaginary guest. At the desk our nerve failed us and we asked bashfully for the Ladies' Room. This was successful for it was up one flight of heavily carpeted stairs with carved mahogany railing. We found ourselves in a dim dusty corridor with flowered wallpaper. Our nose for wickedness was more than gratified when we discovered that the Ladies' included an outer room with a mirror and dressing table on which was a box of spilled face-powder and a dirty puff. This seemed sinister, and even more so a vulgar French print on the wall. The French we could not understand but the picture was obvious, the dog fearing he would be blamed for the umbrella leaking. It seemed to us outrageously scandalous and we tiptoed off in dismay. Molly had lately acquired a new word of horror, though neither of us really knew its meaning. "I bet this place is full of *bastards*," she said reverently.

The regular resort for the high school crowd, on the way home, was the drugstore on the corner where Main Street came into the uptown side of the Square. The Drugs

73

we always called it; I'd hate to guess how many peanut-butter-and-jelly sandwiches we had there, and the usual drink was a Chocolate Glass-A, a sort of chocolate soda poured into shaved ice. *Glacé* was the real name, but I didn't learn that until long afterward. Between three and four in the afternoon the place was full of jabbering kids. The crowd from Prairie College mostly thought themselves too grown up for The Drugs and went to Sparta's, a Greek candy and luncheonette a block farther up Main. I guess getting educated keeps people hungry, anyhow those places where kids collect after school and drink soda and talk their heads off are as important to them as Rotary and Kiwanis to people like Uncle Elmer.

Molly and I quickly formed a hard and fast alliance. We used to grab inside seats in one of the little alcoves; there, with our backs against the wall, we could stand off any amount of kidding. We would be joined by Lyddie Mason or Peg Ramsauer and hash over the day's classroom comedy. As far as I can remember there seemed to be a general underlying joke that burst us into screams of laughter whenever we thought about it. This was that all the faculty, or indeed older people everywhere, had somehow been mercifully shielded against knowing anything about Life. Its secrets, we reckoned, were now being revealed for the first time to us. And not even to all of ourselves; there were some simple souls, like Trudy Weissenkorn or Bernie Janssen, who for some reason would never get wise to the Big Joke. Bernie later on got to be a problem. Although he was at college he broke all the rules by coming into The Drugs looking for us; if he couldn't get a seat at our table he would gloom at us from a distance, but preserving a collegiate touch by ordering Coke instead of Glass-A. I couldn't exactly high-hat him because he was a sort of member of the household at Uncle Elmer's; and also I was rather taken with his military uniform. But he was terribly dumb. It must have been about my junior year, after he had been moping at me in his amiable Swedish way for a couple of years, he asked if he could come to call on me evenings. Of course I had to say Yes, but I had my homework to study. Well, he asked, how often could he come? Oh, I said sadly, every fortnight. So he arrived, all slicked up, the following Saturday. It was pretty awful. Bernie had a room upstairs in the stable where he changed his clothes. When he finished his jobs round the place he would retire there to doll up, and I would fuss round nervously until he had changed character from hired boy to beau, emerge from the stable and come solemnly to ring the front door bell. The first time I was smart and had Molly up to the house and her friend Fedor Vassilly; we played cards and with root beer and plenty of Lena's layer-cake we got through the evening. Except that Lena, who was a kind of aunt or cousin of Bernie's, was so proud of his rise from odd jobs to social caller that she kept coming into the parlor to see if he was doing all right.—But then he came again the following Wednesday and took me by surprise; and then also the next Sunday. I got him to do my geometry for me, but then I protested. His explanation was lovely: he thought that "every fortnight" meant every fourth night.

I learned that way that "fortnight" is a Philadelphia sort of word, not used on the prairie.

Molly also had anxieties about her first swain, Fedor.

75

He was a very nice boy indeed, one of the sweetest kids in the whole town, and unusual because his family had been Russians. The difficulty was he had been the hero or victim of a tragic accident. It was one of those crazy things, still gives me a horror to think of. A bunch of boys were skylarking down at the Santa Fe depot while a train was at the platform. Probably one of those times when Jackie Coogan or somebody was going through. One of the town loafers was leaning against a baggage truck half asleep. He crossed one leg over another just as the boys were running alongside the cars; Fedor tripped and went under the train as it started. He lost a leg. We were all fond of Fedor, a handsome attractive boy, and quite used to seeing him around on crutches and then on his artificial leg. But when he got so attentive to Molly she was a bit bothered, feeling that maybe it was not wise to fall in love with anyone incomplete. It seemed to us rather unfair that Molly's first beau had only half his legs and mine only half his wits.

But Fedor was a swell egg; he used to go picnics with us, but when the weather was warm enough for swimming we got shy about asking him. It was too grim to see him hang up his aluminum leg on a tree so it wouldn't get wet. It was Fedor who put over the good joke on the rough-neck Debaughs out at Plautus. We were having one of the Weissenkorn picnics, and as usual the Debaugh cut-ups making themselves a nuisance, showing off at Fedor's expense because the poor boy couldn't swim so well, and goosing Trudy when they had a chance. Beyond the pool was a rise in the ground, quite a steep bluff, and a few rocks, very rare in that country. Fedor asked the Debaughs

76

if they knew that those were Magnetic Rocks? Of course they laughed at the idea. Fedor insisted it was so. The magnetism in that kind of rock, he said, was so strong that you couldn't stand on one leg, the power of the rock would draw it down again. Especially, he admitted, a metal leg like his. The Debaughs said he was crazy, but Fedor said he could prove it. We scrambled up the hill and Fedor stood on the stone ledge, raised his artificial leg in the air and struggled to hold it so. But the magnetism was too strong; little by little he was forced, apparently against his will, to lower his foot to the stone.

The Debaughs were impressed, but said Oh, shucks, maybe it works on a phony leg like yours but not on regular people. Fedor said that even the nails in your shoes was enough metal to catch the magnetism. I saw the joke by this time and volunteered to illustrate. I held up one foot, and sure enough with many grimaces and gestures of struggle it was slowly attracted back to the ground. By this time the Debaughs were eager to try it themselves. Both leaped on the rock, proudly hoisted a leg apiece, and stood there scoffing. Aw nuts, they cried. We can stand like this the rest of our lives.

Ixnay, said Fedor, winking at us. Like hell you can, and gave a shove from behind. Sam and Sorrel went rolling and slithering down the sandy cliff and landed in a mass of brambles and poison ivy at the bottom.

So there was always room for Fedor in our alcove at The Drugs. I can see him coming in with his stiffleg walk and his dark clever face, awkwardly fitting himself at the table. He would explain that if the leg was in anyone's way we must tell him about it as he couldn't tell by the feel. Not even with all that Magnetism in it, Molly would ask, and we would squall with laughter. I guess laughter came easy in the Middle West.

It didn't take me long to learn the language; to say Chicawgo and gumbo road and you betcha; to know that catfish is maybe as good as scrapple, if you've never had scrapple, and not to notice the soft coal smell and the queer-tasting water, and to hear Uncle Elmer talking about 92-score butter and timothy number 1. I learned to hear the name of Marshall Field with reverence, just as we used to hear John Wanamaker in Philly; and read the *Tribune* instead of the *Ledger*. I'm sure Uncle Elmer took the *Tribune* slogan "The World's Greatest Newspaper" quite seriously, never guessing it was only a regional wisecrack. Just like I never could get it over to Wyn how people everywhere have their own fetiches, hot stuff for themselves. In Nebraska they get a mystical kick out of writing the name backward, Ak-Sar-Ben. That's as important to them as the Shooters' Parade or a box at the Orchestra is to Philadelphia. The Main Line is called that because it's on its way to Chicago (Chicawgo); but I'm sure Wyn thought it was because it goes to Bryn Mawr and the Devon Horse Show. What happens to it West of the Horseshoe Curve he could scarcely imagine.

I loved him for it. I don't mind people being the way they are. Sometimes I think, Oh, if I could just get together all the people I love and give them one perfect day. People's faces are so handsome when they're happy.

Take Uncle Elmer. You couldn't call him handsome, he was too thick and beefy, his neck was reddish, he had

78

pink moss on the back of his hands and he wore carrot-colored shoes with bulging box-toes, but he looked mighty reliable fussing round the place. I wonder what he was thinking about? Either the cornplanter factory or his stomach, probably. When he gets upset his stomach begins to revolve the wrong way. Countergutwise he calls it. He starts to belch at both ends and runs for the bicarb. As soon as Mrs Stillwagon next door came out on our side of the place, trimming her vines or something, Uncle would fill up with gas. There were two things he couldn't take, people who were untidy and people who were talkative. Both were combined in Mrs S. Warm evenings we could hear that hog-caller's voice of hers booming across the lawn as she went on and on at the phone. Once Uncle looked up from the evening *Argus* and said to Aunt Hattie "It's a shame Mrs Stillwagon has that painful disease."

"Why Elmer, what do you mean?"

"I don't mean painful to her. Painful to other folks. She gets started talking she don't know how to quit."

Molly and I thought this was very amusing, we made up a rhyme and got some of the boys to shout it along the street one evening:

"Poor Mrs. Stillwagon, she's full of pop;
When she starts talking she just can't stop."

But the Middle West is a great place for talk anyhow. Every call is a social call, even if it's somebody trying to sell you an eggbeater. Aunt Hattie was a pushover, at the mercy of anybody who rang the bell. She'd ask them in and never knew how to get rid of them. Sometimes Bernie would come in just to find out what he was wanted to do

79

next, she'd ask him to sit and have something, first thing you know it was time for him to go back to college or whatever and he never did get the chore finished. I figure that every woman ought to have at least a year's experience in an office, just to teach her how to get rid of people who call without an appointment and make themselves a nuisance.

It was bad luck that the side lawn, Uncle's specialty, adjoined Mrs Stillwagon's place. Bernie did the rest of the odd jobs, but mowing and weeding and raking the company lawn was Uncle's joy. Mrs Stillwagon was so untidy that everyone who worked for her got that way too. Her hens broke loose from the yard and were always coming over. One morning Uncle went down early for some reason, probably to see if his new grass seed had sprouted. He came out on the kitchen stoop in his dressing gown and found a whole flock of Stillwagon hens gaping at him in their scandalized prudish way. It made him so sore he threw the morning cream bottle at them. That made a thick messy splash on the turf and I acquired merit by going out to sop it up with a big sheet of blotting paper.

When Mrs Stillwagon's hired man trimmed her new privet hedge he threw all the clippings over on our side. Maybe he intended to come and pick them up after, but meantime Uncle discovered them. Belching hard, he gathered up all the cuttings and stuck them in the ground back of the stable as a screen for his vegetable patch. It was sprouting spring weather and in that black prairie dirt they took root and grew into a fine hedge even better than Mrs Stillwagon's. This tickled him so it became a sort of fable in his mind and he used it the time he was called

80

on to make a speech at Rotary.

Uncle Elmer was certainly damn decent to me. It must have been a shock to him to have kids frolicking round the place after that orderly routine of his. Even each of his golf clubs had a little shammy pouch tied over its head so it wouldn't get rusty. He spent so much energy on details like that he had no time left to enjoy the game. He put out a croquet set for us on his sacred lawn, and I can see now how patient he was picking up bobby pins and the caps of coke bottles. He had genius for choosing the wrong kind of clothes, tweeds that were the color of straw and would have given Wyn apoplexy. Sundays he always had an overcoat with a velvet collar, it made my spine creep to see it rub his pink neck. He shaved too close and then put talcum on his face; he carried a show-off handkerchief in his breast-pocket, folded in four points; he'd sneeze all over the room sooner than snatch it out. But what's the use of kidding people who don't even know they're being kidded? He was a Good Provider, and one or two of those don't do a family any harm.

I can't help wishing Uncle Elmer had had just a little more of what Wyn calls frolic. Pop used to say about Presbyterians, it don't prevent them committing all the sins there are but it keeps them from getting any fun out of it. Unless Uncle did it down at the cornplanter factory he never let himself go. Maybe he just didn't have anything in him that wanted to go. I used to think sometimes how respectable he was compared to my Old Man, and blame myself for being disloyal.

All the same you've got to hand it to Uncle Elmer. You might as well; he'll take it anyhow. I'd like to know

81

what he was thinking about, those days on the grass plot. Maybe he saw more than just grass. He liked to make things grow. Maybe he saw his own kind of decent well-cared-for world, with a sizzling platter for Sunday dinner and a snoring nap afterwards and a drive in his shirtsleeves over those straight flat roads to Muscatine or Peoria.

9

But wasn't it grand and gorgeous to get back to Philly that first time, after nine months away. Nine months is long enough for a lot to happen. It must be more than just accident they chose that length of time for the school year?

Aunt Hattie intended to see me as far as Chicago. She wanted to pick out some summer porch-furniture at Field's. We had one of those crazy Illinois springs, terrible hot weather at the end of March and Uncle insisted on Bernie putting out all the bamboo chairs and shays lounges. Then we had an early April blizzard that just about ruined them. That must have been, let's see, '25, and the cornplanter business was riding high. The factory had just got a royalty on some machinery-patent for planters in Ukraine, that was the first time I got the idea Russia really existed, and Uncle said Hell, go on up to Field's and shoot the works. He was always tickled when Aunt Hattie got steamed up about something because except on the telephone she was so quiet about what she was thinking. The telephone was invented I guess for women who never spill their guts any other way.

Just before Auntie was going to take me to Chicago she caught a septic throat and Doctor Witt had to come. It's a funny thing how often doctors are shy and Doctor Witt was the shyest. The screw was loose in the handle of the bathroom door. He was in there washing his hands and when he took hold of the handle to come out, the knob slipped right off. There was no way to turn the latch and he was too bashful to make a fuss, the radio was on, no one heard him knocking until smart old Pattyshells began to bark.

Uncle took me down to that same old morning rattler and I went to Chicago alone. Lena packed a lunch for me because she said the news butcher's sandwiches at Princeton weren't good enough. There were some other high school kids in the car, going to places like Galva and Kewanee, even Aurora, on vacation visits. I sat just behind them and joined in the conversation but I felt very superior, I was going all the way to Philly. Also they had a giggling spell, which is very annoying when you don't feel that way yourself. What is it about girls that makes giggling such a comfort to them? Wyn used to say, they're walking a tightrope over lunacy; their breath comes quicker than boys, their fibres are softer, their whole system is tuned up for comedy like cider in a jug, and something's got to blow. Wyn loved to lay down the law about girls, he'd try out his ideas on me. I supposed girls were just people, but it's nice to be convinced different. Girls don't take girls seriously, no matter what age.

I was feeling too important to really enjoy their cackle. I had a tan pongee dress but the white piqué collar and cuffs were a mistake for travelling on the Q. I was pleased

84

by my new straw hat with daisies on it, but when the conductor came for my ticket a grasshopper that had got on me jumped off my hat and right into his face, which set the kids off in more screams. I didn't like to take my hat off, because I had put up my pigtails and was self-conscious about it. The prairie lay like one of Uncle's sizzling platters and my head felt like a hot cross bun when it touched the plush seat.

I had plenty of time to windowshop the Union Depot in Chicago. That always seems to me the real navel of America. I'm still surprised when I find white redcaps there; of course in the East we take it for granted redcaps should be colored people. At first I supposed they were pale mulattoes but when they scratched their heads I noticed their hair was different. I bought a cheap souvenir ashtray for Pop at the Fred Harvey place and studied the models of sleeping car sections so I wouldn't act like a greenhorn. I hung onto my suitcase until my arm creaked because I was afraid if I gave it to a redcap he'd ask if I was taking the Limited, which I wasn't. The Limited's extra-fare. I got that good old afternoon train, they call it The General now, it makes Philly at breakfast time.

That time I really took in the ride; the first trip I'd been too sick to notice. Probably I didn't realize it all at once, but those different sensations of the trip were registering on me. There's the Fort Wayne feeling, which is not so good because you're still part of what you've left behind. It's too early yet for supper and the soot is working through the double windows. It's not fair to eat till you get into Ohio, and the Lima feeling is mixed up with dining car taste and smell and the fun of writing your order and see if your shaky letters look better after going through the carbon sheet. The Crestline feeling is that you're really getting somewhere and you're not too proud to go to bed. I always wake up at Pittsburgh, I don't believe anybody who says he can sleep through Pittsburgh, and everything has sort of turned over, you're actually in Pennsylvania. If you're young as I was you'll never know about the Horseshoe Curve and Harrisburg; but if you don't wake up by Paoli the porter prods you. After Paoli those Main Line stations go by like a flash but you're too busy dressing to notice. It's still a bit too early for the Nice People to be up; that bunch of Charge Accounts sleep later than Frankford.

At North Philly there were the Old Man and Mac, just like when I went away. Even the platform was still wet, as though that thundershower had lasted all the meantime. They were hosing it for a hot day. The Old Man must have been up most of the night so as to be sure to meet me, arthritis and all. Well, he says, "I've had plenty of training. Watchman, what of the night?"

Seeing him again I noticed he looked old. There were lines in his forehead I didn't know about before. He didn't like the heat and that vein was jumpy in the soft place on his temple. Maybe he noticed soft places in me too, he said "Kitty, you begin to look like a female." We had breakfast in the station restaurant, and as usual I went over to the marble fountain in the waiting room looking for a drink and found no water in it.

Oh it's good, seeing things again you've been carrying in your mind all the while and didn't even know you knew. It's like when you lay down a lighted cigarette; you cruise round the apartment doing this and that but something inside remembers about the cigarette and you always come back to pick it up just in time. At least I do, Wyn always noticed.

Pop had a button off his vest. Now I was the Woman in the family and that sort of thing was up to me. He always put any buttons that fell off in the old pink and gilt moustache cup on the left end of the kitchen shelf. I expected to find plenty of them, and I was right. "Mac's been sewing on buttons for me," he said, "but he figures every other one is enough." I thought Mac looked thin and a bit nervy. "He has a right to," said Pop, "he's moving the earth." This was a joke between them; Mac had got a clerical job with a firm in North Philly that makes Earth Moving Equipment. Most of his off time was spent keeping an eye on the old man, who took some moving himself.

Mac went off to his job. "He's got to go and Move Earth," Pop said. "He don't move Heaven much. He comes home nights with lipstick on his handkerchief."

"It's a pity you aint got anything better to do than study through the laundry basket," Mac said as he was heaving the old man into a cab.

"That's where I keep the Pope's telephone," says Pop. "Myrtle got wise to the corner cupboard."

Griscom Street looked just the same. The sexton at the big gray Methodist church on the corner was out washing off the chalk marks on the sidewalk where the kids had been playing hopscotch. That always got his goat, but it was the only bit of pavement smooth enough. He used to rush out and chase us; there was the time Lena McTag-

87

gart's drawers broke loose from too much hopping and she got tangled in them just as the sexton came out. He switched her on the cheeks and the Presbyterians crabbed about it. Pop said those McTaggarts always had trouble with underwear, they're not used to it. They ought to be wearing kilts like wild Highlanders.

Denny, who was a bit on the prim side, didn't like Pop talking that way. He had gone to live in Cincinnati and married quality, it was always a shock to him to come back to Frankford and find Pop just the same. Denny said: "Kitty, when you grow up you'll certainly be refined just by contrast to your surroundings. There's Ed, he learned so much foul talk making the world safe for Democracy he has to go to American Legion conventions to practise up on it." Pop said: "Sheep dip! Just because you married a librarian, Denny, you can't high hat the family. Librarians know more dirty words than anyone else, they've got cases at the Mercantile that smells so strong they keep 'em locked up." Mac said: "That's research librarians. Denny's wife is the clean-minded sort, she just runs a rental." Denny got sore and said what was the use coming all the way from Cincinnati just to be insulted at home.

Being a girl in a family like ours teaches you the kind of things that make men sore. It's useful to know. What always burned up Ed was "make the world safe for democracy" and "the War to end War." It took me quite a while to get wise to those sayings, they were what people used to write editorials about in the newspapers.

The house was pretty dusty but old Myrtle had done a job of cleaning in my room. I could smell hot shingles on the roof, same as always; and there was the little narrow window over the side entry that gave me a glimpse out on the street. And the old faded photograph of Mother when she was still a young lady in Germantown before she married into Frankford. That's quite a gulf, if you don't know it; though Pop, when he got peeved, would say when you get that far down Wissahickon Avenue it's not Germantown but Tioga. Mother said Nonsense, we even had a station in Germantown named for us, Upsal. Who ever heard of a station called Foyle? Then Pop would call her his little chicken from Wissahickon which always tickled her. I can see now that they once had a private language of their own too, like other people. It's queer when you get a human slant on your own parents.

That little strip of window was what I used to look at when I woke up mornings as a kid. The old wooden bed, with slats, was set so I could just see through it. There wasn't any blind on that window—it wasn't a real window, just a pane let into a jog in the wall. I was waiting for Mother to come and call me to get dressed. It was a nice safe feeling. Now I couldn't quite feel that way again. Mother was gone, and I was sort of split up between Frankford and Manitou, and Pop was getting old and a bit queer. Just for a moment, as I unpacked my suitcase, and that's a queer feeling, if you stop to think about it, the way things change their meaning while they go travelling, the train I'd been on seemed the only real thing I had. Trains, Jesusgod how I love them and how they can hurt. I was rummaging to get out Pop's ashtray and sorry because I hadn't thought to bring anything for Mac or Myrtle and I wanted to cry. I think that was one of the first times I didn't understand myself. Maybe I never will.

Maybe it's better not to. I heard old Pop fighting to get upstairs, hanging onto the banister and cursing; it took him so long to crabwalk up that I got my eyes smoothed out and had his present ready for him. Come to think of it, a kid of fourteen can be a pretty good actress. I couldn't do it now; once you let the flood go over the dam you never get back that tight holding-power.

I think as a matter of fact poor old Pop was lonely to see some female fixings. He was pleased once when I called him a softshell crab. He was just learning to let down his armor. He took a quick look at the picture of Mother on the dresser and then back at me. My trunk was there already, Uncle sent it by express in advance, and Pop sat and watched me unpack. You can usually tell the way a man's mind is running by what he pretends to make fun of. I was proud of some new summer dresses Aunt Hattie and I picked out at the Mode in Paris which was Manitou's big number for Girls and Misses. Pop saw the labels. "I suppose that means Paris, Illinois." He was tickled to death to see clothes again, but what he said was: "When I look at young gals and think of all the crazy things they're going to have to wear before they get through, I wonder they have the courage to grow up."

I probably said "Oh yeah?" which was the new comeback in those days.

Pop lay down to get some rest, and I straightened up my stuff and then I talked to Myrtle on the back steps while she cut string beans. We had Myrtle on full time now; I was glad, I'd been worrying maybe I'd have to do the cooking. I gave Myrtle a full blast about the Middle West, because till I got used to it again Griscom Street looked a bit small compared to Thanksgiving Avenue. I told her about high school, and about Bernie in his uniform, and even about Jess Cornish. "I bet there's not a girl in Frankford as wild as Jess," I suggested. Myrtle wasn't impressed.

"We got some right minxy columbines round here too," she said. "Wait till you see that gal your brother Mac goes out with. He's cohtin' her the way Grant hung round Richmond. They go all the way downtown on the L for fishfood and dancin'. He mus' spend a fohchune. Don't tell yo' Pop, Mac done sold that Libutty Bond the ole man bought him when he was a kid. There mus' be money somewheres, they buildin' a big new bank the corner of Oxford to keep it in. I guess money move uptown faster now they got the L for it to ride in. Tells me Hanscom's goin' start a bakery right here on Frankford Avenue."

Cinnamon buns! Now I knew I was in Philly again.

I went out for a walk. There was the old Friends Meeting House on Orthodox Street, and the milestone that said *7 Miles to P,* which Pop quoted sometimes; and the Library on Frankford Avenue where I borrowed the Little Colonels and *Anne of Green Gables.* How childish I must have been, I thought; I used to think the name of the man who built the Library was Mr Esq because the tablet said "Given by Andrew Carnegie Esq." Pop tried to explain the Esq business, but only puzzled me. He said you can't get to be one of the Esqs in Philly unless you either give a library or chase something in the open air. Mac said, "What do you mean, like chasing a baseball?"

"God, no," Pop says. "A cricketball maybe, that'll help so long as you don't get paid for it, but it's better to be

91

animals. If you can sit on one animal and chase another you get to be Esq."

That night after supper we sat out on the porch, Pop in the old green rocker and me on a mat on the steps. Lena McTaggart and Nellie Simmons stopped by to give me a once-over but I didn't like Nellie any better than I had before. They tried to give me a song-and-dance about big times at Frankford High but I came right back with some Manitou dope. They boasted about their school song and like a fool I hummed *Old Manitou* to them. That was a humiliation because they squawked with laughter and said it was only the tune of *Maryland, My Maryland*. "Never you mind, Kitty," said Pop when they'd gone. "They don't plump out the way you nice cornfed Illinois gals do. Tell me all about Pattyshells and Molly Scharf, and you can throw in a little information about Elmer and Hattie."

You know, the old man was smart. He knew when to treat a kid of fourteen like a woman and when to treat her like a baby. That's not so easy.

10

The old man and I went down to the Shore. We went down by bus to Tidewood. I guess I'm a snob at heart because when I used to try to tell Wyn about the Shore I always found it hard to say it was Tidewood where we stayed. Of course Wyn's kind of people don't think there *is* any Shore unless just the right part of Cape May. Anywhere else the ocean is sort of polluted. Sure, Tidewood's a terrible place and terrible people, but somehow the Ocean seems to have forgiven them. Wyn got the idea afterwhile, because I remember him saying one time we stopped on a lonely beach, God must have loved the ocean, He made so much of it. Wyn, you blessed, how could you quote Lincoln? He was such plain folks, and from Illinois too.

Why did we go by bus, I wonder. It was Mac's idea, he thought it would be easier for the old man. I guess the principal thing was Mac wanted to get rid of us. Madonna of the Lipstick was crowding him pretty hard. He'd done a chore on the old man all winter and he needed his evenings to commute up Torresdale way where the girl lived. I never saw her, but the old man thought she was dirt.

I remember how sore Mac was when Pop said: Don't let her get mixed up in the Torresdale Filters, she'll spoil our drinking water.

When the old man went anywhere you had to make an early start and take plenty of time. Busses were still pretty crude and he cursed so much that women with children complained to the driver. The angle of the seats was wrong for his back. He said he was buttsprung before we ever got aboard, because in the terminal they had regular bus-seats in the waiting room. So you can get used to being uncomfortable even before you start. When the old man built up one of his real grouches he didn't care what happened. By the time Mac left me alone with him I knew this one was going to be a beauty. He made me open his suitcase for him, right there in the terminal, and swigged off what he called some Oil of Ulster.

Must have been soon before July Fourth; we thought we'd get out of town early and everybody else had the same idea. It all ties together in my mind, coming back home and hot weather and the rose rambler on the little wooden porch. In hot weather, riding in a train, I sometimes hum to myself "Philadelphia in June." It goes to our old Blue Room music. Phila-de-he-hel-phia in June. It's unique. Not like that Middlewest heat that dries you up and scorches. In Philly it comes soft and damp and drowsy, clings round you and goes moist in corners and creeps inside and the dear old town just collapses and spreads out flat and says Take me. A woman knows how that feels.

Green country town, Wyn used to say as we drove through the Park. William Penn or Ben Franklin or John

94

Wanamaker or somebody said it. Probably not John Wanamaker.

But Pop was in bad shape. He'd get down to the porch mornings and sit there and stare at the rambler. He was as prickly as it was. Then I figured out what he was looking at. There was a catbird used to nest there. She'd come flying through the whole mess of prickers in one clean swoop and land in her nest. You could see her tail cocked up like a crashed airplane. Yet you couldn't scarcely stick your hand through the briars without tearing it. That was the way Pop was. You had to sneak through a lot of brambles before you found him sitting on his eggs.

Birds are crazy about Philly. I guess everybody is who just wants not to be bothered.

But I'm back at the Shore. We had two rooms in a boarding house out at Tidewood Crest. Pop's peeve lasted three days; partly on account of the beating he took on the trip down, and partly because he didn't know yet where to get a reliable snort. Partly maybe because he decided to grow a beard. His hands had got shaky so he didn't like to shave. He was sore because the beard came out gray and white. He called it his flag of truce, his sign of surrender. I guess he meant he really knew now that he was old and had quit scheming. Women would come toddling out of the house, bending forward to settle the girdle and feel if the stockings are good and snug, before they went parading. If anyone showed a good shaft Pop would wink at me but he didn't really pay any technical attention.

I don't know just how I spent the time. That's a good kind of time when you don't know where it went. There was a girl there had a mah-jong set and I played that quite a lot, and she and I walked on the Boardwalk and tried to win Helene the Beach Vamp, a doll, by knocking down tenpins. We got loaded up with china cats at the Japanese game-boards. I think we were both sore because none of the boys ever took a tumble to us, but we wouldn't admit it and pretended to be amused by the couples we saw. The times I remember best was when Pop hobbled across the sand fields to the beach and I'd carry the old gray shawl and an umbrella and maybe a book.

That was way up beyond the town and the Boardwalk, and the beach wasn't crowded. My swimming that I learned in the mudpond at Plautus wasn't much good in that surf, so I'd mostly sit where it creamed up like meringue on a lemon pie. There was a sunburned young man who said he was a dentist came along one day and offered to give me some lessons, but Pop, who always sat just at the edge of the dune, got nervous if I went in as far as my waist. Sink right back and relax, like you were in the dentist's chair, said the young man. That's a hell of a place to relax, Pop said. I rather enjoyed the way Dr Sunburn, as Pop called him, made a chair out of his arms and offered me plenty of deep water, but Pop used to get fidgety. "What does he think he's doing," he said, "giving you gas? Keep dentists up above your chin." I could have felt almost romantic about Dr Sunburn, for a few days, because his face was rather pleasant and cheerful when seen upside down from below. But he soon discovered more amusing patients. We used to see him farther along the beach, instructing them in the undertow. Dentists have such a tough profession, Pop said, they go

96

crazy when they get a week's vacation.

The sun was good for the old man, and when he wasn't worrying about me we were swell company. It's all just whiteness and heat in my mind now, and the cutting edges of that grass. Funny to hold a thing in your mind and keep it that way always. Pop with his face in the black shade of the umbrella and the rest of him cooking. His beard didn't grow fast enough to prevent him getting burned and the red showed through the grizzle. The place was doing him good; he wasn't drinking too much, and he was taking bicarb for his arthritis or sciatica or whatever it was, and it seemed to help. Oh, he'd get his moods, they'd come down on him like fog, that's the Irish of it I guess. Then all of a sudden he'd snap out of it. I'd feel him looking at me and he'd say: "Be's you got bugs?"

Of course I make the proper answer: "Sure I are."

He says, "Everybody do!"

That was the signal that meant Everything's hunky-dory, let's talk. Maybe I was a little shy of him, because he looked so strange in that half-grown beard. Partly the beard helped because I was the only person there who knew it was really just the same old Pop under that terrible thicket. We heard churchbells and I said maybe we'd ought to go to service.

"Did you ever see a Friends' Meeting House with a bell on it?" he asked.

I realized that I hadn't.

"The Friends got the right idea. The church bells that really matter rings inside of you."

"I guess the ocean's a pretty good church," I suggested, a bit frightened to be talking about such things.

97

"You're damn tootin', Kitty. A tide comin' in and a tide goin' out."

I know what he meant. He meant That's you and me, Kitty. But he knew that would have troubled me if he said it.

I wish I could have thrown my arms round his neck and kissed his spiky old face and said I love you. Why did he have to grow a beard just then, damn him.

He'd always been sort of interested in Quakers, I guess it began because they played good cricket. After Mother died he wanted me to go to Friends' First Day School instead of Sunday School. Something about Mother's funeral gave him a scunner against the regular church. Somebody at the Frankford Meeting House used to send us those little Quaker Calendars, printed in red and blue with religious mottoes on them. Some good old Quaker left a fund for having them printed, and whenever you find them you can be sure there's Friends' Meeting ideas somewhere in the background. I guess that old Quaker would be surprised if he knew how many women use his calendars mostly to check their own private almanac. Maybe that's a part of religion too.

Imagine my surprise, the other day I was looking in the phone book for a Fur Storage and I ran across "Friends Meeting House Quakers." I had no idea there were Quakers in New York City, it don't seem reasonable somehow.

Considering what a lot I use it, the Phone Book really has been my Bible.

A few times we got as far over as the Inlet and Pop took me crabbing. The boatman towed us out a way and we'd anchor there in a leaky punt lowering fishheads on a string weighted with rusty bolts. I wore overalls so I didn't mind the muck, and as long as we kept those big brandishing crabs down Pop's end of the boat I'd forget all about the fishing. Warm salt breeze and the stink of fishheads and once and a while on a gust comes the sound of that steam-piano on the Boardwalk carrousel. I was in a dream, I wasn't thinking about anything, or wanting anything, or scared of anything—just learning what living feels like. It was what they call on the air, Pause for Station Idenni-fication. This is Station K.F., at the Top of the Dial. And here's your favorite Newscaster, Kitty Foyle. This is Kitty Foyle, just beginning to learn about herself; fourteen years old. Oh, lovely things are going to happen to Kitty Foyle. Beautiful blond men with ruddy brown cheeks, shaved so clean, and wearing creased ice cream pants, are going to look strangely at Kitty Foyle on the Boardwalk and she walks serenely by. I wonder if Kitty Foyle sways gracefully from behind, when they turn to look after her, or does she wobble like those women at the boarding house? (It was Pop put that in my mind, he had a trick, puffing out first one cheek and then the other, called Fat Woman Going Upstairs.)

I know now what they call it, Adolescence. What a dumb word for a sweet thing. A skinny kid in dirty fish-smell overalls, black hair sticky with salt under a straw hat, bare brown feet in sneakers, and broken fingernails, leaning over a scow and thinking she's the Lady of the Lake. The hot yellow sun spreads out into the flopping brown water like cream in iced coffee, you can't see far into it, only your crabbing line sloping down in shadow.

You can't see far down, old lady; good thing too; it's sweet, the not knowing; and you couldn't possibly guess how lovely it can all get to be; things that if you knew about them would only scare you or shame you. No one can tell you till you're ready to be told; and there's damn few will ever tell you anyhow; the little silly things we need. Maybe there aren't enough silly things to go round among all the women who need to be told them.

What's the first thing people do when they love each other? They begin to make up a language of their own that doesn't mean anything to anyone else. I guess that's what the Shore was doing to me those times Pop and I went down. It was telling me things I didn't even need, yet, to know what they meant. When I say the Shore, hell, I don't have to be shy with myself, I mean God or Time or my own pelvis. I was getting ripe and I didn't know it any more than an apple does.

As soon as you begin to fret and worry about meanings, you've lost that something in you that makes it possible to know them.

Come to me, my beautiful, and tell me what I mean.

I'm the Lady of the Lake.

"Pop, what's a shallop?"

"They're good with tartar sauce."

"No, a *shallop*. Some kind of a boat. We had it in poetry."

"Canoe, I guess. Pull up your line, Kitty, I'll bet those crabs have ate up all your bait."

"I hope they have, I don't want to smell it again."

Sometimes the skipper was slow bringing his motorboat

to tow us back.

"Jesusgod, aint that old fool coming after us? We'll miss supper at the house. Worse than that I got to go to the bathroom. He don't know what my bladder's been through in sixty-some years."

"You mean the other way round, Pop."

"Quit kiddin' the old man. Listen, Kitty, take off your shirt and wave it at him, maybe he'll see it. I'm too crippled up to peel mine."

I did, but even "short glimpses of a breast of snow" (The Lady of the Lake) didn't hurry that boatman much. I guess it wasn't much of a breast then, but anyhow I was pleased when Pop said "Don't you get tanned all over like those damn Beach Vamps. You got nice white Irish skin. You'll be able to wear thin stockings without showing pelt."

I often think of that in the West Side subway.

I get mixed up which summer was which; it don't matter. We went down to Tidewood several times. I know it was that summer of '25 we made the embarrassing visit to Cape May. It was the first time I suffered the big female problem, Nothing to Wear.

Sunday mornings, like everybody else we sat on the boarding house piazza and read the *Public Ledger*. I used to be fascinated by the society notes and wondered how the papers got to know so much about what Mr and Mrs Swarthmore Comly or the F. X. Haddonfield Berwyns were doing at Narragansett and Bar Harbor. At that time Molly Scharf and I were conducting a makebelieve correspondence in which she played the part of Mrs Rosemont Rittenhouse and I was Mrs B. Cynwyd Lloyd. It was absurd but it was a good game. Molly, writing as Mrs Rittenhouse, would tell me what a time she was having because she and Rosey had to entertain the Prince of Wales and all their hunters had fallen sick and they would have to use their polo ponies to chase the fox; and worse still Sears Roebuck was all out of mail-order foxes and maybe they'd have to chase the Debaugh boys instead. What would the Prince think of that? And I would reply with some social dilemma supposedly agitating the breast of Mrs Lloyd.

But one day I forgot to cover up an envelope I had just addressed to Mrs Rosemont Rittenhouse c/o Miss Molly Scharf, Thanksgiving Ave., Manitou, Ill. Pop happened to see it and said What the hell's this? I explained the game, and Pop was amused but said not to put names like that on the outside of the letter. Some clerk at the post office, who knew damn well Mrs Rosemont Rittenhouse wasn't in Illinois—there never was much secret about where the Rittenhouses were spending the heated term— might put the correct address on it and she'd really get the letter and be sore.

"Rosey's one of the grandest guys in the world," said Pop. "He hit three boundaries in one over, against the Gentlemen of England when they were touring here. He used to be musclebound until I taught him how to loosen up when the bowler's arm rises. I never thought *I* was going to be the one that's musclebound now. You know, Kitty, the Gentlemen of England used to come over here to play cricket. All they come over for now is to pull wool in Washington."

When I would read out some big Society Page name Pop could always place it his own way. Mrs Reggie Montgomery maybe wore a white camellia at the Assembly, and a foaming mass of white tulle, but Pop remembered that he got 56 against Reggie's bowling when Frankford played Merion C.C. in 1904.

"As a matter of fact," said Pop, looking up from a foaming mass of Sunday *Ledger,* "I see Rosey's down at Cape May right now."

I never told Pop, but I myself sent that note to the paper saying that Mr Thomas Foyle and his daughter Miss Katherine Foyle were spending the summer at "Ocean View," Tidewood Crest, while Mr J. McGregor Foyle was remaining at "his residence" in Frankford. They printed it in South Jersey Jottings, omitting the allusion to poor Mac. Pop thought it was very enterprising of the Ocean View to have sent in our names. Of course the whole point was to send the clipping to Molly; it started her on a busy campaign to get her name mentioned somehow in the Manitou *Argus.*

Only a few days after that Pop was hobbling along Ocean Avenue on his way to the bootlegger, he met Mr Rittenhouse driving through to some yachting at Barnegat. Pop was very pleased because Mr Rittenhouse gave him a lift to the bootlegger's, ordered a whole case of pinch-bottle on Pop's recommendation, brought the old man back to Ocean View in the car, and invited us down to Cape May for dinner the following Sunday.

That's when I first had the Nothing To Wear jitters. It was true too, it always is. At a seashore boarding house a kid of fourteen isn't likely to have any Rittenhouse sort of clothes. All I had with me was the old straw suitcase.

"If he'd asked us for lunch," I said, "I could have worn my blue middy and the white linen skirt, but for dinner you don't know what they may pull on us."

"Jesusgod, Kitty, I didn't know you were going to be that sort of a girl."

"Every girl is that sort of a girl."

"It's your Germantown blood coming out," he said. "All right, all right, we'll go downtown and find something chiffoon."

That's exactly what we did, and it was terrible. I didn't know any better, and let the old man pick out for me a kind of yellow gauzy thing with blue flowers on it, what Pop called hysteria blossoms. It was much too old for me, and much too sheer. My poor little camisole I was so proud of showed through like everybody's business. Of course the party turned out to be Sunday evening buffet supper and everybody in outdoor sports clothes; just the exactly correct kind of informality and a colored butler in a white coat passing mint juleps. I felt like a fool and everybody was so terribly kind it made me feel worse. Also I was ashamed of having used Mrs Rittenhouse's name in fun because she saw my trouble and was grand to me. A big South Jersey moon came up and we all went down on the beach, at the foot of their lovely lawn, because, as Rosey said, "something might have been cast up by the sea." It had, sure enough; something with ice in it.

Pop took more than he should, but he had a notable time; Rosey played up to him with cricket reminiscences and we all sang songs and pretended that the bonfire would keep away the mosquitoes. Mrs Rittenhouse lent me a polo coat to cover my chiffon and as long as we were out in the dark it wasn't so bad. But I thought I'd never get Pop to leave. The chauffeur drove us all the way back to Tidewood, and I know I was cross and humiliated.

"Great country, South Jersey," Pop said. "Rosey don't need to talk about Bah Habbah and Newport. We got the greatest air on the Atlantic Coast. Even makes my fingers tingle."

"That kind of a tingle comes in bottles," I said.

I guess now it was probably high blood pressure or something.

It was well on in summer when Pop and I came home. I know the blue morning glories were out on the stone wall of the Pennypacker place. Griscom Street seemed small and dark after all that sunlight at Tidewood.

Those Frankford summers were all pretty much the same. Once and a while someone would come and drive Pop over to Manheim to see a cricket match at the Germantown C.C. I'd try to see that he always had a clean pair of his old flannel pants so he'd feel natural round the pavilion. Usually they asked him to keep score and that tickled him but he said he couldn't do it right unless he had flannels on. It didn't matter they'd shrunk because he was shrinking too.

When you think back you can see it don't matter so much what actually happened as what kind of a pattern it leaves in your mind.

I helped Myrtle with the housework, and I was awfully proud to do the marketing. I'd go round to Frankford Avenue right after breakfast before it got hot. Sometimes

afternoons I'd go to the Andrew Carnegie Esq library and
try to get interested in a book. You could always tell if a
book was any good by the way you didn't notice the L
rumbling overhead. Or maybe I'd iron Mac's shirts for
him, but it was hotter than hell in that little kitchen and
you couldn't work up much enthusiasm about putting a
gloss on collars that the Lipstick Lady of Torresdale was
going to mess up. Matter of fact she faded out of the picture about then. Myrtle, who always did detective work
on the laundry basket, said she was sure Mac had fallen
overboard somewhere in muddy water. We couldn't figure
how, but we kidded him about it and he had to come
clean. He and his girl had gone for a picnic to Neshaminy
Falls and hired a canoe to paddle up the creek. I guess
likely he made a pass at her, or else the other way round.
Anyway neither of them knew much about marine life
and they tipped over. He pulled her out through a swamp
and she had to spread herself in a hayfield to dry. The
girl was so sore she wanted Mac to pay for a new outfit. He
asked her how much and she said fifty dollars. Then Mac
got sore. Pop advised him to stick to Earth Moving instead of canoeing. Myrtle, who entered into any kind of
household argument, said the girl must have lost more
than clothes if she asked that much. "Those mill-hands
never had fifty dollars' worth of clothes on 'em in their
lives."

"Did you take advantage of her?" Pop asks.

"I bet it was vantage even," I said. Mac was shocked,
and Pop tickled. "Kitty, you're smart."

In spite of heat, and the smell of Myrtle in the room
and the smell of chlorides in the yard it was never dull

106

in that old kitchen. Pop would be sitting in the wicker chair under the wisteria vine wondering how he could wait until Mac got home to fetch something from the speakeasy. Myrtle and I wouldn't do that errand for him. When Myrtle had something on her mind she wanted to get across to Pop, but she didn't quite like to say it direct, she'd tell it to me in a way he could hear it. Or she'd wait till she was in the john and grumble it in there. I guess she had a notion that what you say in the closet is kind of privileged utterance.

I have the ironing board across the washtubs so I can look out the window and get a breath of air. I hear Myrtle down below in the backhouse. "That ole man better git less sociable with liquor. He ought to be ashame to encourage bootleggin' on Orthodox Street. I take note there's two ends to that street, there's a speakeasy one end and a unsane asylum the other. He better stick in the middle where that Quaker Meetin' holds forth."

I made a chink in the vine so I could look down from above and see poor old Pop's hand holding his newspaper. If it was shaking too much I'd go down and talk to him. Myrtle brings clothes in from the line and sprinkles them on the big kitchen table. That was a grand old table, white as bread from scrubbing, it was the kind the top lifts up and turns it into a settle. When the top was down I could crawl underneath when I was small and lie hidden on the bench part, watching people's feet. I remember how fast Mother's used to move, and the smell of hot jam. You got to move fast when you're boiling preserves. Myrtle's feet were quite different, a comical flat shape with the heel sticking out behind. They would forget I was under there. Once I called out "Why are colored people's feet such a funny shape?" Myrtle was so frightened she dropped the coal scuttle.

"Lucky I didn't drop that bucket on 'em, they'd be funnier yet. Honey, them's perseverin' feet. Feet tromps out flat wuhkin' in de vineyard."

We used that table for meals. It was handy, over in the far end of the kitchen where the little window looked down the side passage. Anybody came to the door we could see them before they rang and "arrange our defences" Pop said. Under that window was the oldfashioned ice-chest, the kind where the top raises up. Mac could make a long arm from the table right into the ice-chest for a bottle of beer. Over by the stove was the sink, the kind you never see any more, tall curl-over copper spigots. That kind of sink was made for gentry, Pop said, the tall curved pipes so as not to break fine china in washing it.

There's a cursing and a creaking of wicker down under the arbor, and the clatter of a pipe fallen on the brick walk. I go out and give Pop a hand to ratch up from his chair. He'd go through any kind of misery to hobble round the yard, pinch off faded hollyhocks by the back fence. While he was doing that I'd fix him some hot tea and paper-thin slices of brown bread and butter. Butter with bread spread on it, Myrtle called it.

You tell that black woman, he says, there's one advantage in being Irish. If you can't get whiskey you can always make out with a cup of tea.

They both enjoyed kidding, and like sensitive people do, they knew where to stop. Myrtle said once "If yo' Pop called me nigger I'd be like to walk out and quit.

But when he say Black Woman I know he mean it fo'
compliment."

So Pop and I take our cup of tea in the arbor, and
Myrtle has hers leaning on the washtubs over our heads,
and calling down through the trellis. Sometimes Lena
McTaggart came in about that time of the afternoon. She
wasn't so bad when she was away from Nellie Simmons,
and she brought her mah-jong set. When I was talking
to her of course my mind went back to high school and
I'd get a bit mixed up inside. I didn't quite know whether
I was an Illinois girl or a Philadelphia girl. Then Mac
would come home, and Myrtle left to look after her own
family. I'd set out supper for the men, and Pop and Mac
and Griscom Street were all my world and a good one.

11

You can't clean up all outdoors, Uncle Elmer grunted as he savaged over the lawn, trying to collect every stray leaf and twig and rubbish. Aunt Hattie called it taking out blackheads. He had a permanent callus on his finger from using the clippers on the edge of the concrete sidewalk. The grass was trimmed off as sharp as one of those corn belt haircuts.

Unless you've gone through a Middlewest high school graduation you don't know how the world really can be cleaned up and regulated and shampooed to a climax. What Nazis some of those prairie folks would make if things happened that way. How they eat up parades, bar-b-q's, mass doings with flags and silver bands and reassuring statements.

1928 was the first class that had its whole four years in the new building and our graduation was a honey. Maybe someone should write a history of those new high schools that were being built all over the U.S.A., it would be interesting. That was the time the Real Estate Board figured the only serious problem was how everybody on Thanksgiving Avenue was going to have a two-car garage without making the street narrower. From Easter on all of us kids were caught in a rising flood of events. I wouldn't be surprised it's good for people to feel so important; we were regular little fascists. Molly and Peg Ramsauer and I were taken into Gammagam, a secret society that was under solemn pledge to elevate the tone of the female side of the school. Fedor was editor of *Harvest,* the senior annual, and he made us work like dogs. We tramped the town digging up ads from the merchants. It was a thrill when Molly and I cracked down on the Mode in Paris and sold them a full page on the promise we would buy our graduation dresses (white net) there. Some of the girls who had fat legs tried to start a movement in favor of longer dresses, but it didn't get anywhere because of course they wouldn't admit what was worrying them.

Part of the Gammagam pledge was that before being initiated you had to say if you had done anything to damage the school ethics. Like a fool I took this seriously and when the committee hidden behind the screen asked me the question I admitted that at the Princeton game Freddie Unruh kissed me back of the bandstand. I could hear them groaning, pretending to be shocked, then they couldn't help laughing and said Shall we tell her? The point was that most of the kids in Gammagam had been kissed by Freddie; usually at Clubfoot Lake, which was his romantic specialty. I don't guess anybody east of the Alleghanies knows how much innocent kissing can be done in a field of tall corn, except it tickles your ears, the corn tassels. We were all a pushover for Freddie who was our triple threat—football, baseball, and in a coupé. He wasn't much threat in his lessons, he got the idea of wearing dark glasses because he said the light hurt his eyes but actually it was so he could take a little nap in Latin class. He always carried a comb in his vest, you could tell when he was awake because he'd run it through his hair. Mr Sheldon said once, "Freddie if you'd comb the text as faithfully as you do your hair I could give you a better mark." Freddie didn't worry, he was a star halfback and already had a scholarship offer from a State University.

Reminds me how I always had to explain to Wyn that Princeton didn't mean New Jersey. Out that way there's only one Princeton, Illinois. They were our big rival in debating and football and baseball. When the Princeton high school band went into uniform we nearly went crazy until we got one too. We had a girl drum major in silk shorts long before anybody else thought of it; that was Jess Cornish's idea, it was her only contribution to education. Some people said though that it had been done up in Minnesota, some of those big milk white Swedes. But Jess could twirl the old pelvis like a rotary churn, it was really good to see her stepping while the kids would yell:—

Hiliga hoop, hiliga hoop
Princeton, Princeton, in the soup!
S-O-U-P, C-O-U-P, Soup, Soup, Soup!

Seems funny, but I really went to town on my studies. Some ways I was a keep-to-myself sort of kid; both in Frankford with Pop and in school at Manitou I had a feeling I was a little outside of what the crowd was doing, sort of watching the game like what Mark Eisen calls a kibitzer. But I got interested in the work and had more than the 15 units needed for entrance at Prairie. Uncle

112

and Auntie offered to put me through college and old Pop was awfully tickled. What is really comical, I was supposed to be literary, which got me into a tough chore. Every member of the class had to have a quotation to go under his or her picture in *Harvest*. I got Molly to help me because she had a better line on most of the kids than I did. Good old Miss Elliman saved our lives by turning us loose on some dictionary of literary wisecracks. We took it home from the school library and got about 200 index cards from Mr Scharf's store, one for each boy and girl in the class. Then we copied out a nifty quotation on each card and had a grand time finding individuals to fit them to. Molly wanted to hang on me "There is no frigate like a book," which Miss Elliman was always saying, but I wouldn't stand for it. We both rather hankered for "Her pure and eloquent blood spoke in her cheeks," but Molly gave it to me for my habit of blushing. We had one quotation left over and couldn't find anyone to label with it so Molly took it herself: "When pain and anguish wring the brow, a ministering angel thou." There were a lot of opportunities in this job to hurt people's feelings but we managed to avoid them. Our biggest flop we discovered just in time. We were so fond of Fedor Vassilly and admired him so much, we thought the perfect piece for him would be   .

> Come one, come all, this rock shall fly
> From its firm base as soon as I.

Also we remembered the incident of the Magnetic Rock. Then, when it was already in proof, we realized this would look like an allusion to poor Fedor's aluminum leg. We

113

had to make a quick change, so we took one of the female quotes, I forget what, changed *her* to *him* and let it ride.

There was the Senior Prom with its terrible problems. Fedor embarrassed me by asking me to go as his partner, which of course I couldn't do because Molly was supposed to be his girl. Fedor's girl always had a perfectly swell time at any kind of hop because he couldn't dance and so all the best dancers made a point of asking his lady. Freddie Unruh asked me and I was tempted because I knew that would cause heartburn among some of the Glamor Girls; but since I got the Gammagam lowdown on Freddie I wasn't so keen. I went with Fireplug Mason who was Lyddie's twin brother. "But not any longer," he said, "now she's got an appendicitis scar." "Of course if he's as literal as that," Lyddie said, "he never was."

The real problem was to get a partner for Trudy Weissenkorn. None of the boys wanted to be saddled with her, she was heavy on the hoof and a tough one to shake. But it had to be fixed and Peg and Molly and I held a meeting in the Physics Lab one day at lunch. We summoned Freddie and Fedor and Fireplug and said we'd all three walk out on them and go to the movies instead if they didn't get some boy to make the grade with Trudy. There was mercury and kerosene in a glass tube for some physics experiment, and Freddie said most of the boys would sooner drink it than get stuck with Trudy. I got sore and said what the hell was the good of reading all that Lady of the Lake and Sir Scott if they couldn't practise a little chivalry? Molly must have been a bit haywire with what we had been through on literary quotations because she grabbed the tube and said she'd drink it herself if they

114

couldn't be gentlemen.

The boys were scared and it worked. As a matter of fact they came through in good style and gave Trudy a rush, and she never knew. At least I hope not, though sometimes I wondered why she gave me that alligator-skin purse as a graduating present. We had all agreed not to give each other anything.

Warming up for a high school graduation in Illinois would be good training for international diplomats. I wonder if anyone takes Harvard and Yale commencements as hard as those kids do their diploma stuff in Manitou. And were we sore, the clerk of the Board of Education fell sick or something and we were handed dummy diplomas that hadn't been lettered out; just blank rolls of paper tied with ribbon, and we were tipped off not to open them in public. Of course all the parents wanted to look at them as we stood at the reception afterward, and the kids had to make all sorts of excuses. Mr Sheldon, the grand old Latin teacher, who knew about it, winked to me in private and said "Kitty, remember your diploma's a blank sheet of paper, that's the most valuable suggestion in your whole course." I didn't quite know what he meant but I get it now.

One of the tough spots was something you wouldn't expect, Uncle Elmer was on the Board of Education and was to give out prizes so he had to wear his evening clothes. That was always a crisis because he needed a whole bathroom to himself for I don't know how long. He said he had to lie in soak in a hot tub for at least half an hour to get his beard soft enough to shave. With Auntie in one bathroom and Uncle in the other there was hardly time enough for me to get dressed properly. Auntie got peeved at last and started hammering on the door. "Who's going to be graduated, you or Kitty?" Uncle was in there mumbling to himself because he had to make a speech. I think he was disappointed because I didn't get any of the prizes. But I was one of those who had to stand up when our names were read out as Gammagams for High Moral Tone. I was never so ashamed. All the graduates sat on a sort of grandstand built up on the stage. None of us were used to such high heels and each girl as she stood up pretty nearly took a dive. The pure and eloquent blood spoke that time all right, and I wondered if Freddie was grinning.

Uncle's speech was awful too. He had to get in something about Standing With Reluctant Feet.

There weren't any reluctant feet when the Board of Education got through with us and the reception for parents and families was over. The gang got together out at Clubfoot Lake where they had a dance platform right by the water and Gammagams were no longer responsible for community ideals. It was queer to feel all of a sudden so grown-up in our heads and yet so light on our feet. Those wide swishy dresses do make your legs feel independent. But it was really a very orderly little party, somehow we felt the world hadn't changed as much as we thought it was going to. There was a fellow there from Peoria who bootlegged a jug of rum and we all had a shot in our coke which brightened us a bit. But the high school crowd is pretty decent as far as I ever noticed, except when some old goat from the Board of Education itself tries to slip over something swift. The short skirts we all

wore those days had them bothered. But a boy like Freddie
Unruh, all he wants is a little lipstick. They always say it
tastes like raspberry, and that's just what they get if they
act fresh.

Maybe one reason the crowd was so well behaved was
because Jess Cornish was out at the Clubfoot Pavilion. It
was the fellow she was with who brought the demijohn
of rum. We all got a kick out of Jess because she really
was stunning and had that don't-give-a-damn touch, but
also we knew, the ways kids do, that she was headed for
all kinds of grief. She came to our table and gave us one
of her big shiny mascara winks and looked over the nice
boys in their duck trousers. "Don't let any of these men
go too far," she said, kidding. "If they act up, ask why
they haven't shaved lately. They'll be so flattered they'll
forget everything else."

Of course that made the boys sore because they'd all
been busy with the pin-feathers and hadn't expected the
topic to come up again for at least a week. But they
couldn't help following Jess with their eyes as she swung
round the floor with that Peoria pimp. We hadn't ever
seen cheek-to-cheek dancing up to that time, and Fedor,
who sat out watching things, made a good crack. "I understand now why she worries about shaving."

After that one acknowledgement of our existence Jess
paid no attention, she seemed to be selling her partner a
bill of goods of the most confidential nature. She sort of
spoiled some of the good fellowship of the party, because
there was something about her that bothered us.

We all figured we knew everything there was to be
known; but if you're smart you don't hold up your hand

in class and ask to be called on.

I think some of us would have liked a stroll through the grove, just for the quietness of it and think it over in pairs, but Jess had gone off through the trees with that calculating laugh of hers and it took away some of the flavor. What one bitch can do to a bunch of nice people.

I didn't realize I remembered Jess being there. All I thought I remembered was how pretty the girls were, in their white floating dresses under Chinese lanterns hung on the rafters. The music in the pavilion was a big victrola, which tangled up every now and then with the mechanical piano in the Log Cabin dump. Sometimes I'd sit out with Fedor while Molly was dancing and I told him she was the prettiest of the crowd because she hadn't had her hair shingled like most of us. "What I like," he said, "is the way she parts it with that little bend in the middle of the parting. That's really subtle." I didn't tell him Molly has a cowlick, Nicolai himself couldn't part it straight. I love it, it's so much a part of herself and her unexpectedness. Like those dimples on her knees that would drive men crazy if they had as much sense as they think they have. But those things are her business, not mine—or even poor Fedor's, as far as I know.

After Jess went away and quit trying to tickle herself by highhatting the kids, the dancing was smooth. We must have run grooves in that Blue Room record. Dancing is wonderful training for girls, it's the first way you learn to guess what a man is going to do before he does it. You find yourself laughing and say "I'm having fun." With the right kind of partner you don't have to "follow," you know with perfect sureness every move he'll make.

You know it sooner than he does.

Clubfoot isn't much of a lake, at least not by Eastern standards, but there's a good-sized moon that rises over the icehouse and puts a yellow stripe across the water. Freddie thought it would be nice to go swimming and see if we could find where the moon really came from, but we had Fedor along and that was always a good excuse for anything we didn't feel like doing.

Besides, I said, Pattyshells will be sitting up for me, and he's getting old.

12

Pattyshells wasn't the only one who was getting
old. I could tell it in Pop by the way he crabbed about
changes in Philly. The L stairs were too much for him,
but once and a while we'd get on a trolley car and make
the long ride downtown for him to visit his haunts. I
wish I'd listened more to things he said, I could have
learned a lot about the old town. In his big cricketing days
he associated so much with gentry and went around to
the swell taverns, places like Bookbinder's and Boothby's,
and he loved to remember some particular Fish-house
Punch that laid them out in rows; and where to get
Delaware shad and pepperpot and those little pink oyster-
crabs and the Reading Terminal scrapple. But like all
kids my mind was mostly inside my own head and I was
thinking about Me. Molly Scharf and I kept up a big
correspondence about what we were going to do at college that fall.

The Camden Bridge was new then, it always put Pop's
mind on the Camden Ferry. Two big things happened
to him on that ferry. "I saw an old funny fellow with his
beard all sideways in the wind. Kitty, if you think I've

got whiskers you shoulda seen his. He was talkin' to himself and all the kids laughing, they thought he was nuts. His shirt was open and when his beard blew out you could see his neck was dirty, he had a big safety pin where a button was gone. We were all giggling like micks when a fine-looking gent came up to the old boy and says, Mr Whitman, let me tie your shoelaces for you. And he did, yes sir, he stooped right down and fastened the old boy's shoe-ties. I wouldn't be surprised he did it as a lesson to us youngsters. There's something about that in the Bible, about tying up shoestrings. Maybe it means not laughing too quick. Camden Ferry was always lucky for me, I took your mother a ride across the river in one of the new boats, the *Wenonah* I reckon. It was canning season, and the smell of tomatoes was so strong and sweet I proposed to her. Didn't you never notice how she'd wink at me sometimes when we had tomato soup for supper? Jesusgod, that must have been more than forty years ago. Honey, you're too young to know what it's all about. Why the old Jolly Post tavern in Frankford, the one George Washington named on account of a party they pulled when he couldn't get across Frankford Crick, that was tore down the very year you was born. It's almost a pity to be so young, aint it."

I was probably thinking how dumb this kind of talk was but I had forgotten about it when we got out of the trolley. As I was helping him down he said "No, I guess it aint, neither. Kitty, let's go look at the old B & O depot, they aint tore that down yet. That's where your mother and I started for Washington on our honeymoon. I guess that'll stick for a while, the old B & O don't throw

121

things around like the Pennsy does."

But mostly he didn't go out much that summer. Mac was married now and living in Tioga; he got a good opening in a big radio factory. That was how we got a radio at trade discount, we set it up in the kitchen and Pop would sit and listen for hours. But he never got so he could do something else at the same time, and when he wanted to look over his cricket pictures or read the *Ledger* we had to turn it off. Also he said he missed hearing Myrtle sing to herself while she was working. "She don't always know I'm listening. Myrtle, what was that song *Take care, boys, look out for my vaccination?*"

I knew he was a bit shaky when he slowed down on whiskey and even got a kind of religious streak, used to go round to Friends' Meeting. "I 'been down a lot of back-alleys in my time but it's good to come back to Orthodox Street," he said. He was great on the subject of the Sesqui, which was a terrible flop. That pleased him because he liked to remember the Centennial.

"Listen, kid," said Mac, "the old man's sure getting soft, he even said something nice about John Wanamaker."

I didn't get much amusement that summer but I didn't miss it, I was busy reading the Prairie College catalogue and keeping house and once and a while a movie and a dish of ice cream with some of the neighborhood kids. There was a bunch of us dug out our old roller skates and used to go up to the big pavements near the high school on warm evenings. Smart alecs laughed at us, said roller skates were just for grammar school children, but I noticed that after while everybody else took it up. I wouldn't be

surprised the roller skating craze really started in Frankford. One of the good things about Philly is, people do
the way they feel like and don't care whether they're
behind the times or ahead. Wyn said if you get far
enough behind one procession you'll likely find yourself
ahead of the next one because all processions move in a
circle. Then there must be some procession you're a long
way ahead of, I told him, if we could only figure out what
it is.

I used to trim up the back yard, Pop was too rickety
to do it. There was a hot little corner down back of the
hollyhocks, I guess I was kind of dreamy, I used to like to
stand in there and get what I called the be-alone feeling.
In the house I was all the time right up against Pop or
Myrtle or somebody or something. You need that be-alone
feeling. When I had it I didn't feel quite right about going
back to Manitou, maybe I ought to stay home and look
after the old man. But he had set his heart on my getting
a chance at college.

Mac said he didn't think I ought to miss it. Mac was in
great shape that year. Come to think of it, he was just the
same age I am now, and 1928 must have been a good year
to be that age. He married a goodlooker, who also had
sense. Even Pop liked Martha. "She's got a level head and
bumps on her chest. There's too many girls nowadays just
the other way round." Mac had forgotten all about the
Torresdale Trollop and we never mentioned her. He said
him and Martha would come over regularly to see Pop
was O.K., and of course Myrtle was there. I didn't like
the idea of Pop being alone at night but Mac said he
could afford to get a phone put in. Mac figured that all

123

business problems were solved. Radio was red hot, and their machine he said was the Tin Lizzie of music.

Then I got that form letter from the Dean of Women at Prairie saying freshmen would report such and such a date for the week of Registration and Orientation.

Wyn always loved to have me tell about my College Education. Because that week of Registration and Orientation, and a purple felt banner, was about all I got.

Molly met me at the station in Manitou. We had the feeling she and I often have, that even if you could talk as fast as the French you wouldn't get out all the ideas in your head. Molly had fixed things so we could room together in Selfridge, the old jigsaw dorm for women, and worked out a schedule of everything we had to do. We rushed round from registrar to dean and physical examination and course enrollment and some goofy quiz in I.Q. The idea of that was to show how little scholarly aptitude you have before college takes hold of you. The big entrance hall at Selfridge at the bottom of the stairway was a regular scrimmage, girls all unpacking their trunks and carrying stuff up to the rooms. Freshmen always take the damnedest lot of rubbish with them when they go to college first time, things they think they can't do without. We were all toting up piles of favorite books and overstuffed kewpie dolls and window drapes and cushions and photograph albums. Just as Helga the muscular house matron was going through the hall somebody's armful toppled over and she was beaned by a copy of *A Girl of the Limberlost* that fell from the third floor. She only shook that beautiful blonde head and said she was glad it wasn't Webster Unabridged.

124

We sweated all our junk up three flights. Molly said, the original name of the place was Prairie Manual Labor College and we were living up to it. We had all our stuff arranged and Uncle and Auntie down to look it over while most of the other girls were still waiting for Helga to tell them what to do. Molly was a born decorator, she made our room look swell with our special mascots on each bed. Hers was a Winnie Pooh that was definitely super, she'd picked it up in Chicago and nobody else at Manitou had seen one yet.

I had studied the catalogue so carefully that when Dean Bascom gave us her opening blast on Ethics for College Women it seemed like old stuff. There was a bit of a riot about it afterward, because two of the sophomore boys had got in on a bet, dressed up as girls. Of course all that chat about personal hygiene, purity and blind dates, was supposed to be rather confidential.

It was a good talk. I can hear Bascom telling us what all we were going to learn in our academic career. There was self-control, and democratic social relations, an item-ized budget and not too much lipstick and what to do about sororities. She had all the answers in the back of the book. What sounded most educational was something called Extracurricular Load. Molly whispered, That means carrying your stuff upstairs.

It was a big time to be starting at Prairie. The college had just figured out culture into streamlined units, and was sort of airconditioning itself. Respect for tradition with a forward look was the idea. Looking forward there was the new library, just finished; we went and looked at it in reverence and thought of all the fine books we were going to read. Looking backward was the original Sitting Room in Old Founders which was kept just the way it was when Abe Lincoln sat in a rocking chair and figured out a debate he was going to make. It seems like every time Lincoln made a speech in that neighborhood somebody was on hand to contradict him. It's great country for argument. Anyhow the historical Sitting Room still smelled about 1850, sort of lacking in personal hygiene. I don't suppose those old troupers like Lincoln and Douglas had much chance to dust off their clothes, but Molly was mad about the period horsehair furniture. There was a pageant planned, they were going to act out Lincoln and Douglas and everybody appear in costumes. So as a fact the best I remember of my ten days at college was getting ready a crinoline I never wore and a couple of classes in American Literature Before 1870. Wyn said, "As far as I can see you got everything in American Literature down to Cotton Mather." All I remember of Cotton Mather was that he wrote something about magnolia.

The fees were paid, and the notebooks bought, and all the freshmen took a drag at a cigarette in the smoking room just opened for women. The historical pageant was to take place next day, several hundred alumni in costume, and even the Q railroad promised to throw a little less soot on the campus, for one afternoon. Molly and I were up in the room, wearing our new kimonos and feeling pretty bohemian and top of the world. There was a frightful roar outside and a hunk of raw cabbage came whistling through the open window and a paste of ancient carrots flopped on the sill. Some of the boys had amused themselves by loading up the old Civil War cannon that stood on the lawn outside pointing right at Selfridge Hall. They filled it with dead vegetables, packed in a big charge of gunpowder, and touched her off. The front of the building was a macedoine salad, a lot of windows were busted and of course we thought it was a gallant and care-free touch. While the girls were all running round in a thrill of outrage and Mrs Bascom was giving the Dean of Men hell on the phone, my telegram arrived. It was from Mac. Pop had a stroke and I better come home at once.

13

Thank God you don't know beforehand how much you love anything. You don't know till too late, and then because it's too late you've got too much sense to think about it too much. The Q depot at Manitou, for instance. Most always when I took a train at that station it was burning hot weather. You look out from under the shed and see the tracks all run together in a glitter of heat; especially if you've got wetness in your eyes.

Eyes are the last things that dry up. I noticed that with Pop. It was terrible the way he'd lie there, not able to talk, but his eyes wide open and every once and a while one eye would start leaking. We always thought his mind was working same as usual but it couldn't come through in words so he'd cry a little. The tears didn't have far to go before they got lost in his whiskers. Mac wanted to have him shaved, thought he'd be more comfortable, but when the barber came into the room Pop looked terrible and groaned so I made them go away. For a long time Pop couldn't do much but groan and growl, but when he came out with a good Jesusgod we knew he was getting better.

I'm thinking now of the Q depot. Uncle and Auntie

128

drove me down to the train and Molly came. Of course we were kidding ourselves that I'd be back and I guess maybe I thought so too. Aunt Hattie was in such a skirmish about my catching the train she spilled lavender water all over her blouse, you could scarcely notice the old soot and cinders of the depot and even the sandwiches and chicken legs she packed for me smelled of lavender. She was upset because she forgot to put in any salt. "You won't need salt," Uncle said; "she's wept all over 'em."

The toughest part of all that long trip was the ride from Manitou to Chicago. The first stop the train makes is Plautus, it was funny to look over the scorching prairie toward the Debaugh farm and think of winter evenings we had sleighrides on those roads. The Weissenkorns had an old buffalo robe which certainly had a tang to it. Molly said afterward maybe that buffalo smell is an aphrodisiac, the way the boys used to carry on in a sleigh.

Not so far out of Chicago the train stops at Aurora, and something happened that was very important for me. I felt mighty blue, naturally, not only about poor old Pop but about having to rip up and quit college. Just after we pulled out of Aurora I noticed a lady in the vestibule trying to open the door into the car. She was carrying a wirehair terrier under one arm, a suitcase and a bunch of flowers in the other, and had set down a smart-looking black hatbox. I was busy with my own thinking and sort of said to myself, Let someone else help her. There were plenty of men who could have done it. But no one did, and I was ashamed to let her keep wrestling with the door so I hopped up and opened it for her and grabbed her suitcase.

She was very grateful. She said in a French accent she had a wrangle with the conductor on account of the dog. The conductor said he must ride in the baggage, and she wouldn't stand for it. He was only a pup and she didn't want him frightened. Then the conductor said she could take him back to the smoker, but no one offered to help and she was struggling through the train with her stuff.

I still don't understand why all the men in the car didn't run to open that door for her; except that maybe she looks so damn competent you know there isn't anything she can't manage. I think the first thing I noticed, as I carried her bags through for her, was the red heels on her slippers. They exactly matched her lips and fingernails and the dog's collar and leash. As I've often said to her since, I'm surprised Pfui's nails weren't varnished red too.

In one of the fairy tales I read as a kid there was a maidservant who had red heels, it made a great impression on me.

One of the things that was interesting about her was Pfui's complete confidence. Wirehairs can be pretty jumpy, and she'd only had him a couple of days, but he sat there and looked at her in a satisfied way. He didn't know what it was all about but he knew it was going to be all right. She said that French people get along well with dogs.

She pulled out a little red enamel box which was a combination compact and cigarette case. She offered me a smoke but I was too bashful, also I wanted to get back to my own seat on account of my stuff and it was only a few minutes to the terminal. I asked if I could help her when we got there, but she said no, there would be a porter. When I saw her going through the big hall at Union Station the redcap made the final note in that little color-scheme.

Uncle had wired a reservation for me on the Limited. As that long afternoon darkened I felt terribly sad about everything and I guess I was crying and trying to hide it by turning my head toward the window on one of those fat little white pillows they give you. Not exactly crying, I don't cry easily, I wish I did; but just what Wyn calls drizzling a bit. Then somebody was speaking to me. It was the same lady.

"But it's my little friend. Something is wrong? You help me, now I help you."

She sat down in my section and I got a whiff of that wonderful faint sweetness-with-a-sting. Everyone knows it now, the Olympia, she named it for that picture we have in the office. Just then it hurt, and for a moment I lost control. I just blubbered.

"You smell like the front porch at home," I said. Of course I was thinking of that coldcream and brandy love-liness of the old white rambler, and Pop creaking in his rumpsprung wicker chair.

I guess it was one of the silliest things I ever said, and one of the most eventful. She told me afterward it showed I had "educated feelings."

She sat quiet and just looked at me. Even in my Scotch-Irish mist I could see her checking over all my Mode in Paris freshman outfit and my poor little smitch of lip-stick which I'd just started to use.

"You come in my boudoir," she said, "and tell me all about it. Then we will have dinner. I was on my way to the restaurant car."

131

She had the drawing room at the other end of the same car. It was incredible what she had done to that little place. It smelled like her, it looked like her, and she even had the porter calling her Madame. She must have paid someone a notorious tip because she had the upper berth made up for Pfui. You could hardly see the ugly green and cocoa-colored settee for pretty negligees and a Vionnet dressing-case.

It's grand when you're on a spot to have somebody take charge. I gaped at her, I guess, but she was quite calm and commanding. "You go in the dooblavay," she said. I didn't even know what it was; French for the john, the French word for W. She made me sit down on the toilet seat, put a towel round my neck and went over me. She took off my hat and brushed my hair, touched me up with some sort of cologne, washed off the lipstick and did it over with her own, and then gave me a drink from a little crystal flask. I can still hear her saying "Tronkee" (that's what it sounded like) when I tried to speak.

"Now come out and sit yourself," she said. "We take dinner in here and we talk. But first regard yourself in the glass."

If I was thinking anything I suppose I had a dumb feeling this is the kind of thing that doesn't happen. But I was still human enough to be wondering what I looked like. I hope I always am. It seemed almost a pity not to be going into the diner where people could see me. The right kind of sachet and freshener and lipstick can do more than theology for most of us.

"Tell me, then," she said. "And we eat some soup. Soup and cosmetiques, they cure anything."

I tried to. I told her about the old man, and about Griscom Street, and Manitou, and how I had just got steamed up about getting an education and now I would never go through college. As I talked I could see Pfui's paws hanging down over the edge of the berth above, and the Olympia perfume came in waves from Delphine's silk things hanging alongside us over the settee. Pfui whined after a while and at some station, Crestline maybe, we got out and took him for a walk alongside the train. He smelled just the way everything else did.

"Pfui go to bed, you go to bed, we go to bed all three," she said as we got back on the train. I could see the porter admiring the red heels as she stepped up on the yellow footstool. "Don't you worry. Your old man, he has had the good life and the happy life, he is more lucky than he knows. Remember, there is much education that doesn't happen in colleges. I give you my card, some day you come and see me in New York."

When she talked English somehow you could feel the French behind it, and because she had to think to say what she wanted, it sounded more important.

That was the way I first met Delphine Detaille. I did want to tell her how I felt, but all I could say was "I wish I had done better with Abbé Constantin." That gave her a big laugh.

"Even Abbé Constantin did not know it all," she said. "There is a great deal of living and if you are worth while you get hurt. There is an American advice, Be yourself."

Mac met me at North Philly and said they thought Pop would pull through. When we got in a taxi he said "Gosh, kid, if the Middle West smells like that I could take a load of it."

14

THAT LITTLE FLASH FADED JUST THE WAY THE OLYMPIA faded from my fingers as soon as I got back to Griscom Street. Delphine has something in her formula that keeps it from sticking. She always says a perfume must *evanesce;* she makes a cunning little hiss as she says it. "Keety, parfum is like an emotion; it must know how to say goodbye. You must be able to get rid of same when the mood changes. Can you say that for me in the language of advertising, not more than ten words please."

The minute I saw dear old Pop everything else went out of my mind. He was pretty sick. Some kind of blood-clot had been travelling round his system and landed in his speech center.

"I can't make out what he wants to say," Mac warned me. "Something about an owl. Crazy stuff. He mumbles so I can't get it."

Pop opened his eyes and looked at me like he was empty. He was in the big brass bed in the front bedroom, the one we all came out of. In forty years he had worn a hollow in one side of it. It wasn't any use to try to move him over, he'd roll back. "If you've slept with a woman most of your life you don't try to lie in the middle of the bed."

"Owl," he whispered. "Wise old owl."

I knew right away what he was thinking. I was near bawling, but I managed to grin and say it:—

"A wise old owl sat on an oak,
And the more he saw the less he spoke."

I said this into his hairy ear and it hurt me that his beard smelt of medicine instead of whiskey. He nodded and his eyes brightened. "That's right. Wise old owl, sat on oak. Good girl, Kitty. Kitty wise old owl."

That was a rhyme he used to quote to me when I was a kid. "Fine for you," said Mac when we went downstairs. "Gee, I thought I'd go nuts trying to figure what he wanted."

"I never should have gone away. It was selfish of me."

"Don't be silly, kid. The old man wanted you to go. Besides I think he got off easier than we thought at first. Maybe that aint a real bloodclot, I have a hunch it's partly a boozeclot. The old bum went out on a toot a few days ago, he got into an uproar with some of the boys at the ginmill, arguing about Al Smith and Hoover."

"You go on home and look after Martha," I said. They were expecting a baby. "This is my job."

Maybe I really was good medicine for Pop, the way Dr Bartrum said. After a few days we were able to let the nurse go. We had to, she annoyed the old man because she was so homely and as his speech cleared I was scared she'd hear him crabbing because she was fat. He said he'd bite off one of her rivets if she leaned her bust over his face

135

that way. Dr Bartrum said it was remarkable what a come-back he was making; but remember, he added, at 67 you don't come back all the way. Don't let him get excited, keep him in bed as much as you can. If he wants to get downstairs after lunch it's all right.

We soon got into routine. Myrtle was wonderful, Pop minded her better than anyone else. Getting him down-stairs was a problem; if it wasn't done just right he got jit-ters. Myrtle used to take him sort of pickaback on her broad shoulders. "Honeychile, you don't spend all dese yeahs at de washtubs widout gettin' hefty." He liked to sit in the kitchen so we put the old wicker chair in the corner where he could see out the little window and watch what Myrtle took out of the ice-chest. He'd stay there for hours while Myrtle went on working, talking or crooning to herself. Once and a while his eye would study the pantry cupboard where the whiskey bottle used to be. "Mister, you don' need to speculate dat closet any mo'. Ain' nothin' there but groceries, ain' no Pope's tele-phone."

Maybe sick people would all live longer if they sat in kitchens. There's something alive about a kitchen, the way it smells and sounds and feels. Afternoons I was in my bedroom upstairs working on the typewriter, I'd hear Myrtle mumbling away and once and a while Pop answer back. "No *suh,* cullud folks don' drink the way white folks does. Dey don' *need* to drink dat way, cullud people's heart ain' sunk so far down. Don' need to fish fo' it wid whiskey." Pop says something I don't hear, and Myrtle cracks right back: "Don' talk to me 'bout Repeal. You been repealing it yo'self fo' ten yeahs. Dat's what put you

136

where yo' is now. No, don' you holler fer Miss Kitty, let dat honeychile get on wid her wuhk. Mister, don' you black-woman me, ole black woman takin' good care of you."

Mornings, while he was still asleep, I hurried to the Maggie Street station and took the L downtown to business school. I got in three hours classwork before noon, then called up to see if everything was all right. Myrtle always had things under control. There was a little gang of us from the school had a drugstore lunch together on Market Street. Every way of life seems to have its own drink; our shorthand squad specialized on Black and White sodas. We were all pretty serious about it, also pretty damn discouraged by the time we got to Dipthongs and Disjoined Suffixes. That's when you find yourself dreaming shorthand and wake up figuring out the symbol for Indianapolis or San Francisco. Or maybe you fell into a doze in class and trying to catch up you take a page of dictation on top of what you wrote already. Then you're dished. But about then some of the boys were writing out corny limericks in symbols to see if we could read them back, maybe that was a help.

Being in the half time crowd, after lunch I did a little shopping and got home about the time Pop came downstairs. If the weather was good we helped him out in the yard. Sometimes from the window upstairs I practised taking down his and Myrtle's conversation, to work up speed. But Myrtle got wise to this. "Miss Kitty, don' you smirch yo' notebook wid dat dirty ole talk. He say the damnedest things, he think 'em up just to tease me. I had him out in the sunshine, I ask him how is everything? He says he's bleachin' like a dogturd."

I got my school work done in between this and that. Of course I had to transcribe the dictation they'd given us in the morning, and do exercises in abbreviations and copy out symbols for special business phrases. After Myrtle went home I'd get supper, maybe read to Pop a while or we'd listen to the radio, sometimes Mac and Martha came over from Tioga. Pop got quite lively about bedtime and liked to talk about things that had happened to him. We noticed he talked a good deal about Mother. "When we were first married, we took a trip up in Pike County and found a place called Twin Lakes. There was two little lakes with a narrow strip of land between. It was hot and we wanted to go in swimming but we didn't have any bathing suits and we was ashamed to go in together. So your Mom took one pond and I took the other and we had a good swim. Back in those days people was awful sheepish in the daytime. It was getting a job to work nights that killed my modesty." I guess it was Mac's baby coming along that got him thinking in a family way. "I guess most of us aint kind enough to a good wife. It's hard to know; men are selfish buggers. Even some of these Quakers is pretty indifferent with their womenfolks. There aint many women killed with kindness in Philly."

No matter how sore the old guy got me sometimes, I admit he was always good company. Some of his stories he told too often, and Mac and I would wink at each other to hear him hoke them up as he went along. They always got better. The one about the rubber doormat on Frankford Avenue got to be quite a Wild West number. Mother had a new dress; she was going by an open doorway just after the sidewalk had been hosed one hot morning and the storekeeper without looking outside threw down a big doormat. It spattered dirty water all over her good clothes. The way Pop first told it, the man was very decent and paid to have the dress cleaned. But now it got to be a yarn in which the man was rude and Pop went there and threatened to beat him up. They went into a clinch and were taken to the station house. That was the old man's way of justifying himself for some of Mother's hard times. I guess maybe telling lies in honor of a lady isn't the worst kind of chivalry.

He was always tickled about the time he mended a broken rosebud with adhesive tape. "It was that big pink La France rose, that was your Mom's favorite bush. The biggest bud got broke in the stalk, and she carried on about it. That bush come with her from Germantown; brought a lot of rose-lice with it, too. Her old man never knew nothing about how to treat flowers. Anyhow I straightened it up with surgical tape. Mother said it wouldn't work, but it did. When it come to flower I put it in a creamjug on her dresser. She was mighty pleased. Now I'm the broken rosebud myself."

If he thought he was going to pull some pathos on us he was mistaken. Mac and I laughed and I said, "Rosebuds don't have whiskers like that. I'm going to get in the barber and have you pruned."

Myrtle too was good for more laughs than she knew about. One day she had to leave before I got home, one of her daughters had a miscarriage. She left a note for me: "Miss Kitty, theres mice in the Popes panty closet, better get some trap cheese." I told Molly about this in one of the long letters we exchanged, and she still calls her lingerie drawer her panty closet.

It must have been funny to see me trying to ease the old man off to bed, because I'd be tired as hell by ten o'clock when he was feeling talkative. I read him the sleepiest things I could find in the *Ledger,* where there was plenty to choose from, but they only put him in mind of adventures of his own and I'd pass into a stupor. At last he'd say, "Well, Kitty, give me the three steps of decency." That's the three steps you're supposed to go along with a friend who's leaving. I'd help him upstairs and fill his pipe so he'd have it ready to smoke in the morning—and likely burn more holes in the sheets. Then I'd go back to the typewriter and wonder what those damn symbols meant.

I must have been rather a solemn old owl for a kid of eighteen. But I knew that if and when anything happened the pension would stop, there wasn't much insurance, and I'd got to be ready to back up to the hairbrush. . . .

15

. . . Backing up to the hairbrush is what Molly calls it when we sit down for a Milkman's Matinee—which is coffee and cigarettes at midnight and hair down all over the place.

I wonder what we'd do without coffee and cigarettes, the career girls of our generation. As a matter of fact the milkman doesn't get much out of his matinee because the girls take it black. No cream because that adds just one more complication; and no sugar because it's fattening. Something of the strong taste of black coffee has got into our thinking.

Nothing brought home to me the mess the world has got itself into like a piece in the papers a while back. It said the German women couldn't get any coffee, and if they tried to, their government called them Coffee Hyenas.

Molly says, "I suppose if a woman can't get what every woman needs, and tries to, they'd call her a Love Hyena."

There's such a grand lot of comedy running around loose, but who's to enjoy it *with?* Comedy isn't really comedy when you're all by yourself. At least not for women and Irish. Pop used to say, when they talked about settling the mischief between Ireland and England, what will the Irish do if they've got nobody to be Irish *at?* It's like that with women. Every woman in the world has some Irish in her.

Pop comes into the Milkman's Matinee because I use the old Dooner coffee spoons. When Dooner's closed they gave some of their stuff to the faithful customers. Pop got some knives and forks and spoons and a plated fish salver, what they used for the Friday finnan haddie. He must have been a mighty good customer because they also gave him a little painting of a bull terrier that hung back of the bar. When Pop died that went to Denny. I don't think Denny's wife liked it because when I visited them in Cincinnati he had it hanging in his workroom in the basement.

Mac asked why we didn't get a good nude, but Pop said Dooner's was the only bar in America that didn't have any paintings of women. There's too many priests visits the hotel, he said.

Molly and I don't see each other often enough. Once and a while she mails me anything she finds in the papers that strikes her funny, and I do the same. Somehow you find more of it in Chicago papers though. She gets some good laughs out of the advertising. She sent me an ad about an all-in-one that "carries the bosom proudly high and deftly separated." That's us, she said. It's a little too close to facts to amuse me. Sure, I've been deftly separated but I'm not always so proud about it.

Kidding the world is a lonely kind of fun and I don't

think women are exactly cut out for it.

Molly says that because we have to be smart kidding the customers we don't have to take ourselves for a ride. She sells them the latest trick in stylized interiors; settees made out of nickel pipes or padded barroom stools. Every time she puts over a streamlined living room on some rich dame she figures there's another Man been fooled. He'll come home from his downtown clowning, she says, and won't have a chair to sit in. That's as much fun to her as big game hunting. She sees a big Charge Account on the skyline, heavy with bone as a moose, and she drills it right through the forehead.

Molly says her racket is cleaner than mine because she only cripples the Man and I work direct on the women. "What you sell them, you fiend, is the idea of Staying Young. It isn't fair."

I tell her all about what a great chemist Mr Detaille is, and how our face powder is exploded so fine it can be blown through silk and she laughs like Little Audrey.

I'm not trying to justify anything, I'm just thinking. Sure, I know it's an attempt to make things so complicated you won't remember how simple they might be. If any of my customers came in my bathroom wouldn't they be shocked because I don't use the things I sell 'em? That's all grand talk about the vanisher and the cleanser and the freshener, tissue packs and astringent pads and double-chin gymnastic and milkweed massage and Bathsheba Shampoo. Beautifully packaged too. I can stuff a dame's toilet cabinet so full of gadgets she's afraid to open the mirror for fear they'll all fall out. And my own equipment? A box of salt and a bottle of cologne and a jar of cleansing cream. With a toothbrush and a hairbrush and a lipstick, what more do you need?

What happened to me with Wyn was a kind of salt gargle. It's good for teeth and sore throat and it leaves you feeling clean. I'd like to be in the salt business. It's Bible stuff, it ought to be fairly honest.

"I hope you don't say that kind of thing to your customers," Molly remarks.

Sometimes I do, and they want to buy all the more of the line because they think I'm so wonderfully frank. You got to be cagy, though; there's some things you can't say. We got in deep when we listed a face powder as ranging from Porcelain Blonde to Oriental Brunette. The Jewish trade thought that word Oriental was a knock at them. We had to call in our literature and change it to Languorous. If you're not sure what word to use better say Exotic.

"And be sure it don't get misprinted," Molly says.

Another cup of coffee. Just fussing round in a kitchenette helps. Molly says that, for her, gin is the best medicine. Learning to drink gin gave her a new start in life, and better than aspirin for a headache. I never cared much for it, probably because Wyn didn't. But when Molly and I let our hair down she works on gin and I take Scotch. It seems to come to pretty much the same either way. By myself I stick to coffee.

Things come through on coffee. Instead of getting amusing and hazy they get clear. Too damn clear. When I find so many people trying to make me think something special I just get cranky and won't think it. This patriot-

144

ism business, for instance. Molly and I were trying to figure it out. The U.S.A. just isn't the home of all virtue and foreigners crazy. It doesn't add up. People are like other people. I work for a foreigner. Delphine has been over here fifteen years and made a fortune out of DD products.

But, Molly says, you always tell me how different she is. She's not the least bit like an American.

True enough. Usually I haven't the least idea what she thinks about outside business. She wears the most perfect mask. There must be something behind it. Isn't that the only reason for wearing a mask, you've got something behind it you want to conceal?

Molly says maybe not. Wearing a mask can get to be a career in itself. If you take it off you may find there's nothing there. What a thought.

I can't imagine anything about Delphine being less than perfect. Her figure, hair, clothes, makeup, all fit to drive any other woman crazy. But what for? That funny little deaf husband of hers? It can't have any allure of mystery for him, he's her chemist, he knows the formula for all the DD products. I wonder what they talk about? I guess they have the French passion for a balanced budget. When I've been up to have dinner with her and Mr Detaille, the minute you get inside that Park Avenue apartment you know you're in a special world. I've never been to Paris, but I imagine that's what it's like? Everything a bit shiny, a bit flimsy, a bit fragrant, and beautiful legs and perfect manners. Even in her last rag of underwear I can't imagine Delphine less than formal. Even Pfui so well bathed and plucked you could imagine him wearing little striped pants and button shoes.

Please, for God's sake, *let* France be like that, the way I get an idea of it from magazines. Let something in this world be the way I imagined it.

She must be over fifty but I swear you wouldn't put her past thirty-five. Unless you got very close, and no one is likely to.

Molly says maybe that's the perfect score; to build up such a front it gets to be your whole life. Delphine would have a contempt for muddleheads like Molly and me if she knew how we get puzzled and scared. Or if she heard us screaming with laughter?

We were wondering if foreigners talk to each other like Americans do? I can't imagine Delphine ever spilling her inside thoughts to anyone. Or is it they're more grown up than we are and too smart to have bull-sessions about things you can't solve?

But some of the sitz gadgets in Delphine's bathroom showed me that even if the French haven't solved everything they've done a lot of thinking. If French women are as practical as that they ought to have more to do with the government.

If you let your mind go it certainly takes you places. I'm going to quit harping on women. Maybe it's because the cosmetic business keeps me tied up with females all the time. But I get fed up with the screwy way things are going, and some of the White Collar Girls are starting to wonder. I used to smile when I saw nuns and sisters going around in their robes. I was sorry for them, thought they must be unhappy; hoped they wore something pretty and sheer underneath so as not to forget they're still female.

146

But maybe that's what they want to forget. Maybe they're just as sorry for the rest of us. They've quit thinking and started believing. Maybe they've got something there.

Wyn could always help me when I got this way. I see it now, Wyn's happy because he believes; he doesn't think. He's a kind of nun himself; monk, I mean. He obeys the rules of his Order. He's taken the vows of the Main Line or Rittenhouse Square; Philadelphia Proper. He doesn't question them; just accepts.

I saw in the paper about a bank that failed over in Jersey. Somehow the big depositors were tipped off and drew out their accounts in time. Listen, if the Bank of Civilization is going to shut down, can I draw out my poor little deposit before the crash? It's not much but it's all I have. It's me, my happiness, my belief in things. It used to be Wyn.

This was a good Milkman's Matinee, even if it'd turn to cheese if he overheard us. God bless Molly, her good cagy sense helps me more than she knows. She says not to take the New York jitters too hard; New York always gets panicky too quick. She says remember the old Midwest, with its feet planted in corn and manure. She still reads the Chicago *Tribune* on Sundays; anyone who can do that isn't likely to be doubtful about things. Can you imagine the old *Trib* being uncertain about anything? Marshall Field's is still busy, and there's a Furniture Show on at the Merchandise Mart. Molly remembers one Sunday we went to the Shedd Aquarium. There was a tank marked "Common Sucker, Habitat Eastern Half of the U.S." "That's you," says Molly.

She was glad I picked out an apartment on Riverside. At first she was a bit ruffled by race prejudice, but I get quite a kick out of it. They're so different from the Main Line. Jesusgod, I might even marry one of them. They think about the future, and they're good on the fiscal end. Sometimes I wish they weren't quite so hairy.

I told Marcus Eisen, you know you'll be miserable if you don't marry a girl called Shirley, and he said "I can't marry the whole Upper West Side."

Honestly, I'd rather have one window looking across the Hudson towards America than a whole penthouse over on the East River where people have to live to remind themselves how well bred they are. When I get home about sunset I like to think of Molly hiking up Michigan Avenue and across the old bridge and by the Fur Trader tablet and the Wrigley Building. I know that even if she gets the jitters too, she'll snap out of it. She never fell for anyone quite the way I did.

I had a notion to send her a subscription to the New York *Times* for a birthday present. It would do her good as an alibi against the Chicago *Trib*. I won't say the *Times* never loses its head, but at least it has a head to lose.

I didn't do it. Molly, you keep your feet in corn and manure.

16

THAT SPRING POP WAS SO MUCH BETTER THAT HE'D AL-
most forgotten how ill he was, though I hadn't. I remember the hot afternoon I was doing speed practice on the
typewriter, amusing myself to try how quick I could make
the little rings on the bell come after each other. I heard
a hammering at the bottom of the stairs. It was Pop
thumping with his cane.

"Katherine!" he bawled. "KATHERINE!"

I was scared, for he didn't call me that once a year. I
thought maybe he was taken sick again, and ran out on
the landing. He looked up with his beard bristling.

"Jesusgod, are you deaf?"

"I'm sorry, Pop, I was working. Are you all right?"

"I'm fine. I want to know how you spell Katherine."

"The regular way. What's the idea?"

"Somebody wants to know."

Of course it seems ridiculous to me now, but while I
was at Manitou I flirted with the idea of spelling my name
Kathryn. I guess it had a sort of moom pitcher touch. Pop
and Mac had been kidding me about it and finding so
many Kathryns and Cathryns at the Business School cured

me. I wondered why Pop was bringing it up now.

"Who wants to know?" I asked, but he had gone back in the Front Room. I looked out the window and saw a weatherstained old station wagon, and painted on the side of it in small green letters DARBY MILL, OLD ST. DAVIDS. In the car were some big piles of shingles baled up with wire. Pop had been saying for I don't know how long that we must get new shingles for the backhouse roof, it leaked on him when he was sitting in there. I supposed he ordered some without telling me, and ran downstairs just to see he wasn't getting cheated.

"Is that the man for the backhouse?" I said as I went into the room. Pop cackled with laughter and the visitor rose politely. I could feel my pure and eloquent blood doing its stuff. It was Wyn.

"It's Wyn Strafford again," said Pop. "He didn't want to interrupt your work, but he heard the hell of a pace you go on that machine and he wondered if you'd like to type the cricket book."

"I was going to write you a letter," said Wyn. He was a little pink himself, but he's always so beautifully bronzy you'd scarcely notice it. "You sounded so busy I didn't like to bother you, but I wanted to spell your name right."

"K-I-T-T-Y usually works," I said; then I felt worse still; it sounded as though I were being too familiar. I got out into the kitchen to make them some iced tea while they went over their cricket dope. By good luck I'd brought home some cinnamon buns not long before.

"I really came round to apologize for helping to burn up your waste basket," Wyn said. "But when I heard that typewriter going I couldn't help asking about it. Gosh,

150

Miss Foyle, we haven't anybody down at the bank that can make the keys move like that."

I suppose somebody must have called me "Miss Foyle" before that; the registrar at Prairie College maybe, or the Dean of Women; but it never struck in before.

I went the three steps of decency with him myself when he left, as Pop didn't get off the porch much. Oh Wyn, my sweet, how adorable you were in those old gray pants and the soft shirt and the cricket club blazer. But I didn't guess it then; I only thought "My God, does he work at a bank in that outfit?" Darby Mill, Old St. David's, meant nothing to me. How could I guess how much swank there is in that intentional shabbiness. He was so serious about his big portfolio of cricket stuff and the chapters he had already written.

"I guess I'm not a very good writer," he said, "but the cricket people won't know the difference."

I could see he wasn't a very good speller either, but I didn't say so. I don't know anything that makes you feel more maternal and lovely towards a man than correcting his spelling for him. He was trying to say something about what rate should he pay for getting the stuff typed, but he simply couldn't get it out. I was embarrassed too, because this was my very first paid job of any sort. And Pop kept talking at us from the porch.

"Don't forget that century Not Out your uncle made against Marrowbone in '96," he shouted. I know now it's not Marrowbone, it's Marylebone, but that's the way I heard it.

"I tell you," Wyn said, "I better not leave these chapters with you now. I've got to read 'em over and get in

151

some more dope your father has given me. I'll send them back to you and meantime you can think it over. I guess I better go now, I've got to get these shingles out to the farm, we're mending the kennels."

After he'd gone I got Pop calmed down. Too much cricket talk wasn't so good for him.

"I thought Mr Strafford must be in the lumber business," I said.

"Jesusgod," exclaimed the old man. "Don't you ever read your *Ledger?* Strafford, Wynnewood and Company, the oldest private bank in Philly. Darby Mill, that's the name of their country place; there's an old sawmill on the crick out there, where they cut up the logs for Washington at Valley Forge. Honey, those folks are so pedigree they'd be ashamed to press their pants. They hire someone to drive the Rolls for a year before they use it, so it won't look too fresh."

"I think that's just as silly as the opposite," I said. I think so still.

I was pleased at getting the typing job. Otherwise I honestly didn't think about the incident one way or another. Myrtle was ready to go home, and I wanted to fix a stew for Pop's supper. Mac was coming over that evening to tell us about the baby, and sit with Pop a while so I could go out with Marty Bockmeyer, a nice dumb boy from the Business School, but a good dancer. Once and a while I'd manage time off and Marty would take me to some dance hall.

Naturally I thought at first Wyn was just hellbent on that book of his. That seemed a fair enough reason for his coming. It was too damn silly to suppose any other reason. I did a good job on the typing too. I believe short-hand and practise getting things down condensed might be good training in literature. I could see right away how Wyn's sentences scrambled all over the place. When I wasn't sure of his spellings and checked him in Webster he was usually wrong. Bless his heart, he used to say "It's wonderful how much better it reads when it gets typed." He had no notion how much editing had been done on it. I really got a good deal of education by watching how simple Wyn was about anything that needed thinking. But in anything outdoors, or engines, or animals, or getting along with people, how perfectly swell. Like all the nicest people in Philly he had a terrible inferiority complex about anything outside his familiar routine. But watch him on his own ground and he'd surprise you. Pop took me over to the cricket club one day to see Wyn play. It was wonderful to see him. He was different. Every movement, every look counted. When he waved to the fielders where he wanted them to take their positions I could have kissed him. He knew just what he wanted, and had reasons.

I'm mixed up thinking about Wyn, because it doesn't matter now what came before what. Darling, let me think and just see how it feels. My blessed. My boy.

Funny, when we met he was 25, seven years older than me, but I always think of him as almost a baby. He said he'd been at Princeton, and he didn't mean Princeton, Illinois. What he did there except play games and drink beer I can't imagine. Wait though, there was some prof there put a kind of notion of being literary in his mind; he bought expensive books at a bookshop in Princeton; once and a while he talked about first editions, but only like something he'd been told was pretty important. Not the way he talked about cricket and beagles and that little olive-green Buick roadster. She was his darling all right. The first time he turned up in her, instead of the old station wagon, I suspected something was happening. It was right after lunch, I guess he knew Myrtle would be there to look after the old man. He asked if I wouldn't like to go for a ride. We went up the Oxford Pike, to Fox Chase and Huntingdon Valley and all the way to Sorrel Horse. I didn't know what lovely country there is round Philly. It's no wonder the right people settled down on it and keep it to themselves. He took me to have tea with some artists who live at Bethayres and showed me off as if I was somebody. I had such a good time I forgot to be shy. You couldn't be shy when Wyn was around because he was shyer still. Not exactly shy; I mean sort of ashamed in secret, because where he was concerned everything had been done beforehand, and the things he knew about didn't seem to be important. He was ashamed of being such a small potato in the banking business. He said they'd started making money by lending it both ways in 1776 and they'd made money out of every war in the world ever since. All he did in the bank, he said, was what some Higher-Up told him to do; he would never think for himself what might be done, nor give a damn whether it happened.

"Some day I'm going to do something nobody ever told me to do," he said. "What's furthermore, I'm going to do it now." He stopped the car and kissed me.

I wasn't in the least bit surprised. It seemed perfectly

154

natural. Everything that ever happened to Us was that way. We never knew what was coming, but when it came, there it was.

"I get so damned interested talking to you," he said one time, "I almost forget about kissing you. Almost; not quite."

It's a fact. We had fun just gibbering. Maybe he hadn't ever really talked about what was inside him. "I had to look up some bird in Who's Who," he said. "They listed him as a patron of the arts. Gosh, Kitty, that went big with me. Maybe that's what I ought to be. Maybe I could get somewhere helping people that are cleverer than I am. Maybe you would help *me*. Maybe I would help you too if I told you you're beautiful."

When I blushed like that it used to give me a pain in my stomach.

The real miracle was the way all of a sudden we just crossed over some kind of a boundary line and everything was different. The first couple of months it was all strictly business, Wyn turning up at the house with a bunch of copy about twice a week, and Pop always remembering something new that ought to go in. They'd dictate it off to me and then of course I'd fix it up the way it ought to go. Wyn said he was getting a lot of work done because he'd taken leave of absence from the bank and his family were all away at their summer cottage in Rhode Island. He had a funny phobia about saying "Newport." I soon got to spot that habit of the Main Line crowd, kind of ashamed to let on how swell they are. Jesusgod they don't even brood on it in secret, they just know. It wouldn't even occur to most of them to notice that there are a lot of people who live on a different scale. That's what made Wyn so sweet. He noticed it. He even tried to think about it. It was bad for him.

He noticed more than I thought. "Kitty, do you know when I first adored you? When I saw you didn't wear your stockings rolled under the knees."

As a matter of fact, my knees are too nice to let 'em run round loose the way some people's do. Molly and I used to have what we called knee-parades. We'd size up each other's and figure out what could be done with them.

"I saw the back of your knees before I ever saw the front. That's unusual, the way dresses were then."

"How was that?" I asked. Of course I knew perfectly well, but there are some things you like to hear fairly often.

"When we were hunting for that picture of your father, to put in the book. Thomas Foyle, Last of the Great Coaches, 1861-1930. Remember, we were leaning over that bamboo table in the Front Room going through the photographs. They slid off and you leaned over to pick them up."

"Wyn, you're a hound. I love you."

That's the way we talked in August. We never talked like that in July. As a matter of fact it wasn't till the cricket book was finished that he ever brought the Buick to Griscom Street. It was sort of honorable of him. When we were working we were working.

The first Buick Day I had the typescript all ready for him. I thought to myself, the book's going to the printer, and Wyn's going to Rhode Island to sail in some yacht races, and where's Kitty Foyle going?

We were kind of silent on the way up to Sorrel Horse. After while he said "You've been awfully kind to help me out with that book. I think we make a good author."

I couldn't say anything. I had one of my dumb spells, and the hot leather seat of the roadster was burning my shoulders.

"I don't suppose you and your father could come up and visit us in Rhode Island. Gosh, I'd love to take you sailing."

I thought he was just being kind. Of course the old man couldn't make a trip like that. And I couldn't go alone.

It's really comical, I sometimes think, how many things people have invented that you can't do.

I looked hard at the dashboard. There were two buttons there, one said Choke and the other said Throttle. I felt like both of them. "It would be wonderful," I said. "But I've got a friend from Illinois coming to visit me. Molly Scharf, we were in school together." I was going to tell him about Molly, anything to talk about that would make me feel easy. He'd be amused how Molly and I used to pretend to be Mrs Rosey Rittenhouse and Mrs B. Cynwyd Lloyd. I stopped just in time. My God, Mrs Lloyd was his aunt.

"What do they do at the bank," I asked, "when you all go away?"

"They sharpen up the scissors and cut coupons."

That cut me too, somehow, but I was able to be quiet while he told about the bank and how he hated it. Not long after that he stopped the car, and Before Us turned into Us.

157

We were able to talk about anything, without hurting or being ashamed. But even then I still thought he was just being kind and sweet. How could I guess how he needed me? We had to learn about everything together.

"When I get back from Rhode Island," he said, "I've got an idea I want to go to work on. But I don't want to talk too much about it now, first I've got to sell it to my father. I think he'll fall for it, he knows I'll never be any good as a banker and he's tickled to death about this cricket book. He's not a bad egg and he loves to think we're a literary family because Weir Mitchell was our doctor."

Fortunately I'd heard of Weir Mitchell, there were a lot of cards with his name on them in the index of the Carnegie Esq Library.

"And Bayard Taylor signed a book for us one time when he came to tea at the farm. Isn't it wonderfully Philadelphia to be still living on ideas someone else had in the 70's?"

He seemed a bit sore about this. I didn't know who Bayard Taylor was. I used to run round to the Library and look things up when Wyn mentioned them.

Poor darling, he had an idea of his own, one he couldn't possibly put across but I can see now that he wanted somehow to justify his existence.

He dropped me at Griscom Street and said goodbye to the old man. "We've been celebrating the finish of the book," he said.

"Well I'm glad you took the girl out for some fresh air," Pop said. "She don't get out much. We'll miss you now the job's done."

I got just the slightest bit of a wink from Wyn on this. That made me feel better, because I was really a bit puzzled. He roared off in the little car and I tried to imagine him sailing at Newport, white trousers and brown skin and gray eyes. I didn't know then how the light on water changes the color of his eyes, they turn silver green.

17

Wyn got out of town just in time, because it turned terribly hot. That little bedroom under the roof was like a furnace. I sat there working because the typewriter bothered Pop if I brought it downstairs. One day the keys of the machine were so warm they were positively uncomfortable to touch. I sat on an old kitchen chair in nothing but a slip, and I left two damp patches under me when I got up. Anyhow, I wrote Molly, they were symmetrical.

I think I'd have stripped to the buff but I was so simple it didn't seem modest, somehow, to sit naked while I was working on Wyn's manuscript. He had said something about reading proof and preparing the index. I learned a little about printers' proofs working on the Manitou *Harvest* so like a jolly Judy I offered to do it for him. The index had me stumped until I had the idea of asking them at the Library how it was done.

The Library was a good friend to me. They knew I was keen to make use of my business school training and they recommended me to the Frankford Historical Society, which was putting on a drive for their new building. I typed a lot of letters for them.

Wyn sent me a postcard of some beautiful yachts. When it came Myrtle and I were spraying the back yard with the hose every hour, and old Pop sitting under the arbor with a palmleaf fan, Jesusgodding. Once and a while I got a good breeze going downtown on the L and tried to imagine what it was like on a sailboat at Newport. The ads in the *Ledger* telling about places in the mountains were enough to make you grind your teeth. But Dr Bartrum didn't think it would be wise for Pop to travel. We couldn't afford it anyhow. Mac had bought a second-hand car, one of the old model-T Fords, to give Martha and baby Kitty some air. Sometimes on hot evenings he'd wabble round from Tioga and take us a ride along the Schuylkill or through Fairmount so Pop could tell us again about the Centennial. Martha was played out with housekeeping and babyminding so I'd do a turn of duty for her. They'd put me in the back seat with the baby and the old man and I got dictation from both. When the infant had to be changed it seemed to put ideas in Pop's system too and he'd say he must go to the bathroom.

"Gosh sake, Pop," Mac said, "can't you wait till you get home? Is it stand-up or sit-down?"

"Reminds me of your Mom," Pop said. "She was so used to looking after boys that when Kitty come along and said she had to go Mom asked her that same question. She forgot it's always sit-down for girls."

"Listen," I warned him, "none of that backhouse talk when Molly Scharf gets here. She wasn't raised Irish and she's not used to that kind of family conversation."

As a matter of fact he couldn't really shock Molly; but

161

those kind of things sound ornery when your own folks say 'em, and I thought he was getting too damn careless. Of course I was really thinking about Wyn, who had given me a new slant. I didn't ever want him to hear that sort of talk.

I'll say this for Pop, when Molly came he really tried. More than once I heard him say Conshohocken.

Molly did us good, and how grand it was to see her. She said it wasn't hot compared to Manitou and told us how the editor of the *Argus* got tired of hearing about frying an egg on the pavement, he really did it. Molly said the whole town turned out to watch; they cleaned off a patch of sidewalk, and smeared butter on it, and broke the egg and sure enough it cooked and the editor ate it. They took a picture of him and the Chamber of Commerce got it into the Chicago *Trib*.

Of course it took quite a while for it to get well cooked, they had to stand back and let it simmer and some of the Q soots got into it, but they left that out of the story.

Molly said I looked different; I guess we were both in a quiet mood. I didn't tell her about Wyn; there wasn't anything to tell, except that I'd done a job of typing. It was hard to keep my feelings all to myself because of course we got talking about the old paper doll days and Molly wanted to see where Mrs Rosemont Rittenhouse lived. I looked up the address and also on the sly the address of the Strafford town house. On one of our sightseeing trips I showed her the Rittenhouse place on Walnut Street. It was all boarded up for the summer and I remembered my adventure at Cape May. At the same time I managed so we walked by the Strafford house on the Square and I took a look at it sideways. Just as we went by a colored butler in his shirtsleeves and a green-stripe vest came out on the front steps smoking a pipe and looking across the park. I didn't think he ought to do that while Wyn was away. I knew it was the house all right because there was an old silver name-plate on the door, the name was almost polished off but you could still read it.

Molly was all set up about seeing the houses where the Paper Dolls lived. She said "I always thought you just made up those names." When she saw something in the *Ledger* about Cadwalader Shippen she said "My cup runneth over." The Liberty Bell and the Betsy Ross house didn't give her nearly such a bounce.

A good deal of the time we sat in the back yard and sewed and just talked. It was good to get my mind back into Manitou again. After I left Molly didn't have any room-mate till mid-semester, then a redhead from Chicago called Pat Kenzie was put in with her. "She's got big brown eyes like caramels," Molly said, "and she's as red as those cows out at Debaughs'. In fact she's red all over. She's a swell kid but she thinks college is a waste of time. Her mother is a buyer in one of the big stores and thinks she could get jobs for both her and me this fall. I'm enrolled for next year but I've got half a mind to quit. Most of the kids in college are just playing around. Honestly Kitty, all I got out of freshman year I could have learned in six weeks hard work on the books. Except for the bull sessions in the dorm. I think it's mostly a racket to keep kids from being a nuisance at home before they're fit to earn a living."

This was a new idea to me. I'd been biting my nails

thinking what a lot of good culture and education I was missing.

"It's different for girls like Trudy Weissenkorn or Ida Meagher," Molly said. "They're just dumb clucks, and they haven't any ambition to go off on their own. And it's fine for a boy like Fedor—say, did I tell you he won the medal for Freshman Oratory. He's a natural scholar. But I'm not so sure about me. Jeeminy, I'm nearly nineteen and I want to go places."

"You betcha," I said, just by good old Manitou habit.

She had with her a book on Great Periods in Furniture that she was reading on the train and the things that pleased her most in our sightseeing were Colonial sideboards and fireplaces. Even some of the junk in our Front Room, which I thought was awful, amused her, like the little blue glass shaped like a top hat, to hold the old sulphur matches. "Kitty," she said, "some of this goofy stuff of the 70's and 80's is going to be a curiosity, I bet it'll be fashionable when they get wise to it. And Philadelphia, why the town must be loaded to the muzzle with unconscious comedy. Think of Godey and Mrs Hale."

I couldn't, because I didn't even know who they were. I looked them up afterward. When people tell me things I like to follow through. I was a little jealous of Molly's year in college. Even if she sniffed at it I thought she'd learned a lot.

What really made me homesick for Thanksgiving Avenue was her telling about Pattyshells. She said he didn't bother to get up now when you went to the front door. He just lay there sprawled out on the porch, but he thumped his tail a bit louder as a kind of apology for not rising,

164

Bernie had graduated and was going to work for Uncle Elmer at the factory. Aunt Hattie was trying to get Hugh Walpole for a lecture at the Woman's Club, but almost hoped he wouldn't accept as she felt she'd be frightened of him. One of the Debaugh boys, I forget which, had got into trouble with a waitress at the Manitou House. And Trudy Weissenkorn hadn't been taken into any sorority, which her father was very sore about and threatened to make a stink to the trustees.

While Molly was with us I got the letter from Wyn telling about his big idea. His father had agreed to it and would put in some money. Wyn said he was coming back to town in September to get started and wanted me to help him. Of course I was thrilled and naturally I told Molly an outline of the scheme.

"He thinks Philadelphia is a big enough town to support a sophisticated magazine of its own, something like the *New Yorker,* but written for the Philadelphia crowd. He says they'll call it *Philly* and begin publishing about the beginning of November. Plenty of wisecracking stuff about football, and hunting, and cricket, and the Orchestra, and famous food and drink, and little articles about picturesque history. Think of all the schools and colleges round Philly, they ought to eat it up. He wants me to be his secretary. Gee, Molly, what a chance."

Molly was cagy.

"It sounds like fun," she said. "But if I get the town from what you've told me I don't think it'll work. The *New Yorker's* grand because it's edited by a lot of boys who are both smart and ambitious. You haven't got 'em like that here. If they're really peppy they clear out. And the *New Yorker's* got a readymade public of all kinds of people who have an awful yen to be In the Know. It's a kind of inferiority. But I don't believe Philadelphia gives a damn about being In the Know. It prefers not to be, or it thinks it's there already. The people on top are so damn sure they know it all they don't want to learn anything new; and the people underneath know they haven't got a Chinaman's chance. I think it's rather swell to have one town that simply doesn't give a damn except be comfortable. Why does your friend want to give it the needle? If I were you I'd let Philly be like old Pattyshells. Leave it wag its tail on the porch."

Shrewd gal, Molly. The last thing she said when I saw her off on the train was "If I land a job in Chicago you better come out there and see what's doing."

18

Wyn called up the first of September. I remember the date, it was Sunday, and Pop was grumbling because he couldn't get oysters till next day. Wyn had taken a floor in a little old house on Sansom Street for an office, and bought furniture, and we were to move in next day.

I was up most of the night going over my wardrobe. My God, Wyn never guessed how I worried about my clothes. To work in an office with Wyn Strafford, and help get out a smart magazine, that means some female overhead. Do I laugh on the wrong side when I read pieces in the papers about the Working Girl's Budget and how if she lives home she should get along on $1072.06 a year or something like that. I suppose the six cents is for an air mail stamp if her sweetie happens to be in Rhode Island or somewhere. She might blow herself to that once a year? They allow her 185 bucks a year for clothes.

I'd like to see some employers go blind before they read those stories. I was practically a millionaire because Wyn put me down for $30 salary which was a lot more than I rated right out of business school, but even so and with all the meals he blew me I had to skirmish to look the way the office of *Philly* needed me to look. I was relieved one day when Wyn told me he'd been to the office of the *New Yorker* and said they were a weird-looking crew.

I was on the L before 8 a.m. that Monday. All the way downtown I could see the fresh-painted R signs in oyster saloons. Wyn was on Sansom Street already and the furniture being put in. I felt very bashful because I didn't know just what line to take, probably Wyn had forgotten all about me. While the men were busy heaving a big desk upstairs he suddenly took me behind the door and kissed me.

"Today we'll start opening our oyster," he said. "I hope it won't give us ptomaine."

"Maybe we'll find a pearl in it."

"I've found one already."

After that everything was all right. The rooms were filthy, I was sorry I'd worn a new dress but it was worth it for that first look Wyn gave me. I hurried over to Gimbel's and bought a housewife apron and some dusters and took the broom away from Wyn and got busy. No woman can resist that combination of office-work and housekeeping. It's about the best feeling there is. You know you're doing things men do, just as well as they can, at the same time you're doing women's kind of things that men are so lousy at. In between sweeping and settling filing cases Wyn would get an idea and say Take a Letter. Down at the bank they didn't even trust him to dictate so he was crazy about seeing his own words go down in a notebook. He'd bend over and watch me so close while he was talking that I'd get rattled. Also I was afraid, after all the furniture wrestling we'd done, he'd smell perspiration. Women think of everything.

We certainly worked. It's comical to think back about it. Those three rooms were a madhouse. They were up one flight and we had to use the landing as a reception. Wyn's father said he'd risk ten grand up to the time we could get out a first issue. It didn't take long for the news to get round that Sansom Street was the place for a hand-out. All the broke cartoonists and newspaper paragraphers in Philly were round there by the third day. With Wyn's pals in and out the place sounded like an item in the *Ledger's* social columns. Parry Berwyn and Bill Cynwyd were out in the front office trying to stave off bums and timewasters, and Wyn was fighting with printers and paper merchants in the middle room, and I was in the little coop at the back trying to make Wyn's letters more concise. Nothing was ever so much fun, and I think I knew in three days that it was all hooey. It was good clean sport for Bill Cynwyd and Parry Berwyn and Coxey Narberth to quit polo and racquets for a few weeks to amuse themselves by being Editors, and Staceylea Bitch-Bala had herself a grand time trying to imitate a New York shopping column. But poor Wyn somehow figured this was to be Philadelphia's literary comeback. The old town had once been tops in journalism, why not again? His greatgrandfather had staked Edgar Allan Poe, to drinks, probably, and why shouldn't Wyn Strafford VI be another dower house for the Muse? That's what some smart alec from the *Bulletin* said when we threw out his lousy pun, Adam and Evesdropping, for a Gossip Column.

Later when I started working for Delphine I had to go to town on class magazines and see what makes them tick.

Naturally I smile when I look back on *Philly* and its amateurish attempt. Everybody, even Wyn's father, has forgotten it by now, it must have made a useful writeoff in Mr Strafford's 1929 income tax, but I wouldn't have missed the experience. Just getting a look at Stacylea's clothes when she came in to talk to Wyn and not notice me sitting at the typewriter put ideas in my head.

Wyn was so happy it was lovely to watch him. Even with the typewriter in rapidfire I could steal a look at him once and a while. First time in his life he was doing something besides cricket or sailing that seemed to answer back inside him. Parry and Bill were so easy that most every caller got in to see Wyn anyhow, and he accepted all their ideas as the quickest way to get rid of 'em. Meanwhile he'd forgotten to do anything about distribution and I had to rush round to the News Company myself and try to get some cooperation. I gave Myrtle $5 extra a week to stay home until I could get back to Pop, we never cleaned up at the office before eight or nine o'clock.

We had an old accountant who came up from the bank to keep our books. He was bald as a china doorknob. After he'd been watching our doings a few weeks he said "Miss Kitty, the only reason my hair don't go white is because I haven't got any."

Wyn had a habit, no matter how busy he was, of writing me a little rhyme now and then, maybe on the back of an envelope. I'd see him very tycoon and intense at his desk and be afraid to interrupt him and then he'd say "Kitty, Interoffice Memo," and pass me some simple verse he had sprawled out in his college-boy handwriting. One day when we worked late he took me to a French hide-away up on Pine Street, he said a drink would be good for our morale. As a matter of fact it was the first speak-easy drink I ever had. There was a confidential little bar at the back of the house and we stood there for a highball. Wyn thought the first snort was a bit pale, so he said the motto of the Racquet Club, "A bird can't fly on one wing," and ordered a second. "Be a little more liberal this time," he said to the bar-man. The proprietor happened to overhear him, I guess he knew Wyn was an important customer, and as the barkeep reached out with the bottle old Monsieur Duval said "Soyez gentil avec." This tickled Wyn so he often quotes it when anyone's pouring, and the next day when he'd had time to think it over he handed me a slip of paper:—

> Waiter, that highball looks skinny, by heck.
> Don't let your bottle get clogged at the neck,
> Next time you pour, soyez genteel avec.

You always had to wait till next day for Wyn's poetry to come through.

After that first oyster-opening kiss he scarcely looked at me except in a friendly way, he was so absorbed in the idea of getting out the magazine. It wasn't long before I wanted to try to tell him I thought we were shooting up a blind alley. The drawings that came in didn't seem to me funny, and most of the articles were about on a par with the Manitou *Harvest*. In order to really kid Gentle-men you have to have people who aren't Gentlemen and when the Main Line tries to kid itself it's just committing suicide. But I couldn't tell Wyn, he was so happy. It

171

wouldn't have done any good.

Wyn, I tried to tell you afterward, a hundred times a day I'd look over at you and want to straighten your necktie or pull up your socks or just kiss the hem of your shirt. I even brought a little sewing kit down to the office because I thought maybe some day one of your buttons would come off and I could sew it on. I thought God damn those swell custom shirt makers who put buttons on so tight.

Remember, our first issue was to be on the stands on Hallowe'en, and the very day we made up the page proofs and sent everything in to the printer your father called up and told us about the Market Crash in N.Y.

We sent off the last batch of stuff by messenger and Parry was going to see it on press. Remember, you said Parry must know his stuff because he edited the school paper at Groton. You put your feet up on the desk and leaned back, I could hear the creak of that swivel chair. When I happened to turn round you were looking at me quite different from ever before.

"Kitty," you said. . . . "Kitty. . . ." I remember how you spaced it out.

"We've put the magazine to bed, why don't we go to bed ourselves."

I didn't even know what you meant, at first.

That was the afternoon I phoned Myrtle to stay with the old man, and you took me to Harrisburg.

I was so frightened I said to you "Soyez gentle avec," and you'd had too much whiskey and passed out.

Wyn, Wyn, I was so sorry for myself. I know more now, and I'm sorriest for you.

19

I HATE TO THINK ANYONE ELSE IS AS SILLY AS ME. OR MAYBE I like to think they all are. "Be's you got bugs?" Just now I got looking at this damn phone, I was thinking it never talked to him. All I'd have to do would be lift it up and ask the operator to get that number. I did lift it up and whispered Old St. Davids 31, just to hear what it would sound like. Old St. Davids 31. But my right hand, I guess that's the practical hand, kept the crosspiece pushed down, so's electricity couldn't leak through.

Easy, Kitty, easy old girl.

It's good you don't remember bad times like you do good ones. When I think back about fun, love, happiness, I feel strong, as though I was printed in bigger type somehow, in capital letters. Misery just pushes me into a little frightened knot inside. It makes you feel small. I guess that's why you don't remember it so well.

I wouldn't look again at that magazine for anything in the world. I have the four issues wrapped up in tissue paper and they're going to stay that way. When Wyn and I got back from Harrisburg the first number was lying on the desk, and we looked at it like it was a dead body. So it was. Wyn's old man was on the phone saying the stock market had jumped out the window and no more jack.

I guess I didn't have enough chin to take it on. Even Myrtle noticed the black rings under my eyes. I guess colored people don't show them. I wondered was I a huzzy, a slut, or worse just a plain damn fool. To do something I never dreamed of and not even get anything but misery.

Everybody who told us the magazine was such an amusing idea was now saying of course Philadelphia wasn't the kind of town for that sort of thing. Some of the advertisers cancelled their contracts, others wanted to insist on our getting out the number of issues they bargained for. Wyn called me into a conference he was having with Parry and Bill and a lawyer from the bank. He said they had arranged a compromise. I thought, I've been compromised myself, and it didn't seem funny. Then I noticed how unhappy Wyn looked. It started me thinking more about him than about me. I could tell he was feeling lousy because he had taken the trouble to put on a blue pin-stripe and look like big business. That meant the end of his career as Patron of the Arts and return to the bank. Parry and Bill looked like a couple of big airedales that had been whipped but they were both wearing their Racquet Club neckties so I guessed they'd live. Bill said he'd bought a new fur coat so as to make a good show when he covered varsity football practise for the magazine; could he put it on expense account? The lawyer asked who were those bohemians sitting on the stairs, he had to climb over them on his way up. We explained they were artists with drawings to sell. Parry said he'd heard that Detroit was going to get out a magazine in imitation of the *New Yorker,* maybe we could sell it some of the stuff we'd bought for our own paper. "Just change a name here and there, put Grosse Point instead of Bryn Mawr and Radnor, the Detroit smart set won't know the difference."

"I didn't know they had one out there," said Bill.

Wyn got sore at last. "You boys go and have your lunch at the Ritz," he says. "Leave Kitty and me clean up the mess."

We dictated letters a while, and we did a good job too, but we both knew what we were thinking of. Poor baby, I can see now, maybe he felt he was committed to make good with me. That's the way a man would feel. Thank goodness, I got to know later that wasn't the way of it.

After while he stopped and we really looked at each other, the first time in several days. I didn't like him in that dark suit, even his eyes were darker, and his necktie was sort of downtown and Bourse-looking.

"Kitty, when I was at school they gave me the louse part in some Shakespeare play, As You Like It. I had to be an old fool in a long white beard and my big line was, In my youth I never did apply hot and rebellious liquors in my blood. You might remind me of that sometimes. Put it in the tickler file."

I wanted to say, "Am I going to have a chance to remind you of things?" but Choke and Throttle were both working. I had to turn sideways because I didn't want him to see me drizzle. That tree in the backyard looked like a windmill in a fog.

"What are you looking at?" he says.

"A girl that tries to take dictation from you needs to

175

keep her handkerchief handy," I said, and ran to my desk drawer where I'd left it.

I knew I was acting rotten and spoiling everything. I tried hard for a comeback. "That's one of the things they don't teach in business school," I said. "Never take dictation without all your equipment."

He didn't say anything, just looked, then he grabbed the big file case we'd put behind the door. He pulled it out from the wall; maybe it wasn't so heavy, we hadn't used it much yet.

"Damn it," he said, "I didn't mean that filing cabinet to go there, that's *your* corner. Now stand in it and I'll kiss you like I did before."

After while he said "That old bird in the play, the guy who didn't drink hootch, said he was frosty but kindly. That sounds like juleps. I bet no one ever had a julep in November before. We'll go round to market and buy some mint and have Duval make us one."

Mint julep was only a name to me, but I let him go and do the marketing for it while I got on with the letters, and he phoned me from Duval's when it was ready. "The frost is on the punkin and the fodder's in the shock," he said and I didn't know what he meant till I saw the glasses. "Hop a cab."

Three nice words, "hop a cab." To me that always means Wyn, calling from somewhere with some crazy idea.

It was mid afternoon and the back room at Duval's was empty. I guess Wyn had crept up on one already, he was looking better. I was all set to tell him not to be too sorry about the magazine being a flop, and maybe the stock market crash gave us an alibi for what would have

176

happened anyway. While I was figuring the right way to say it he came out with the same idea. So I was holding back, not letting on that I'd been thinking just that. It's good for Wyn not always to be told somebody else has had his ideas first. Maybe holding anything back sort of shows through on your face, he said "It isn't fair."

"What isn't fair?"

"Making your eyes so big."

"It's this julep. It's almost as good as a chocolate coke."

Somewhere at the bottom of that julep, maybe it came up through the straw, Wyn found the idea of our going to Pocono.

Wyn, is it all right to think back about Pocono? You don't need to, I expect they keep you busy, you've got too much sense to think back about things. The Main Line's too social. You don't have those long pink summer sunsets out at Darby Mill; the big trees dark them off maybe. But Jesusgod, summer evenings when K.F. works late at Delphine's office and looks over all those midtown terraces and penthouses and the whole town brightened up with a touch of sunset cosmetic and a little flicker of pink light on some man's shirtfront if it's been laundered just a smitch too shiny. There's a roof of some hotel I can see right from my office desk. The women come out on the terrace and I can see them pause just an instant in the doorway to feel beautiful and sure and to know the dress will float just right as they step off the sill. Their escorts, just like it might be you behind me, following politely right after. You wouldn't be wearing a dentistry coat and a cummerbund, though, and looking like something in café society. Did you make a snob out of me, big boy! I could wring Mark Eisen's neck when I see his clothes, poor sweetheart; and how hard he tries. Always too nifty, always too shiny like cellophane, that's them.

Something certainly was working for us, that warm spell in November. Things always broke funny, somehow. Remember, it was the first time I ever saw mountains. I knew then I'm really a Pennsylvania girl; not Illinois. The Middle West can't do that to you. It's all right for me to think back about Pocono because I'll never see it again as long as I live. I wouldn't see it on a bet, it would hurt too deep. But you will; you'll fish there week-ends and go on up there whenever you feel like it and only once and a while a little funny sharpness in the back of your memory, like putting your tongue in a bad tooth.

I was so excited when we got as far as Manunkachunk in the Buick; Pop used to tell about how he and Mother had a visit there once but I always thought it was a word he made up or a kind of an oath. You said I hadn't seen anything yet; and I hadn't. It was always something just more I must see. When I was so mad about the Water Gap then I must see the Wind Gap; or the Buck Hill Falls, we called it Buick Hill Falls; or Dingman's Creek or Tobyhanna or Lackawaxen or the ride from Milford to Port Jervis. I didn't know the world was like that. How would I get to know the world's like that?

And that other world of ourselves we learned about, I thought you were teaching me and began to guess it was the other way round. We didn't need to have two different ponds to swim in like the 1880's. Remember how we laughed until the echo came across the lake, and I'd never heard an echo before. Little Sir Echo, damn it. You told me about the different summer colonies and I wondered what started all the Quakers up that way. "It was a profitable route for getting coal down to the Delaware River," you said. And you said "It would spoil this country for a lot of nice old Quakers if they knew what a good time we're having up here."

It was more than a good time. It was goodness itself. I must have been a dumb little thing but I was learning how people need each other and how a woman needs a man to make her complete. Maybe it's a mistake to learn things you can do so little about.

We sat in bathing suits in the sun on that big log down by the edge of the water. The autumn leaves blew out over the pond and the air had a sting to it as soon as the sun got low. Wyn said the Pocono country was a great place for snakebite, we better keep a flask handy. That's the way I remember Prohibition, the whiskey was always warm from being carried on someone's hip. But we didn't drink much, not after Harrisburg. "I wouldn't go to that town again," Wyn said, "not if they made me governor of the State. I was so plastered that night I didn't even see what you look like. You look lovely."

Like that touch of chill in the air, remembering the misery made being happy all the sweeter. It's good to remember us talking, we were simple and sweet. We went out in a canoe and he called me The Lady of the Lake.

"That's funny you should say that, it's my favorite poem, I was just thinking of it."

"We're funny people. We just click, don't we. I'll be

your stag at eve."

"We had a parody of it at school, we used to say

> The stag at eve had drunk his fill
> Where danced the moon on Monan's rill,
> And brushed his teeth and combed his hair
> And took a whiff of the mountain air."

"Hold steady now, I'm going to dive overboard. See how nicely I can do it, won't even splash you."

"But Wyn, how will you get back?"

"I won't. I'll tow you in."

"Let me swim in too."

"It's too far for you. The water's cold."

It makes me feel clean just to think about it. His lips were awfully cold after swimming, so he built a big fire in the cabin for us to get dressed by. How he laughed the first time he saw me wriggle into a girdle.

"Is that how it's done?" he said. "I always wondered."

"But Wyn, you must, I mean you must have known about girls before."

"I went to a whorehouse one time, with some of the boys from college, but I didn't like it. That was in Trenton. Come to think of it, I guess I don't like State Capitals."

"When did you first think about me?"

"You know perfectly well."

"Tell me again."

"It was a fine day in the spring of 1929 and Mr Wynnewood Strafford was talking with Mr Thomas Foyle about cricket. And a girl with dark hair came in and brought some iced tea and I liked the shape of her blouse. Or maybe I mean shapes."

"Why did you like the shape of her blouse?"

"I won't tell you. I don't want to embarrass you."

"I like to be embarrassed. It's good for my pure and eloquent blood."

"And the story ends," he would say, "Mr Strafford made up his mind he'd never marry a woman unless she had pointed breasts."

"But Wyn, that's not enough reason."

"Even the State of Pennsylvania's got 'em. Look at that map on the wall. See, one at Port Jervis and one at Bordentown. I never thought of that before, and Bordentown's just the right name for it."

It was perfectly crazy the amount of geography we found round there that fitted into our private language. You might think Wyn picked out that part of the country on purpose. Maybe it's the same all over. I wonder, does everybody talk like that when they're by themselves? I think it's good for them. I guess it only happens once?

As good almost as mountains and waterfalls and the canoe and the firelight on the cabin rafters was Wyn remembering to bring along a whole case of coke for me because he knew I didn't care much for liquor. I tried to keep him company with drinks but it only put me to sleep. What sleep that was too, lying on a mattress in front of the fire, your body singing with exercise and cold mountain water and love, and watching the light on Wyn's face while he was reading me a little book of poems he brought along. It's funny how you can't listen with your eyelids closed. I tried hard, it won't work.

Being in love makes a woman feel quiet and a man

feel talkative. Wyn was quite indignant when I said he had drugged me with love so he could make speeches at me. He was wonderful, when he got excited he walked up and down, as I lay there I saw his feet going to and fro in moccasins like he was wading in firelight, and I could go shut-eye without his knowing it. He talked about the magazine, and how it might have been a chance to escape the banking business. He said his family had lived in Philly for seven generations. "What a humiliation! Think of it Kitty, people that in seven lifetimes didn't have gumption enough to pick up their skirts and move on. Just because they were born with a silver spoon in their mouths; or in their heads. Jesusgod" (he was catching it too) "we've stuck in the mud so long, we stink. Your old man is worth any three of us. The original Strafford, over in England, was beheaded, and they haven't had a head in the family since."

I had my mouth open to say "You *don't* stink." I tried to form the words, but I was asleep.

Once and a while I'd wake up in his arms. Each time the firelight was a little duller.

"Kitty, is it really you?"

"Who else could it be?"

"I don't mean is it you or anyone else, I mean is it the most You of you."

I guess it was. If there's anything more Me, I never found it.

We were there three days and three nights. I had a kind of pain in my mind once and a while when I thought

I had told a lie to Pop and Myrtle, but if you're going to live your own life without hurting other people too much you've got to lie sometimes. We drove to the village every day to phone and see if everything was all right at home, and get milk and ice. I was crazy to learn to drive and Wyn gave me some lessons. It was lucky he did, because the third night he was taken sick on a can of corned beef we had. He insisted on doing all the cooking; I think if I'd smelled that beef I would have known it was bad, but he mucked it all up with some tomato ketchup and eggs we wanted to finish and made a kind of chowder and then he ate most of it. Middle of the night he was vomiting and had terrible cramps. I was scared to death and said I would drive to town myself and get the doctor, though I don't believe I could ever have found the way through those lanes and woods, and only half able to drive. Wyn swallowed about half a bottle of whiskey, and then spewed it up again, I rolled a blanket round him and was able to get him into the Buick. He was in bad pain but he had just enough sense to tell me what turns to make, and somehow I drove to town. One wheel went over a sandy edge on a steep cliff, and I thought we were licked, but we pulled through. He loved that Buick so, she might have been jealous of me. Anyhow we found the doctor, about three in the morning. Of course he knew Wyn well, and he must have wondered who I was, wearing a pair of blue cotton jeans Wyn had brought along for me, with a silver flask of whiskey in the pocket. But he didn't waste any time wondering and went to work with a stomach pump. It was a queer way to end up what you might call a honeymoon.

Wyn was pretty shaky but he drove us down on the Monday. I checked my bag at Reading Terminal and suddenly felt like false pretences. I wondered if anybody had ever done anything dishonest before at Reading Terminal, it always seems like such a well-behaved station. People who wouldn't live on the Main Line for fear of being highhatted, go out to Oak Lane and Elkins Park. You wouldn't believe how complicated social life can be till you know about the Philadelphia suburbs. It's a riot. Wyn had a theory about how certain kind of people wouldn't dare live further out the Main Line than Merion.

I think it's damn sensible of the Main Liners to be so careful of themselves, because if they aren't who else will be?

Wyn said he felt so pooped he'd go out to the Mill and ease off, I said I'd take care of the office. "If you need me," he said, "call Old St Davids 31." That was the first time I heard the number.

20

THE WAY SOME SIMPLE LINE WILL COME INTO YOUR HEAD
and go round and round, and sort of sum things up. It
was only a few blocks to Sansom Street and I kept saying
to myself "America's a beautiful country." That seemed
like a great new discovery, no one ever thought of it before. I guess what I really meant was, Wyn's a beautiful
boy.

Still and all we don't notice beauty enough, I guess
that's what's wrong with us. I felt more like religion that
five minutes hike to the office than I ever did before.
Just a window of doughnuts frying on Ninth Street was
wonderful, there was a chef there mixing batter and I
wondered if he knew about things, if any woman loved
him, if he had a thrill when that dough begins to turn
brown and crispy and full of diabetes. Jesusgod it's a good
thing women don't often let on what love does to them.
They must be meant for it, they've certainly got the equipment. I wondered if those three days really happened.
When you can't believe a thing really happened I guess
that means it was worth happening. Anything sour you
don't wonder, you know damn well it happened.

A girl certainly has to be ready with a change of pace. Somehow I don't think men shift over so quick from one gear to another. Remember when men thought they wanted them to act bawdy and tough and roll their hose, then business took a dip and overnight the girls had to go demure and fluffy so as to cushion the hardworking sire. Whatever goes wrong downtown the dames are expected to be able to iron it out before dinner is served.

But I'm thinking of a different change of pace, I mean I had to switch fast from Pocono to the mess at the office. Bill and Parry were still nursing a hangover from a football week-end and a lot of artists and printers and wouldbes of various kinds were plowing through their line for big gains. "Godsake, Kitty," they moaned, "where's Wyn? We can't get him on the phone, the paper company says we've got to order more stock, we don't know if the magazine's going on or not."

"Wyn went to Princeton for a reunion," I said. I figured that would account for anything.

"Nuts," they said. "Reunions don't happen this time of year."

"This was a very select reunion, just the men in his class that got a straight A all through college."

I always had those boys buffaloed because they never knew if I was ribbing or not. The Main Line girls Bill and Parry were accustomed to have to spend so much time on clothes and stuff they don't have a chance to figure out a good line of hidden-ball formations. The Assembly gazelles know they're practically doomed to the clutches of someone in their own set, why waste good energy in broken field running? Bill and Parry always made me think

186

in football terms, something they could understand if you'd bother to tell it to them.

We got out four issues of *Philly*. We were committed to a big number for Thanksgiving and the Penn-Cornell game. As a matter of fact we sold a lot of that number. People at Franklin Field were snapping it up and it came in handy to sit on when the rain started. The ink wasn't really dry on the cover and the copies all stuck to the seats —either the seats of the stadium or the seats of the customers. There was torn bits of our beautiful back cover ad all over the stand when we left, and CAMELS stencilled on many a social rump.

We had seats in the press box, I was glad because I didn't have to put on an act for all the Blue Book entries that would have been swarming over Wyn if we'd been down front where his friends have a right to be. I always got on fine with the newspaper crowd, even after they get a by-line or a syndicate they still know what people are talking about and you don't have to waste time explaining. But after the game Wyn wanted to take me out to Darby Mill. He had planned it all beforehand, they were throwing a house-party out there and I'd had a note from his mother. Naturally I had some sense, I could even see in the way her handwriting went up and down it was a fever chart, but Wyn wouldn't take No.

It was a mistake. Of course Wyn had done what any man would, told everybody to be lovely to me and they were so god damn lovely I could have torn their eyes out. I was the only one that wasn't in the union. That crowd, if they stopped to think about it, would reckon that Ben

Franklin was still a boy from the wrong side of the tracks, so what would they think about me. Somebody wanted to know if I was one of the Iglehart Foyles from Baltimore or the Saltonstall Foyles from Pride's Crossing. I said no pride ever crossed our family, except when the old man carried his bat against Merion C.C. That was Wyn's fault, he tried to ease the situation by making everybody drink too many oldfashioneds. But it helped because good old Rosey Rittenhouse turned the talk on cricket and said he wished he could get more girls to show some intelligence about it. After a few drinks they got up an indoor cricket game in the tennis house, rounders they called it, and acted that way. Coxey Narberth got one of his ass-slapping spells. I knew either I or the rest of them didn't belong, and the embarrassment went round the dinner table all wrapped up in a napkin like that wine bottle the butlers carried.

Even in a Thanksgiving rainstorm, what a lovely lovely place. When I saw Wyn's old faded station wagon out in a hitching shed I asked him to drive me home. Of course he wouldn't and he couldn't. I was supposed to stay the night and I had to go through with it. "I hope you'll rest well," Mrs Strafford said, "will you want the maid to undress you?" Jesusgod, I blushed like one of those Cornell chrysanthemums. I wanted to say there's only one person here who's good enough to undress me. Wyn saw me turn red, he kept his eyes on me all evening bless him, and came across the room to see what was going wrong.

"You mustn't try to get up in the morning, we'll all sleep late," said Mrs Strafford.

"I've got to get to the office," I said. "We're closing up

188

and I want to leave everything clean."

"Oh, I'm so glad Wyn is giving up that dreadful magazine," she said, "I don't think Philadelphia enjoys that sort of persiflage."

Either she or I must have been pronouncing that word wrong up to then.

"We know damn well they don't," was what I had a yen to say, but by God K.F. had herself under control.

"I don't know what I would do without Kitty," said Wyn, trying to help. "In fact I *won't* do without her. Maybe she'll come and help me at the bank."

"I'm going to Chicago," I said, unexpectedly. I didn't know myself I was going to say it. I'd had a letter from Molly a day or two before. All of a sudden I saw what came next. Wyn was terribly startled, and what a flash of, well, thankfulness, I saw in Mrs Strafford's eyes. Poor lady, she was only playing on the signals they'd taught her. I could see that down under she had a respect for me, she'd like to have me around if it could have been allowed.

"Really, that's very interesting," she said. "Do you know people in Chicago? We have some very pleasant acquaintances in Lake Forest."

"My best friend has a job at Palmer's, she's in the furnishings department."

"The modern girls are so courageous, I think it's wonderful how enterprising they are."

I looked around at the enterprising modern girls. They were showing a good deal of knee sprawled on the sofas with brandy and sodas and members of the Racquet Club, or they were screeching at ping pong in the game room, or playing some baby chess they called b'gammon. I felt homesick for a good filing case somewhere.

Wyn was worried, I could see he wanted to get me off in a corner but his father said to come look at his First Editions and I did. I guess that was the only time I ever really tormented Wyn, but I was sore, I hadn't wanted to come and he made me. I slid off up to bed and left Wyn mooing after me as I went up the stairs. And I knew my legs looked pretty as I went.

I was bitchy. I locked my door and I heard scratching on it some time in the middle of the night and I turned over and buried deep so he couldn't hear me crying. Wyn, my blessed, did you know how I wanted you?

That was enough and plenty. Molly had written asking if I wouldn't come out and see her, she was so tickled about the job at Palmer's, which I could always get her goat by calling the John Wanamaker's of the Middle West. She and Pat Kenzie had a room together and could put me up on a day-bed. Pop seemed well enough so I could leave him, and Uncle and Auntie had been urging me too.

I needed a chance to think about things. The world the way it is now brings lovers so close together they cramp each other's style. I mean telephone, taxicabs, telegrams, florists' delivery anywhere, you're always in touch. Wyn said once that the reason there aren't so many good sonnets written any more except maybe by women is because he can most always get her on the phone and he tells it that way. I had to make him quit sending flowers to the house because I couldn't always pretend they were for the old man and I didn't want to start Pop thinking.

He was kind of in a doze a good deal of the time and it was better that way. Of course Myrtle knew something was going on, and I broke down and told her about it. You can't lie to colored people, they're just open wide for everything that's really so.

"Honey," she said, "you ain' tellin' me no astonishment. When I see you comin' down in de mornins lookin' so female I know it aint just because we got scrapple fer breakfuss. Don't you let nobody cut corners on you, dere aint nobody too good fer Kitty."

Wyn and I went over in Jersey one night, we had so much to say to each other and of course we didn't get it said. He suggested I should come and work at the bank but I didn't like the idea. There was another reason, perfectly cockeyed, for me to get out of town. Wyn had been running me ragged about how he wanted to take me to the Assembly as his partner. I don't know how he thought he was going to work it. Even if he took it right up to the Committee of Mesdames it would only make trouble, you just can't do that sort of thing to the Philadelphia Assembly, not even if you're Wyn Strafford, it hasn't been done since Benedict Arnold, and it would just about crucify his mother who was one of the Mesdames herself.

I tried to explain all this to Wyn but he wouldn't listen to sense until I put it to him from my angle. I said "you're really being selfish though you don't know it. You want to make a gesture of defiance and use me as the weapon." I guess most men would have been angry but he was sweet. "I never thought of that," was all he said. "Listen, you darling," I said, "the ballroom of the Bellevue wasn't planned for gestures of defiance. Nor you neither."

We settled all the magazine accounts and closed the office. Wyn had given me a bonus of $100 above salary and I didn't see why I shouldn't accept it, I knew he'd be miserable if I didn't. I used the money to buy some clothes but Wyn thought my Chicago idea was lunacy. He thought it would be nice if I went to South Carolina for a little holiday, which gave me a laugh. I arranged about having Myrtle stay at Griscom Street nights and got myself on a train without letting him know.

I wrote him a long letter as soon as I got settled in the car. I remember I was just choosing between Darling and Sweetest Boy in the World and deciding to use both when the train went through St Davids. Damned if there wasn't the old station wagon parked where he'd left her. Life does things like that to you. Why couldn't *I* park somewhere and wait till he came?

I was going to mail my letter when the train stopped and was on my way out to give it to the porter when all of a sudden I realized it was Harrisburg. I opened it again and wrote some more. I wasn't going to have him get that letter with a Harrisburg postmark. Not Harrisburg.

21

It's pretty decent of me to keep riding the Pennsy after what it did to me that trip. Maybe what was wrong, it was the first time I ever went a long ride and nobody saw me off. No one went with me the three steps of decency, not even Mac or Myrtle. I guess I was running away from Me, that don't get you anywhere.

When I finished that letter to Wyn I had the M.P. all right, what we called the Mortal Pang. I hadn't told him hardly anything. Do men know about what turns over inside of you when a letter goes down the slot and you clank the slide to be sure it don't stick and gets a good start. I couldn't clank the porter but I gave him two bits and he said he'd mail it at Altoona.

That was the first time I ever wrote Wyn except Inter-office Memo. I learned a lot about letters in the office of *Philly* because when I addressed one to Parry I remembered Pop's talk about the high-toned Esq and I wrote it Mr Parrish Berwyn Esq which Wyn said was wrong. If you're Esq you can't be Mr at the same time. I think I was rather cute, I said suppose I'd ever write You a letter would it be Wynnewood Strafford Esq VI or Wynnewood

Strafford VI Esq? He said at Old St Davids or even at Rittenhouse Square it was his father was really the Esq and he himself was only Wynnewood Strafford VI, but if writing to an office it was better to put Mr because there you were just the honest tradesman. It seems a man can't properly be Esq away from his inherited private property. To put Esq on a business letter is New York phony or the Nouveau Long Island touch, he said.

O.K., but suppose I'm writing to him at the bank, how's about it? The bank is a regular safe deposit of private properties. Anybody but Wyn I'd say apple strudel but I wanted him to think I knew what was right by instinct. I wrote it Wynnewood Strafford VI just like he was King. I was worried after, I should have said Personal on it, but if anyone else opened it they wouldn't need to go far to see it wasn't theirs. Sweetest Boy in the World is no way to ask for Ninety Day Time.

I sat there and took it hard. I was going round a bend as tough as the Horseshoe. Oh I suppose I was only a kid but everybody is as grown up as the feelings they have at the time they feel them. It was crazy to be on that train, what was I there for? The porter started making beds and shutting everything up in those damn green curtains, just the look of them always gives me the preliminary cramps. A couple of cunning little boys were being put to bed in an upper berth, I could see them scuffling up there in pyjama suits with feet. Everybody else had some good sensible reason for going somewhere but where am I going and why?

I'm walking out on the Philadelphia Assembly, I bet nobody else ever did that.

194

I'm running away from home, the only home I have, it won't last long now, the old man is cracking up, Mac has a home and Myrtle has a home and what has Kitty got? I'm running away from Myrtle and the kitchen stove with a broken lid and the ice chest that don't latch tight and the little entry window and the smell of wisteria-chlorides and the bamboo table the photos fell off of where I had pretty knees. Even that coon porter has a reason to be here, this car makes sense to him, he has a little homey cupboard of linen and stuff, no wonder he can jolly those kids, he's doing a job and got someone like Myrtle to think about. Maybe not though, he's not black enough for Myrtle. Do they check up on shades of blackness before they get too fond of each other? Oh, I'll bet they do, I'll bet somebody has figured things out to make it tough for them.

Why haven't *I* got some place to stick to where we've lived for seven generations?

Kitty you better behave, you'll have rings under your eyes, you'll have rings under your mind.

I'm not running away from anything but Darby Mill, Old St Davids 31. I didn't know people lived in places like that, I thought it was just frontage for the movies. Long and low under the trees, that grand old brown and silver Pennsylvania stone and late roses, you wouldn't think roses could hang on like that, I bet it takes seven generations. Chrysanthemums so strong in the wet they make you sneeze. And that clear water over the dam by the old mill, they use it for a game room now but I bet Wyn Strafford Number 1 really sawed wood, wood with knots in it. Down by the stables is smell of chrysanthemum mixed up with smell of horses, their rear ends polished like antique furniture on Walnut Street and a fire in my chintzy bedroom and nobody to wade in firelight in moccasins. And fox heads and bear heads and moose heads and deer heads like a stockyard and somebody's red coat flopped in a corner like the battle of Bunker Hill. That family certainly raised hell and havoc among animals and British.

I get a notion why the Main Line is so British nowadays, they start the little boys dressing like English gentry soon as they're old enough to stand up in the bathroom, they don't even know it's English they think everybody dresses like that. It's their way of apologizing because they were so ill bred in 1776.

Those little boys better keep away from Manitou, Illinois.

I could get off the train at Altoona and still get back to Griscom Street and cook Pop's breakfast. Sure I could, I looked it up in the timetable.

Kitty you're crazy. Listen Kitty, all those people going places, looking so intentional and doing things on purpose, I bet every one of them has a soft spot in him somewhere, poor dubs. Listen sister, don't bear down too hard on that soft spot, you'll break through. Get yourself a club sandwich and a glass of milk, do something sensible there's a swell kid, read the *Saturday Evening Post* founded 17-something by Benjamin Franklin. What was Wyn Number 1 doing when Ben Franklin was founding things? I bet they were a couple of tough old cronies. Wyn said to Ben, go fly a kite, and look what happened. Telephones and stuff.

I love him. I'm a woman and I love him. Nothing can't

196

ever take that away. I've held his love in my body. It's
wonderful how wrapped up just four arms can make
people feel. Once I said to him Now you're Esq, you're
on your own private property. Does he love me? Maybe
Straffords go hunting for women like they hunt animals,
put up their heads on a panel somewhere with glass eyes
shining in the firelight. Oh, once and a while they catch
a nice one out of the stud-book and tame her and let
her live there, just for breeding.

All I asked was to be allowed to love someone.

Nothing can't ever take that away.

Porter I'll go in the diner while you make up this berth.

We're past Horseshoe Curve, past Johnstown. Brush my
teeth and comb my hair and take a whiff of the mountain
air. If you can't sleep you can sit up in the berth and hunt
where the light turns on. You can rearrange your clothes
and count your money and buff your nails and listen to
snores. I wonder how I'll wrestle into that new girdle in
the morning. If hips ever come back I'll sure qualify for a
dress model.

There's a man who can snore through Pittsburgh. It
takes seven generations to learn that.

I guess I went to sleep through Ohio and Indiana. What
would you lie awake for when you get outside Pennsylvania? When the porter punched me there were the good
old strings of Swift Refrigerator cars. I had wired Molly,
I picked that train so's we could have breakfast together
before she went to the store. She met me, I could see her
waving at the top of the little slope that goes up from

the tracks. She said, what would we do without trains to meet each other at. Just the same I didn't want to see that one again. And by the time we got set to eggs and bacon at Fred Harvey's we were happy as fools. I hate to admit it.

Molly's grand. You can't take it easy with a man, not even Wyn, the way you can with a girl. I guess you don't want to. You're always trailing your airial out the window to pick up some music or other.

People must get bored stiff when they've got only sex to interest them in each other. Wyn and I would always have something to talk about, he's so simple and sweet I could spend my whole life educating him. The beauty of it, he wouldn't know when I was doing it, and I would always know when I was learning something from him. It's bad for a man to know how much he needs to learn. I guess every woman is a schoolmistress in her heart.

That kicks a goal for Mark Eisen. We'd always have the hospital to think about, and the cripple children. But I couldn't ever give Mark what I gave Wyn. I told him that, but he's so sure of himself. He says, how do you know what you can give till you give it? He's quick.

Molly said once, It's good we're only thinking.

But a woman hasn't got seven generations to find out what's beautiful.

Chicago's different from Philly. You don't worry about how many generations. Why the scalp wounds are scarcely healed. Out there anybody who even has a grandfather is an oldtimer, practically a Daughter of Fort Dearborn. I had to laugh at myself, I was almost ready to highhat the town because I came from a clapboard house in Frankford and a brass bed with a forty year trough in it. Molly and Pat Kenzie had a room in a comical old dump near the Water Tower, it made me feel at home right away because they had a tin bathtub like Griscom Street. Pat Kenzie was old Chicago all right, she said she was related to Kenzie the Fur Trader, the one they put up a tablet by the Wrigley Building. We used to kid her about it, if she was legitimate old Kenzie must have been a trader in red fox. Both the girls were all hopped up about their new jobs, Pat was in lingerie and Molly in furniture. Business was fine and Molly said everybody in Chi was laughing about the market crash in N.Y., the Middle West don't get jitters like that. "Hoover comes from the Middle West, don't he? He's got his feet flat on the ground." Pat said Chicago was the best town in the world for lingerie, on account of the soot people have to change their underwear more often. Molly was all big-eye about teaching the furniture department good taste, she had reference books out of the Library. She had a scunner against the twin bed suites they were selling and I wouldn't be surprised it was the big double bed and the daybed they had in the room that started her on her Two-and One idea. She went to town on it later. "It's terrible nonsense people always buying two little twin beds. Sure, people want to sleep single once and a while but even if they want to sleep double they need room to spread out. At least that's what I imagine. Why not make up your bedroom suite with one double bed and one single, then you can cover any kind of situation, they both got a bed to themselves when they want it and they got a big one for romance and cold weather."

Pat said since she was sharing the big bed with Molly she felt all this was aimed at her somehow, but Molly said it was a good commercial idea. She got herself embarrassed though, because after she thought it over a while she took it up with Mr Krebs the head of her department. She said "Mr Krebs don't you ever get tired sleeping in a twin bed?" and if he hadn't a sense of humor she might have lost her job or else got one she didn't care for.

I have to laugh when I think back about the things White Collar Girls talk about when they live together. When you're working on 18 a week like those kids you don't go out evenings unless someone takes you. You sit home with what Pat called a Confederate Highball, that's lemon coke, and wash stockings and iron a slip and buy the evening paper in turns and set the alarm clock so there'll be time to walk to work in the morning. Nowadays when things are different with me, living by myself and I even took to curling up with a book, sometimes I run on some philosophy about Women and Behaviorism and so forth and I wonder where those writers get their ideas. I guess no woman ever bothered to put them wise.

Men are good about Telling the World, but pretty often some woman whispered it to him first.

While the girls were at the store I trouped round the town, and got a big kick out of Michigan Avenue and the Art Institute. When I was with Molly and Pat I kept pretty quiet about my own problems, I didn't want Molly to get upset about my going off the deep end and I didn't know Pat well enough to come through with much inside stuff in front of her, though I never knew a redhead that wouldn't understand. Somehow I didn't want to let Uncle and Auntie know right away that I was in Chicago, I just wanted a few days out in the clear, no strings on me. That's the way you feel on Michigan Avenue, open to the Lake on one side. And the names of the buildings, so different from Philly, imagine Carbon and Carbide or People's Gas. In Philly it would be the Contributionship for the Assurance of Granting Annuities on Lives. The names of streets too, sound like they were going places, not just named after take-your-time things like trees. But it's hard to remember the order of those President streets. In Philly all the children learn the important streets from a rhyme—

> Chestnut, Walnut, Spruce and Pine,
> Market, Arch, Race and Vine.

So I made up a song of my own for the streets I'd come to after crossing the Michigan Avenue bridge:

> Randolph, Washington, Madison, Monroe,
> Then Adams, Jackson, Van Buren we go.

After that you come to the good old Congress, usually that's about as far as I got. Or if you're going West through the Loop, from Michigan you can figure on

> Wabash, State, Dearborn, Clark;
> LaSalle and Wells, not after dark.

Going north from the bridge are those streets named for Great Lakes, Ontario, Erie, Huron, Superior. They made me think about the old missionaries and pioneers and want to study more American history, then I'd see something in a window and find myself back at the Water Tower. Chicago always makes me feel anything might

201

happen. The trouble with history books is they don't know about things till afterward.

Molly and I planned to go down to Manitou after the store closed on a Saturday and spend Sunday. I was going to meet her at the store and we'd do some shopping before catching the train. I remember what a happy day I had, I didn't think once, just enjoyed myself. I took a bus up to Edgewater Beach and bummed around, wondered what happened at the Saddle and Cycle Club, came back and had a bath in the tin tub and packed my bag. I was coming out of the house to go downtown and there was Wyn.

Wyn, west of Paoli! Just the few days I'd been away I'd got used to the way men dress in Chicago, pressed very sharp and neat, and provincial snap-brim hats, and Wyn looked almost foreign. He'd gone from the train straight to Palmer's where he knew Molly worked and found out our address.

Poor darling, I was sorry for him, but I had to take that train, I wasn't going to let Molly down or disappoint Uncle and Auntie, or even Pattyshells.

"It's all fixed," he said. "I've arranged it with your friend Molly; she's a grand girl. I'll take you to tea somewhere and then I'll ride you to the station to meet her. I'm going there anyhow to get my bag. I'll take a room at a hotel and wait till you come back on Monday. You little fool I love you and I'm going to talk to you."

"Wyn," I said, "didn't you get my letter? I wrote you saying I wanted to think about things."

"Yes, and what the hell do you mean by mailing me a letter from Harrisburg?"

"Why Wyn that's just what I didn't do, I specially didn't. The porter said he'd mail it from Altoona."

"Well then maybe he handed it to a trainman and it didn't get postmarked until Harrisburg. Look here." He showed me the envelope, it was stamped *R.P.O. Harrisburg*. I guess that proves how it isn't much use to try to figure things out.

"You better tell me the name of a good hotel in this madman's town. All I know is when my father was here for the World's Fair in 1893 or whenever, he stayed with somebody called Potter Palmer and they had silver dollars inlaid in the floor. They must chew an awful lot of gum out here, they've even got a building named for it."

He must have been talking with the taxi because he had it figured out already where he'd take me for tea, and it was like him to discover the most Philadelphia kind of place in the whole city. It was a chop house tucked away in a back alley that looked like a street in Philadelphia, there wasn't anyone there but ourselves that time of afternoon and they had English waiters wearing red coats, all ready to shoot some foxes.

"I was counting on getting some dancing with you tonight," he said.

"Not tonight, Wyn. I've got to go to Manitou, I'd love to take you along but it would mean too much explaining."

"Tonight was sort of special," he said.

"Why tonight?"

"Have you forgotten? It's the date of the Assembly."

I didn't know whether to laugh or cry, so I guess I laughed.

The ride to Manitou always makes me feel good. There's something strong and decent about that dumb flat country. Also, if I'm riding with Molly, there's just about enough time for a good talk, and we had it all the way to Plautus, before the quiet spell that hits you near the end of a long journey. I only remember one thing she said, just after Wyn saw us off on the train. "Is that boy an American?" That hurt somehow, so I let it lay; I mean I put it back in my mind to think about later.

I guess Americans don't have to be all alike, do they?

The visit with Uncle and Auntie wasn't quite what I expected. I guess I'd counted too much on it. There wasn't enough time, we had to go back to Chi late Sunday so Molly'd be on time for the job; and it was snowing, and Auntie asked everybody in town to come for coffee Sunday afternoon and I found I was just being polite to people I loved. Lyddie and Fedor and all the rest of them were full of college doings, naturally, and I felt such a long way away from that. Wyn called up about lunch time and said he'd changed his mind about Chicago, it was a swell town. We told him when we left that if he was lonely to call Pat Kenzie and sure enough he had. Pat junked her usual stable of Saturday nighters and he took her to Chez Pierre. That's a swell night club I'd always wanted to go to and I guess I was a bit sore.

I was mixed up anyhow. Things in Manitou seemed sort of simple and straightforward and I was all tied up in knots. Pattyshells was so feeble he made me think of Pop, he had the same look in his eyes, puzzled and a bit frightened. Uncle would pick him up and carry him in beside the kitchen stove at bedtime, and that made me homesick. I telegraphed Mac to see how things were, he wired back *Old Man Grouchy But Okay You Better Enjoy Your Holiday*. That's the only poem Mac ever wrote and it was just ten words accident.

Molly and I got back to Chicawgo late Sunday night, and damned if Wyn wasn't there at the station, he figured out what train we'd have to take. All of a sudden I was happy again. There are a lot of tough things happen but Jesusgod there's nothing like meetings.

"How did you get clearance papers from Pat?" I asked, but he only grinned.

"She's gone to bed," he said. "She takes that job of hers seriously."

"So do I," said Molly. "You can ride me home. Kitty, here's the latchkey."

Wyn had certainly learned his way round town in a day and a half, he had a taxidriver called Potatoes who was a wiseacre. He had even put a different curl on the brim of his hat so he wouldn't feel so foreign. It was my first idea how the Colonial Families open up when they get away from Philly. Potatoes took us to an all-night speak that had a sign on the door "Agricultural and Machinery Service." Wyn's idea was that this sort of thing wouldn't do at all in Philly but it was all right when you were slumming.

He said he went to the Palmer House but he couldn't find the silver dollars on the floor so he moved to the Congress. "That's a grand old place, Kitty, wait till you smell it. It's something like the Bellevue at home, but more cheerful in its ideas, they've got some perfume of their own they sprinkle round the lobby and along Peacock

Alley, it leads you to the Balloon Room where they dance. They call it an antiseptic but I don't think that's the idea, they've got it in the elevators too."

"You learn your way around, don't you." It was on the tip of my tongue to say something, just kidding, about Pat being a good tutor, but I held back. It's a bad mistake ever to give a man the idea you can be jealous.

Then Wyn surprised me the way he always could when he was really Wyn.

"I found my way to a jewelry store," he said, and pulled out a little box from his pocket. It was a funny little silver ring, a snake eating its own tail. He had made a bad guess, it didn't fit the third finger but it slid right onto the pinky as though it was made for it, where it is this minute.

"That's the snake that bit us at Pocono," he said.

I wonder how many Philadelphia girls ever had a proposal of marriage in a Chicago speakeasy.

Next night we followed that perfume down the long alley to the Balloon Room. Even Delphine's Olympia can't mean to me what that old Congress flavor did. Wyn said he thought it was left over from the Chicago World's Fair; it was the Lust of the Nineties. I guess they gave it up when they went into a chain. Even the bedrooms had old clocks in the walls, so the patrons wouldn't miss the legshow out at the 1893 Midway; they were all stopped and broken by then.

Molly and Pat, the hardworking wenches, must have thought we were crazy. It's good to have been that way maybe once a lifetime. When they came back from work they found me getting fixed. Wyn came to the house that morning and said "Get a move on, we've got to get our outfit." We hadn't either of us any swish clothes with us, and he'd set his heart on doing the Balloon Room in style. He said it was really the Philadelphia Assembly. This hurt me inside but I wasn't going to take time to let anything hurt just then. He took me to Palmer's and bought me an entire outfit. Pat picked out the lingerie and he mannequin'd me around until we found a gold lamé dress and I was never so dolled up in my life. I knew it was dishonest and unfair and all that but it was giving him such a kick to fit me out as he said from the bottom up. When I was all equipped he sent me back to Molly's in a taxi and got himself a readymade evening suit. I bet it was the only time Wyn Strafford wore readymades and he looked almost too Ritzy. He said he did a few somersaults over the bed to take the shine off.

Once and a while I think of those colored lights on the floor that ran around under our feet, and flocks of balloons that came from somewhere like shad roe. We were very dignified, sort of wondering if anyone admired the distinguished-looking couple. The headwaiter did all right, and it was a profitable evening for him. I wonder what he thought when Wyn kept telling him that this was the Philadelphia Assembly. I bet no Assembly was ever so perfect, because we had that wonderful feeling of being alone in a crowd that doesn't know or care who you are except that you're happy. It's wonderful not to know who anybody is, and I guess Wyn hadn't had much experience of that. "It's like being a god," he said. He said things that were like colored balloons and floated right into my ear. "Mouth and ear ought to be close together, like those

207

new French telephones." When we'd do a spin and wonder if there really was a floor to that room ("What have you done to the Law of Gravity?" he said to the head-waiter) he'd maybe steal a kiss and if I was worried he said "The lip is quicker than the eye."

"I think getting away from Philly is good for you," I told him.

When he called me Baby Girl I could feel the sap running like I was a sugar maple.

"Kitty," he said, "you look like something wrapped round the neck of a champagne bottle."

"I look like something wrapped round your neck."

"I got it fixed, we can have a glass of champagne up in my room."

We went up there, and sure enough from somewhere he'd got a champagne bucket. We drank each other's health, maybe a little too much for really good health, and then I saw the label on the bottle. Piper Heidseck. It brought back the old man's song, "In came Piper Heidseck and handed him a glass of wine." I cried and cried and Wyn couldn't understand. Oh I'd been hoarding up that crying spell a long while.

Wyn, I said, I've got to go home. No, I mean Home, Griscom Street. I want to see Pop and Myrtle and the Pope's telephone booth. I want to get back, I can't pretend myself into happiness. I guess I've got snakebite."

He saw I meant it and called the porter for a reservation. We didn't even go down to the Balloon Room again for a last dance, Wyn called the headwaiter up to the room and settled the bill. He told him we were the King and Queen of Bulgaria and Al Capone was jealous of us, we had to leave. I wouldn't be surprised he believed it, as much as a headwaiter believes anything.

We parked our beautiful clothes at Molly's, in case of another Assembly, and went home on the train together. It seems as sad as a fairy tale. They're pretty sad if you read them again after you're grown up.

22

Mark Eisen said something I don't forget. He was talking about an operation he watched. "She won't need to worry about a scar. Of course in a man it don't matter, but for a young girl it's important. The surgeon took plenty of time to figure it out and put it right in one of the natural creases of her neck. It's lovely."

"Mark," I said, "that's just like me. I've got plenty of scars in my memory, but I hope they're in the natural creases."

I'm thinking of those last days with the old man. It's always queer watching anybody say goodbye. I didn't quite know it then, but that's what he was doing. He took a habit of humming to himself, used to lie abed crooning The Low Backed Car. He had that tune and Mother and the old hollow in the bed all tied up together in his mind, and he would say things that made me cry. That was the only time I was grateful for his beard because sometimes if I didn't pull away fast enough the tears would fall in his whiskers and he wouldn't notice. Then he'd get downstairs and sit in the Front Room and his temper would come back on him and Myrtle and I were pleased. He liked to hear my typewriter going, I guess it made him feel that I had something to fall back on. I got some typing jobs to do at home, and even when I didn't have anything on hand I'd go and beat the machine, just practising, to make him feel good, or maybe to give him something to crab about.

I didn't see so much of Wyn for a while. That was partly because I told him I better build up some conscientiousness at home, and also I dare say his family were working on him and maybe he promised he'd try to shake me out of his system. He never said so, but that's my hunch. The problem was, the old man kept asking why Wyn didn't come to see him. That put me on a spot but it was Pop I was thinking of most, so I wrote Wyn a note and told him what the old man said. He called up and said he'd come on Friday. It *would* be like that, Friday was my birthday, of course he didn't know. I made up my mind that when he came I'd go out to the movies so's he could concentrate on Pop; but it seemed tough to be chased out of my own home on my birthday by the man I loved. I made Pop and Myrtle promise not to tell, and I went and sat through some pictures but they were pretty blurred. It didn't strike me till afterward that Wyn would think I did it just to be ornery or difficult.

I suppose if you always knew what everybody was going to think about everything life would lose its savor. The hell it would.

But there was a few weeks in there somewhere that had a feeling of peacefulness. They were just kidding, I guess. What I mean, I was so happy doing for the old man; it was cold winter and the house was warm and packed tight with familiar habits. When Pop got tired talking or reading he liked to sit by himself in the Front Room and Myrtle and I had grand talks in the kitchen. There's something about an ironing board that makes you say things. I doubt there ever was a household got so well ironed up, nightgowns and curtains and bedlinen and Pop's Sunday pants, everything I could lay hands on because it was good to spill things to Myrtle. Next after Molly she's the best conversation for a woman.

Myrtle never was outside Philadelphia in her life except to some African Methodist fresh air farm in Jersey. She was born and raised on South Street, and I think she had a kind of idea that was where the South begins and everything from there on down is a solid Black Belt, the best of which is called Virginia. She was very proud of the fact that her father came to Philadelphia from Virginia for the Centennial, "He wuz a pioneer in de wool-straightenin' business, nobody dat can straighten wool is goin' starve. He had a kind of sweetenin'-gum would take kink out of an iron cable. Every black Sheba on South an' Bainbridge want to comb out her frizz wid dat cunjur-lotion. It thin out varmints too. One day someone touch a match to it and it burn down de whole alley. Too much turpentine into it."

She was curious about Chicago, which lost nothing of its pride in my accounts. She considered carefully my description of the lake front. "Ef you cain't see across it, dat ain't a lake, dat's ocean." She wanted to know about colored people in Chicago, and I had to admit I'd not seen many. "Dat's natural, honey. High class cullud folks all comes to Philadelphia. Virginia niggers won't go nowheres else." I realized that to her Virginia was the Main Line.

"Dey live mighty highfalutin down there until Government strangle it. My father use to tell me. Gentry all smoke cigars because kitchen and backhouse smell so strong, and ladies' dresses all whipped up wid ruffle. An' blue ribbon in eve'y pair o' drawers. Honey, dat must have been a struggle fo' de ironin' boa'd. You think dem times ever come back? Not in Frankford, I reckon."

Something, maybe seeing the old Manitou crowd again, put in me a yen for education. When Pop heard the typewriter going I was likely copying out bits from the freshman textbooks I had bought and not used. I wished I knew some Abbé Constantin who would tell me the answers. Myrtle was as near as I ever found one, I guess. When you're pushing the iron to and fro you're not embarrassed to ask questions. "How am I going to learn about things that are beautiful? I don't think those Manitou kids are really getting it in college. They're too young, too well fed, too secure. Can I learn it in books? Or newspapers?"

What I wanted to hear Myrtle or somebody say was "You can learn it all from Wyn. He's beauty itself; he's truth and kindness and everything lovely. You worship him, and you should."

"Dat's what *I* calls beautiful," said Myrtle, taking a pan of beaten biscuit out of the oven. "Dat make me feel good."

A funny little thing happened. Somebody at the Library gave me a ticket to go to a lecture at a Club over in

213

Germantown. There were a lot of dames hopped up with culture and good grammar and nowhere to park it between 3 and 5 p.m. I could tell by the way they chirped and rustled they were all set for a big shot of high-pressure literature. What shocked them was, the lecturer talked just like he might to a crowd of men, as though they had a sense of humor. First thing they knew, they were laughing, and they hated it. They hadn't come there to laugh, and it threw them off balance. I heard them afterward saying it was an insult to a club like that to come there and just be jocular. What they didn't get, and it made me so sore I wanted to shout out about it, in between laughs that man was in savage earnest, he was really trying to tell them things. He was feeding them laughs to shake up their opinions. I guess it's risky to tell people anything except the way they count on hearing it.

"Listen, babygirl," Wyn said one time, "you weren't put here to reform the world."

I asked Myrtle, was she ever in love. "Maybe not, honey, not the way you mean. Anyhow, not to make me mizzable. 'Pears to me, colored folks aint persecuted by love the way white folks is. The only real misdemeanor in our family is when my ole man cut his wrist off wid a sickle. He was sicklin' on a grasspatch while he had hiccups. A big hiccup throwed him forward just as the sickle was comin' up at him an' he like to amputate himself. All the grip in that hand is clean paralyzed, I tell him it's lucky it aint the hand he use for drinkin'. Oh dat's a long while ago, it heal up nice, new meat come through as pink as white folks."

Come to think of it, when things happen to other

214

people it's always a while ago. When they happen to me they're happening *now*.

My being out that night Wyn called started up some new campaigning. He invited me to dinner at Rittenhouse Square and I couldn't hurt him by ducking it. He said this would be different from the house-party at Darby Mill. It was, it was lovely. It was just family and a few old friends. Myrtle was disappointed I didn't get the social dope on the colored butler, she thought maybe she knew his folks; I didn't let on I'd seen him light a pipe on the front steps. They had me at Mr Strafford's right, and Wyn was across the table next to his sister who is just as darling as he is. There must be something to Englishmen because she married one of them, but he was killed in the War. On my right was Mr Kennett, a perfectly delightful old Quaker who called me *thee* and started to talk about music. There was a Russian musician there and his wife, he played the violin after dinner and his wife at the piano.

I never talked to anybody who got more out of me than old Mr Kennett. I guess you just can't resist it when they say *thee*. Naturally I was nervous and made a bad start, I said my favorite tune was that theme song that starts the Tasty-yeast program on the radio because it put Pop in a good humor for his supper. But the Russian came to my rescue, he made me hum it and then said it was a phrase from an old Russian balalaika or something. We got on to Pop's Irish melodies, and college in Manitou, and business school, and I spilled a lot of my simple ideas before it struck me the old Friend was maybe pumping me to see what kind of a girl I was. I thought afterward he was probably a kind of spiritual adviser for the Strafford family, they confided their anxiety about Wyn's feelings and he was put there to get my number.

Anyhow it was better than Darby Mill, there were no dead animals around the house, no drinking except some sour wine, and I could catch Wyn's eye whenever I needed to. Rosey Rittenhouse and his wife were there and Rosey said wonderful things about Pop. I had some ammunition in reserve, if any highhatting started I was going to come through with the fact that Pop's father was wounded at Gettysburg. When he did his shooting he did it at people that shot right back. But I didn't need to say it, and old Mr Kennett being a Quaker maybe it was just as well.

They have a wonderful big drawing room with a greenhouse opening off of it, full of flowers. Several people, who probably didn't need the meal, came in after dinner for coffee and music. One of them was Staceylea Bala; I wondered was that to tip me off that she was still runner-up. If so she was a little late, Wyn had me on a sofa together with Rosey Rittenhouse who didn't mind or notice if we held a few hands. You've got to do something with your hands when they play that Russian music. Even Stacey was on her good behavior and actually made out to recognize me— "Why yes, from the office. How delightful!"

They talked a bit about the poor little magazine. Mr and Mrs Strafford said they were so glad Wyn had got over it, as though it was a disease. Staceylea said she

216

thought it was putrid luck it hadn't gone over, it would have been such fun, as though it was a game. I said I didn't think there was really much fun in imitating other people's ideas; it was a New York kind of idea, not a Philadelphia one. Rosey whispered to me, what would you call a Philadelphia kind of idea? and I whispered back "Wondering how much of what you think it will be safe to say." By the time it was right to go I was beginning to enjoy myself, there was something unreal about that big warm room smelling of flowers while I could hear tire-chains in the snow outside. That was sort of appropriate while the Russian music was playing inside, like prisoners clanking on the way to Siberia. I could see there was a certain number of things that had to be said, after that they felt free to go ahead and talk. Something had to be said about the Community Chest drive for charity, and about the Orchestra, Stokowsky has so much magnetism, and about the Depression, has Mr Hoover got it under control? You can't help being impressed by those sort of things, they say them so comfortably as though they know they've got a warm bed waiting upstairs and a bank account to go to in the morning. Once, in the pause after a piece of music before anyone thought of just the right comment, I could hear that good old Philadelphia sound, very faint like church bells, the butler somewhere down in the cellar shovelling coal. It sounded so homely, it surprised me. I guess I don't get far enough away from myself and when they were talking gently about unemployment I almost wanted to holler out "What about K. Foyle? Suppose your old man might die any minute and his pension stops and you're thrown out on your ass." Rosey would have understood, there's something human about that bird, in between chukkers he must have heard about what goes on, maybe he talks over long distance.

I said to him, and I meant it, "I think they're wonderfully kind." He said "Kitty, we're the kindest people in the world, and don't we know it."

I was worried about Wyn, he was pretty quiet, I could see that his family had him swamped and I guess he felt himself sinking back into the banking business. Even old Mr Kennett, who turned out to be Wyn's godfather, seemed to have something to do with banking. Everybody called him *thee*, but I doubt if it would make him any easier if you wanted a loan without security.

Mrs Strafford explained that she and her husband were leaving for South Carolina so she was afraid they wouldn't see much of me for a while, but I hadn't really been counting on it. They had a big limousine waiting to take me home. Wyn went along, but I didn't feel like talking much with a chauffeur right in front of us. "You made a great hit with old Godfather Kennett," Wyn said.

"He almost had me calling him *thee*. But I think I'd have to love someone very much before I could do it. I'm like the French that way."

"Kitty, does thee love me? I told them I considered myself practically engaged to thee."

"I thought they all acted scared about something. I figured it was only the stock market."

"Oh Kitty, we can't seem to talk in Philly. Could we go somewhere else some day and get confidential?"

"I'll let thee know," I said.

218

That was a funny time, now I think back. There isn't any better thinking than you do at the hairdresser's, and sitting in one of those orchid-colored booths of Nicolai's puts a new light on all sorts of things including complexions.

Everything was in the oven and the heat turned on and the yeast ready to go to work. And the Main Line was out chasing fresh air and foxes as though nothing had happened or ever would.

I get a pay-off on things sometimes from Nicolai. He's a Russian and if he gets fond of your scalp he talks about it. What I mean, he knows that revolutions really happen; he saw one. He says he was raised in the Imperial Institute of Hair Culture in Saint Petersburg, and Russia is the place to study hair. He says when Russians shaved and shingled they went crazy. He was brought up among the whiskers and coiffures of the Romanoffs, who were the Main Line of Holy Russia. He thinks maybe I'm not fair to Holy Philly. He says "they worked hard."

Well, I guess they did. Sometimes it strikes me life has been ugly these past ten years and maybe the Strafford-Rittenhouse crowd were more faithful to an ideal than most of us. They were kind and generous and sweet and they didn't even mind a little modernism if it was limited to music. No wonder they were sore when Franklin Roosevelt came along and acted up; one of their own crowd too. It was like a fox turning around and chasing the beagles.

Rosey Rittenhouse was really super. He had me and Wyn out to his lovely place for dinner, he apologized for his wife not being there. He said she went to bed with a headache, which is good sense when you don't understand what's going on. They have a farm out beyond Swarthmore, down Rose Valley way. Of course this isn't Main Line, Rosey kidded me; we've been corrupted by a lot of strolling actors and Hicksites. No one would ever have a scunner against liquor if they could see what a lot of good it does to a man like Rosey. He's careful and proper and sort of Knox Hat when he's on routine, but a couple of Scotch bring out the very best that's in him. He says he was born two Scotches below par. He said something while Wyn was out of the room: "Kitty, don't forget maybe Wyn has his own hell to go through too."

Jesusgod, I've thought about that, my poor darling. And something else Rosey said. "Don't be too hard on patterns. Remember your father was head of the pattern-shop for a good many years."

We sat by a big fireplace and talked. I guess Rosey is a good man because he hasn't any yen to solve things. He said Philadelphia went to bed with a headache fifty years ago. We talked about religion. Wyn said what he liked about Quakerism was the idea of salvation piped direct to the individual, what they call the Inner Light, everybody has it for himself. A kind of neon tubing I guess. Rosey said he wasn't so sure, there was something to be said for Indirect Lighting too, like the Catholics. "But don't quote me, I'll be thrown out of Swarthmore Meeting."

I told him I was getting a new slant on him. "I used to think, reading the *Ledger,* you were the kind of person who wasn't interested in anything but horses and tally-hos."

"What first got Rosey interested in horses," said Wyn, "he saw they were so good at pulling beer-wagons."

I think of Rosey's voice sometimes, that easy well-bred Philadelphia accent that seems to fit them like a suit of good tweeds. The kind of voice people only get when they've had good meals and good sleep for several generations and horses in the stable.

"There's nothing wrong in associating with horses," he says. "They're better animals than we are. And I never saw a woman yet who had legs as pretty as a good pony's."

While Wyn was getting his car to drive us back to town Rosey said: "Kitty, I'm on your side. But that means I know there's another side too."

23

We came in on the train at dusk, rumbled through the long tunnel, walked up some stairs, but still underground because I could hear subways overhead. Then there was quite a hike down another tunnel; I remember how far ahead of us the redcap got and he was still going on. That was my first view of New York, that long passage, a sort of gloomy yellow color. "What do you think of our skyline?" Wyn said. Still we had to go up in an elevator before we got into the hotel.

It was specially sweet because Wyn had thought everything out beforehand. The room was high up, about thirty stories, and I got my first view out over the city. He put his arms round me as I stood there at the window and I said "Wyn, let me take it in. Let me memorize this so I never never forget it."

Just the same it doesn't always work, to try to tell yourself what you're going to memorize. I always remember the craziest things. It's not altogether my fault, because every time Wyn and I went anywhere together, things happened that seemed completely invented for us. They were just plain goofy. After we made ourselves comfortable Wyn thought we might go somewhere and have a drink. He'd been given the address of Giono's, Snorty West Forty, so we hopped a cab. We didn't take a table, just had highballs at the bar as Wyn wanted to go somewhere more swell for dinner. Giono's was just a run-of-the-mine wopeasy and I dare say the kitchen wasn't any too clean; first thing we saw was a roach running along the top of the bar. Wyn put the little whiskey glass upside down over it and called Giono's attention. "That ought to rate us a free drink," Wyn suggested. Giono wasn't upset, he said he was sorry but lots of newspaper men came to his place and the roaches followed them in. "All the roaches in town have got fresh on account of Don Marquis writing about Archie." This was certainly an elegant specimen because when he tried to climb up the inside of the glass the push of his legs would slide the glass across the wet bar. No one had seen anything like that before, all the people at the bar were watching and crowding round, and they kept the roach pushing the glass along and pouring out little puddles of highball to make it slippery for him until I guess the fumes were too strong or he got discouraged. He folded his feet and laid down. That was amusing for a while, then Wyn wanted to go where we could dance with our dinner. Part of the fun was for Wyn to order without my knowing what was coming; it was wonderful the way he could pick out things I liked, or things I didn't know about and wanted to. So without telling me he ordered sweetbreads sous cloche. When they came in, under a glass bell, I said it was a coincidence. We begin with cockroach under glass and we follow on with sweetbreads under glass.

I wonder if there would ever be any way to check up silly little memories with Wyn. Maybe if I was in jail, or dying, he'd be allowed to come and talk to me. Even if I couldn't touch him it would be something to see if he remembers the same things.

I guess that was the night I got the crying spell because Wyn was so dear, he was always different as soon as he got away from Philadelphia, and it came through to me that we never would be able to be really Us except outside Philly. At home we were too tied up with all sorts of inhibitions and influences. I loved him so I couldn't really kid myself about that. And I'm not going to kid myself, even now, thinking about it, by pretending that it was just Wyn who was chasing me. I didn't know it then, but it was just as much me chasing him; why even when I'd stall him off it was done so as would make him want me all the more. Jesusgod, how hard it is for people to be square with each other. I wanted him, I wanted him more than anything in the world, I wanted him enough to slip away from home even when Pop was so sick. When we were alone together it seemed like the answer to everything, and I know he wanted me too. He needed me and I gave him joy. It's good to know you gave someone joy. From outside our room there came a pale sort of shining from the lights of New York, and he said it was as beautiful on me as Pocono firelight.

As a matter of fact I agree with Rosey Rittenhouse, there's damn few girls as well shaped as a fine horse. It's a great piece of kidding Nature put over on men to give them the idea that females are so beautiful; but it's mighty satisfying to hear it said.

Take Molly Scharf, and somebody should; one of the loveliest shapes anyone ever saw, and men never even suspect it. They all go for Pat Kenzie. Pat used to call up from downtown, "Don't wait for me, I may be late. I've got a cocktail date, but I think I can stretch it to dinner."

Wyn, blessed, you and I had a cocktail date but I never tried to stretch it.

Wyn had to go down town next morning, errands for his bank. I sneaked out on a little idea of my own. I'd never forgotten Delphine, so I looked up her address in the phone book and went around there just to see where it was. I didn't want Wyn to know about it, but in the back of my mind, the part that keeps cool, I knew the old man wasn't going to last much longer and I'd be hunting a job. It would be better for me and better for Wyn if I was away from Philly. I didn't go in, I thought it would be better to write Delphine and prepare her mind, but I fixed the geography of it in my head, and it was right across the street from Giono's.

Then I walked up Fifth Avenue all the way to the Plaza and back again, looking in windows and trying to figure out whether women looked different from Philly. I was kind of disappointed. Of course I didn't know then what I do now, you don't see the really smart women on Fifth; they're mostly on Madison and Park Avenue. As a matter of fact Fifth Avenue isn't as smart as the right blocks on Chestnut Street. There's too much of it, and a Public Library and Woolworths and clearances of Philippine lingerie certainly drag it down. I could sense that most of the crowd on the Avenue were from out of town, and I felt quite superior about it. I forgot I was from out of town myself. It was comical to feel my Philadelphia patriotism raring up all of a sudden, something I didn't know I had. When I met Wyn at the Ritz for lunch I could see how much more like a gentleman he looked than most of them. The men I'd been seeing on the pavements probably never saw a fox except round somebody's neck on instalments.

I wondered why Wyn picked out the Ritz, that's not the kind of place he goes for much. He said he always wanted to find out what the doorman had in that leather satchel he carries slung round his neck. "If I knew what he carries in that wallet I'd really have the lowdown on the big town. I thought maybe it was code messages from foreign diplomats, or suggestions how to meet fragrant beautiful women."

"Probably it is," I said. "Did you get some good numbers?"

"Well," he said, "it took guts, but I asked him. All he has in it is small change so people can tip the taxi and a bunch of little cards."

"The cards must be your fragrant beautiful women."

"He said they're to write down the address when people drop dead."

"Why would they drop dead right outside the Ritz?"

Wyn was getting the lunch check when I asked this.

"They've just paid their bill," he said.

As a matter of fact, I guess the doorman was kidding him; but I always think of that when I go by the hotel.

It was cold early spring, the air very clear, it made you feel you had collyrium in your eyes. The whole blue sky's just a big eye-cup, I told Wyn. I guess it's love gives you that clean and washed and rested feeling. It makes you feel good, I mean with a line under it, good. I said to Wyn "I feel so virtuous, I really feel kind and sweet and when I'm with you I seem to see things. I guess that's the way poets are all the time."

"Or musicians," Wyn said. "Take a sheet of music, I look at it and it doesn't mean anything, but a musician runs his eye over it and sees all the harmonies and tricks that are there in code." Like shorthand. We practised seeing things that no one would notice unless they knew the signs. I wanted a ride in the subway so we went all the way up to Columbia University, which Wyn hadn't ever seen. When a Princeton man first sees Columbia it naturally opens his eyes to all sorts of things. We took turns trying who could get what we called Flashes. Mine was in the subway. There was an elderly man sitting across the car, you could see he was all buried in his own thoughts and he looked as though he might have had a hard time. That was when lots of them were jumping out of windows. All of a sudden, sort of written under the lines on his face I could see a look of the small boy he had been once, before anything battered him. I got a thrill out of that, I still watch for it sometimes, that kid expression that peeps out of a man's face. You don't find it often on older women. I guess they went too far down inside. You don't find it on animals either, I suppose an animal gets disillusioned early?

I was watching Wyn when he didn't know it, wondering

if I could see what he would look like when he's old, I couldn't imagine it. Just then he was being shocked by the advertising cards in the subway. "My God, Kitty, this is certainly a vulgar town. In Philly most of the car cards are about food or cigars. Here all they seem to worry about is their physical humiliations, dandruff and bad breath and head colds and diseased gums and hair in the armpits. When did New York get so anxious about personal hygiene? Well bred people don't get public about things like that."

Wyn was always adorable when he came to N.Y., he told me how lots of his friends in Philly used to come over on the sly once and a while just to get shocked. When they went home they said "I wouldn't live there if you gave me the place." He said New York even had to start a Racquet Club and a Union League to take care of the Philadelphia members who needed a place to rest after lunch. "New York has an inferiority complex," was his theory. "That's why it does such marvellous things. It's so worried about its bad breath and its complexion it builds an Empire State Building to take its mind off its troubles."

He was amused by a leaflet we found in a taxicab, it said "Reassurance to Lady Patrons. The Driver of this cab is a Married Man."

"That's pretty naive," said Wyn.

I didn't think it was naive at all. It was a kind of flattery. "Don't you know, my sweet, every woman loves to think she's travelling in terrible dangers?"

I guess the supply of married men ran out in the Depression, or else the lady patrons got more hardboiled; I haven't seen that notice for years. Nowadays they build the cabs with an open top so you can climb out on the roof and yell if you need a chaperone.

We went back to the hotel about dusk, and dusk comes early that time of year. Looking out the window you wouldn't need to believe all you read in the papers. Mostly women don't anyhow, except the advertising. With all their boloney about it sometimes I figure the ads are the most really honest and restrained things you find in newspapers. You have to play pretty square with people when you're selling an actual article. It's only when you're selling ideas you can run fast and loose. There was a lot of church bells in the air round that hotel at dusk; I don't know how, because we could never find any churches in that neighborhood. Just as well too, because I was nuts enough to have gone in one with Wyn and got married if he'd caught me unawares. Honestly it's a miracle we didn't. I don't know where those church bells came from, I thought maybe it was really ferryboats but Wyn said he regarded it as a kind of ceremony.

I don't know why I said to myself life was ugly those years. Well, it was in lots of ways, but I'm telling myself no one ever had more beauty to be grateful for. The right time to be living in is the time you live, and I haven't any hankering for what they call Mauve Decades or any other decades. Suppose we'd been living in the 80's and Wyn and me bathing in different ponds.

It's going to be uglier too unless people show more sense than they seem to have, but I'm here to say that I've had joy and given it and I was in there fighting.

Wyn said, why didn't we think to have our Assembly clothes sent on from Chicago, he could have wired Molly to forward them.

I said, let's not worry about clothes for a little while. Besides, you needn't think I'd wear that dress again until I'd had a chance to steam out the wrinkles.

I suppose Wyn has to do a good deal of dancing in his Main Line routine, even the Quakers shamble a leg nowadays, but he'll never find anyone who knew every slide he was going to make, and what made him think of it. Mark loves dancing too, but it isn't the same. I try to keep my mind off dancing. Some art museum somewhere I saw something called the Dance of Death, I see it in the papers every day. The whole damn world dancing with Death, and Death knows beforehand.

Maybe women take life too seriously. Maybe it's not as important as all that, just to stay alive.

Oh Wyn, it was *good*. Would there be any way to tell other people to believe in the goodness of it? No matter how it hurts. When we got away from Philly we felt the same things at the same time. There's something about New York makes you do that. Philly doesn't want to feel things until they've had a careful okay from yesterday. Sometimes I think if Wyn had to live in New York he could have been a clever man. It certainly stepped up his ideas. Think, if he'd gone to Columbia, how he'd have had to study to keep up with their economic wisecracks. It wouldn't have been good for him. I'd hate to see that Little Boy look of his all hardened over with ambition. It don't sit well on old Main Line families. Jesusgod, he'd likely be wearing balloon pants and polo shirts in the subway, the way those Columbia boys were. Wyn said it made him feel faint; that's why he had to look at the advertising cards.

I wouldn't turn a Master of Foxhounds into a stock exchange finagler, or the other way round. It's been tried. Maybe it's a comfort to the fox to know he's being chased by the right kind of people.

There was always something idiotic to make us happy. One time we were in a cab, we saw a truck marked Mutual Mattress and Bedding, The Bronx. Wyn thought it over, because next day I had a telegram from him. It said: *Send the address of that firm in the Bronx and fix a date for the wedding I am done with brothels and honkytonks I want mutual mattress and bedding.*

24

I WAS PROUD OF POP, THE WAY HE DIED. HE JUST PASSED out asleep the same as if he'd taken too much hootch. I guess that's what life is anyway, pretty strong drink. The last few weeks he was gentle and easy in his mind. Like Pattyshells, Auntie told me the old mutt had got too tired even to bark at the hand-organ man. That's funny too, a few days before there was a hand-organ on Griscom Street. They always came around about the same time as bock beer. Pop says "Ask him to play the Low Backed Car." That's the same for Irish as Swing Low Sweet Chariot for colored people.

It was good to see that dear old face of his, so rested. In spite of beard and sickness there was still some open-air color on him, and it was good cricket weather, the first smell of cut grass, weather he'd like to be out in his old green-stained flannels with a red ball. Denny said he wished the old man could be buried in his cricket pants with the club sash round his waist. Even Ed turned up, poor Ed I think that was when he was peddling hardware on commission. I know he made us laugh telling how he was demonstrating an aluminum skillet and when he lifted it up to show the customers how rugged it was the bottom fell out. Ed was always our hard luck baby. He talked rough but I can see now it was likely to hide his inside feelings. When he saw Pop laid out he said "People with beards don't seem as dead as the others. I noticed that with those Frenchmen in the War."

I think myself Pop would have liked to go out through Friends Meeting, but Denny said we better stick to the old batting crease and I will say the Presbyterians gave him the three steps of decency in a big way. All the cricket clubs sent flowers and the *Bulletin,* the paper that never forgets, had a little piece on the Great Days of Philadelphia Cricket and how Pop bowled that Indian Prince Ranji for a duck. Wyn and Rosey Rittenhouse came to the service, and the Orangemen's Lodge turned up in their sashes and tail coats. Ed said they wore tails to hide what they had on their hips. The minister worked a lot of cricket phrases into his tribute, something about "appealing to the wicket-keeper." Denny was peeved, he said the reverend got his cricket all mixed; the old man wouldn't appeal when he knew he was clean bowled, and anyhow you don't appeal to the wicket-keep but to the Umpire. That was mostly Greek to me, I was thinking of all the things I'd have liked to ask Pop if I'd thought about it. While the talking was going on I could imagine him saying "Teach your grandmother to suck eggs." I always wondered why anyone would want to suck eggs; it seems a messy way of eating them.

Aunt Hattie stayed a while to help me close things up. She was more hindrance than help because of course she ganged up with the Upsal crowd from Germantown and they all wanted to plan my future for me. Either I'd ought to go and live with Uncle and Auntie in Manitou, or I'd ought to take a room at the Y.W., or I could be nursemaid for some of the Upsal cousins who were all much younger than me. Those Upsals were always slow about making up their minds on anything, even in bed. Auntie got Mac so sore, always wondering how come Pop lived so much longer than Mother, poor Mac would scarcely come over to the house. And every time I talked to Wyn over the phone, which was often because he had plans for my future too, Auntie would have kittens.

I knew perfectly well what I wanted, and had it all fixed up in a couple of letters while Auntie was trying to make up her mind what ought to be done with the old mahogany dresser.

Auntie never could forget that Mother was her baby sister, and I guess she felt this gave her sort of squatter's rights on me. It was difficult because I love her very much except when anything's got to be decided. I promised Myrtle the old brass bed and mattress from Pop's room, for some reason of her own Myrtle thought they would bring her luck. Auntie seemed to think this was a kind of sacrilege. "What does she think we'd ought to do," Mac said. "Put 'em in a museum?" Then Auntie would bleat "My baby sister's marriage bed," and Mac whispered a short word which would have given her hysterics if she heard it. Mac was very proud of a rubber doormat he and Martha had in Tioga, made out of strips of old automobile tires. He said Auntie should come over and wipe her feet, maybe she'd rub a little speed off it. "Tell her to step on the exhilarator and get the hell out of here."

It was a pity to be squabbling right after Pop's death, but the old man would have understood it and loved to get his word in edgeways. His words had plenty edge.

"How come Miz' Taswell get herself so *muddled?*" Myrtle asked. "Muddle's catchin', she got me all wrenched out o' shape. Ef she come in here wid any mo' o' dat babysisterin' I'm like to work loose. Lissen, honey, babysisterin' all bleed out in one generation."

I guess it was partly the strain of what I'd been going through. I got the house sublet, and all the stuff stored or disposed of, and Auntie off on the train, and Myrtle and I had a howl and a hug and how good that old black cheek of hers tasted. I knew I hadn't played fair with Wyn, I hadn't told him anything and hadn't given him any chance to help me though God knows he tried hard. I couldn't. I was wound up tight and I just had to keep on going or I'd crack. He's almost psychic in his own dumb way and that warm morning he turned up in the Buick when I was packing my things. I was feeling pretty sorry for myself and went out in the yard to throw some chlorides into the backhouse and thinking what was the use. The front door was open, Wyn walked right through and found me there. Oh it was good to see him, like finding one more cigarette in the middle of the night when you think you're all out of them.

"Well, darling," I said, "once when you came here I thought you were the man to fix the backhouse, now you can do just that. Sprinkle some of this in there, it'll break my heart if I do it."

Always the gentleman, bless him, there wasn't anything

he wouldn't do if you told him.

"It's a good thing you came," I said. "I've got something for you."

It was Pop's old cricket bag, all scuffed and worn and the labels of Canadian hotels still on it that time he went on tour up there with the Gentlemen of Philly. I hadn't opened it up, we looked in it, his two favorite bats and the pads with grass-stains on them and those funny rubber-backed batting gloves. And a red ball and about half a pint of Scotch that I bet he'd forgotten it was there.

I only cry when I try to say something, so I just pushed the bag at Wyn and looked hard at the corner of the room where the glass toy used to stand, the little girl in a blizard. I'd packed her in my trunk, but I could see her clear enough with her red scarf flying and she's laughing as she goes down the hill. There was something about that old leather bag made me think of Pop out on the field the way I sometimes saw him, or how he'd watch them playing and chew on his pipe and say "Well played, sir. Well hit indeed." He always talked kind of English when he was watching cricket, I guess you have to, it's what they call cockney. That bag was part of the dearness of Philly, grand homey old town and I was walking out on it. I could see Broad Street Station and the Bellevue and Chestnut Street and all those sweet satisfied people. It must be terribly comfortable to be so pleased with yourself. Isn't it hell, when you love a thing most you're always bitchiest about it.

Wyn didn't say much, just patted my shoulder, but I knew he'd treasure the bag. He took a look at the dusty house and the old bamboo table pushed in a corner and the grass not cut in the yard and said "Jesusgod, let's get out of this."

I knew he was right, Oh how I knew he was right, but I needed to contradict somebody. Besides it was just the wrong time for Us but I wouldn't tell him that, he'd think I thought that was all he wanted.

"I can't," I said, "everything's in a mess, I'm just trying to get straightened out. I'm going away."

"Now wait a minute. I've got something for *you*. Let me show you." He took me out to the Buick and there he had a little overnight bag with my initials, and he'd bought and packed in it what he thought I'd need. "It's got everything," he said. "When I say everything I mean everything."

"It's funny to have all this fog in May," I said. "Lend me a handkerchief." There's nothing like a big man's handkerchief when you're on the way down. I still have an old one of his in my bureau drawer.

Men are so sentimental they've pretty near taught women to be sentimental too.

We drove down to the Shore. Maybe it's healthy to be cruel to yourself thinking back. I guess we thought then how bright and initiative we were, acting on our own. It looks to me now like the whole thing was doped for us like a story plot. Or like that damn dream, marching in someone else's parade trying to get to where *we* wanted to be.

Partly the weather, one of those first hot days of spring, so lovely you would figure everything must really be all right. Remember, Wyn, over Haddonfield way you said

the trees looked surprised, they got caught by summer
before the leaves were ready. Like the little girl that sat
on the steps and had forgot her underwear. Wyn knows
the roads through the Jersey Pines and along the Mullica
River, we went through places he liked because they had
funny names, I remember Bat's Toe and Stop the Jade
Run. He had some joke about that, I forget. I think it
was Ship's Bottom Beach he went swimming, I sat and
watched. That clean way he had of going through a big
green wave just before it would curl over on him. Then
it would all lift and spread behind him like a full skirt
in a wind and flash white along the sand like petticoat
ruffle. Where did all this hooey get started about women
being beautiful, they'd ought to see Wyn play tag with
surf. He'd run up the sand with wet sparkle all over him
and bring me a shell or something. He was so simple and
sweet he thought the only reason I didn't go in was because the water was cold.

One time out on the Dunes near Chicago, Molly wondered why I got so homesick, I nearly bawled. I had to
tell her it reminded me of the Shore in Jersey, but without that smell of salt. It's a beautiful world if your nerves
aren't too close to the surface.

After smell of salt you get smell of pines. I was mostly
asleep because I had to shut my eyes to keep sunset out of
them. If you can't sleep in Jersey I don't know where you
would. Wyn must have been looking at the map because
he reminded me of the shapes we noticed at Pocono and
said Jersey is just a kind of brazeer for Pennsylvania.
That's the last I heard until I woke up and found Wyn
looking at a little hotel that was asleep too, buried away

in the pines. He took a road he didn't know, to get the sun out of his eyes, and that's how it happened. "How did we find this?" I said. "What do you mean *we*," he said.

I scarcely know afterward if there really was such a place. It wasn't officially open yet, but the proprietor and his wife were getting things cleaned up for the season and of course Wyn persuaded them to take us in. He could persuade anybody anything because you couldn't bear to see him look disappointed. I told him one time he could sell copies of *Fanny Hill* to the Vice Society. "They've got most of them already," he says. He got his at college, together with that manly poem *If* that somebody at Princeton wrote.

"All we need is a double whiskey, a double ham and eggs, and a double bed, but don't tell anybody in Moorestown." I don't know what was funny about Moorestown, maybe Wyn had relatives out that way who got crowded off the Main Line.

Everything was so perfect you couldn't believe it. The sunset was sliced up by the pine trees, and there was a dog like Pattyshells who lay in the sand and made a fan pattern on it wagging his tail. We were all alone and when it turned cool they made a fire for us. Wyn said Burlington County hootch was always all right because the revenue agents got lost in the pinewoods and never found their way back. The proprietor pretended for a while that he didn't know what we meant about the whiskey, but after Wyn mentioned the names of people he knew, he came through all right.

Sunburn and tiredness and Griscom Street troubles and in love and being unwell and whiskey on top of all that,

I guess made me dopy. I was like somebody walking in somebody else's sleep.

"This doesn't count," I said.

"It gets hold of me all right," said Wyn.

"I don't mean the hootch. I mean this place. It's not really happening. I feel as though I'd got my fingers crossed. This is the one place, maybe, where you could do whatever you want and it wouldn't be held against you."

"We'll call it Fingercross Inn."

We were so happy, we both fell asleep sitting in front of the fire. I wish to God we could have stayed there, but the proprietor, who had got all dewy-eyed about us, woke us up and sent us upstairs.

"Wyn, my poor sweet, there's something I haven't told you."

The next day I guess fingers were crossed the wrong way. It wasn't anybody's fault; what is? I had the queerest feeling, as we drove back to town, that Wyn was sort of talking from dictation. He said he realized now he needed to get educated and he was going to do some serious reading. He said he thought people were more upset about the present economic and moral breakdown than they needed to be because they didn't know enough history. They didn't know that almost every period of history had been on the edge of a breakdown. He said old Mr Kennett had been riding him about being ignorant. "By the way," he said—and just the way that "by the way" sounded tipped me off he was working up to something. "By the way, he wants you and me to have lunch with him."

"But Wyn, I'm going to New York, I've got a job all

set with Delphine, I'm all packed and ready."

Poor Wyn. God help him, I suppose he was jumpy like I was. He seemed to think the Delphine idea was just silly, that I could dismiss it offhand. He said I could come and stay with his family for a while and think it over.

And after all I'd struggled, dear old Pop dead, and the home broken up, and me ready to go out and fight for my life. Of course I got angry.

"Well then I've got to tell you," Wyn said. "Uncle Kennett has a big idea, he wanted to explain it to you himself. He says you're just exactly the girl for me, Kitty, and the girl the family needs, and he wants to send you back to college for a year and then maybe go abroad a year and meanwhile I'll try to get some education myself and be ready for you."

Oh Jesusgod I don't know exactly how you said it, Wyn. It was something like that. My poor baby, how could you know what that would do to me the way I was just then. Maybe that nice old man with his *thee* talk could have sold it to me; I don't know. I had a kind of picture of some damned family conference and the Straffords and their advisers trying to figure out how the curse was going to be taken off Kitty Foyle. So that was it, they were going to buy the girl with an education, and polish off her rough Frankford edges, were they, and make her good enough to live with stuffed animals' heads and get advertised in the *Ledger*. I can still see your face, my poor baby, when I turned on you. I felt hot inside my throat and on the rims of my ears.

"You can tell Uncle Ken he's a white slaver. Listen, Wyn Strafford, I'll be your girl whenever I feel like it

241

because I love you from hell to breakfast. But I wouldn't join the little tin family if every old Quaker with an adding machine begged me to. No, not if they all went back to college and got themselves an education. So they tried to sell you the idea they'd trim up Kitty so she could go to the Assembly and make Old Philadelphia Family out of her, hey? Cut her out of a copy of *Vogue* and give her a charge account and make a Main Line doll out of her. They can't do that to Kitty Foyle. Jesusgod, that's what they are themselves, a bunch of paper dolls."

Remember, you stopped the Buick just before we cut down a tree with it. Better maybe if we had. You just looked at me, and tried to light a cigarette and your hand shook pushing in the dashboard lighter. You were so rattled you threw the lighter away, you thought it was a match. I loved you specially because you hadn't shaved. I thought how the old man would rise green from his grave if he heard a proposition like that. I felt tears coming like those waves you swam through and I had to hurry to say it:—

"By God, I'll improve *you* all I want but you can't improve *me*."

25

I HAVE TO LAUGH, OR I GUESS MAYBE I LAUGH, WHEN I think what a solemn little bitch K. Foyle was when she came to N.Y. and took a room in the Pocahontas, Residence for Women. It sounds like a cat house but that's what the West Side called an economical apartment hotel for dames only. The reason you take your thoughts so serious when you're that age, you honestly don't know they've been had before by a billion other people. Honestly you think it's the first time this ever happened to anybody.

I guess I should have been lonely and miserable. Still and all it doesn't feel that way in my memory. It was hot and I didn't know anybody but Delphine and living in a house for women only is terrible on morale. A neurosis to every room. I can see them yet in the dining room, poor souls, with the twice a week chicken croquettes and those rocky little peas, sort of crimped so they wouldn't skid. They couldn't even have men waiters to remind them what a pair of pants looks like. They called themselves bachelor girls, but a bachelor is that way on purpose. One hot evening one of them must have gone haywire, somebody yelled out into the courtyard "There's a man in my room!" I know what Mark Eisen would say about that for psychology, but anyhow it turned the place upside down and gave them all a good purge. Matrons and janitors were roaching the corridors and everybody saying how they'd seen him, the sinister fellow. Of course he was just what Wyn used to read in some poem, the pale phantom of desire.

It was a change of life all right. For me, I mean. I got out of that house as soon as I could afford to, but it wasn't so bad. I got a notion, looking them over, how many breaks I'd had. A good home till I was going on 20, and business training, and love, and a lot of good laughs, and a job. What else is there? I studied some French all by myself, I could see that would help me with Delphine, and I wrote a long sort of diary letter to Molly every week. I stuck to the West Side because it felt closer to Philly. Once and a while it got in my hair, I almost found myself saying Long Gyeland. Working with Delphine didn't help me any out of being a snob because her whole racket is pointed for the ultras. I didn't see it then, but it's comical how after I ran away from the Main Line idea I found myself working for it.

Molly was tremendously excited about my jump; of course she didn't know all the details. I wrote her, If it's smart to be thrifty I'm the Tattooed Countess. Delphine was no pushover. Her business had only been going a couple of years and everything was deep in the red, but there were symptoms. She had the guts to keep her stuff to exclusive outlets and hoke it up with all sorts of restrictions and show it was the Secret of the Champs Elysee and

So You Smelt It In Paris. It was something too utterly subtle for vulgar Endorsements; what great lady would commercialize the mystery of her boudoir? Besides those endorsements coûtent cher. She started me on her own personal stenography because Pearl Velour her first help was to go on the road demonstrating. It was $20 a week but I had just a little backlog in cash from the break-up at home. Mac turned in poor old Pop's Liberty Bonds to pay for the illness and funeral and there was about 200 bucks for me to thumb my nose with. I figured that would see me round the bend.

I didn't waste much time moaning to myself in my bed-room at the Female Falansteer, Delphine called it. She has a phrase about doing her parsley, which means in French getting your fresh air, going for a walk. I did my parsley after office by taking a walk in the Marguery-Maillard region to see what the dames were wearing. I wished I could afford to get near enough to see how they smelled, that would have been good trade dope. Delphine was tickled when I told her that. She said "But your young man, delegate that to him." Of course I had told her about Wyn, and how he was getting over his shock. There wasn't anything I wouldn't tell Delphine. I was always disappointed when she left off giving me personal dictation and did her stuff to the dictaphone, because when I sat alongside her it was grand to study the details of her outfit and get a whiff of the Olympia. She studied me too sometimes, I could feel her doing it. We were making up our first big drive on the Olympia and she had proofs of our mailing pieces, circulars for the trade and so on. I guess because the ink was fresh I noticed the smell of it and I said why don't we perfume all our promotion matter, give it a whiff of the Olympia?

She looked at me with those big plum colored eyes. She was always kidding me about my having blue eyes with black hair, she said it was the belle sauvage touch. "Keety, you always astonish me. You are the first blue-eyes I ever know who has brains. Now let us think. That is a superb idea. It won't do with the Olympia, that one evanesce too queek. That is our whole campaign for Olympia, it evanesce. It is parfum for when you have got your man, you are sure of heem. You do not need to cloy heem. But the Cinq-a-Sept, now that is competitive. That is how they say in the Far-West, for roping your steer. You are in there fighting. We can try the Cinq-a-Sept on our mailing pieces, it has the carrying power. Keety, you were born for this business. I see on the Chicago train how you notice my make-up and my color scheme. Be very careful not to use too much lipstick yourself. Do not distract from those eyes. It is good you live on the West Side, you can see what not to do. That is how the religion of beauty begins, commandments what not to do, Thou shalt not."

"Why don't we make up a list of Ten Commandments for the Religion of Beauty?" Jesusgod, I thought I had a big idea.

"No, Keety, that would scandalize. But I make them up for you if you like, a private list."

She fed me work in carload lots, but I couldn't help loving it. If I stayed as late as six she'd give me a dollar for dinner and that was a fortune. Of course she was trying me out to see if I had guts; I've done the same to others since. Usually they haven't. Things I thought at first were gaga I can see now how smart they were. She could talk perfect English when she wanted to but she made capital of a kind of half-French dialect in writing to the Trade because she knew it impressed them. I got to learn how to write a letter myself that sounded like it was sort of translated from French. She paid for me to have a typewriter in my room and lent me French phrase books to study and practise. "Keety," she says, "you have the educated ear. The educated ear is, How will it sound to the person that gets the letter. Read these letter to Mr Fargo at Palmer's, tell me how it sounds to heem? Is it too much high in the hat?"

"I have a friend at Palmer's," I said, "she's in the Decorating Department. Why don't we send her some of the sachet and the cologne and the Olympia, she could drop into the Cosmetic Salon and let Mr Fargo get a load of it by accident."

"No, Keety. I am sure your friend is a lovely smart girl but I want Mr Fargo to get his load from someone in a drawing room or at the Opera."

You can't beat her; she's got all the reactions figured. By the time I realized how much hooey all this is, I loved it too much to care.

Oh I had my foul moods all right. That Olympia nude picture behind Delphine's desk, she had it there as a kind of good luck, and it does sort of suggest the damn-your-eyes note of the perfume. So sure of herself it must make a man want to fight back. But I couldn't help taking it personally in a way, the lady lying there with nothing but mules and a ribbon round her neck the way it's good in a hot little room at the wigwam; and the old colored servant very like Myrtle, handing her flowers. She looks so damn satisfied with that pointed chin and hard mouth, not paying any attention to the bouquet. "Why bother about flowers, I smell sweeter than they do." When Wyn got a little cooked he wanted to draw pictures. One time he said he'd pose me as Olympia and do a sketch, but he wouldn't know how to bring Myrtle into it without embarrassing her.

That picture might get you wrought up until you're used to it. It was tough, after working nine to six, to come out on the street in summer sunlight and see Giono's across the way. Wyn wrote me some heartbroken letters, and sometimes I felt rotten about what I'd said. It wasn't *his* fault, poor baby. I got so low I even used to read letters to the Woman's Page in the evening papers. I consoled myself sometimes thinking anyhow I wasn't as bad off as some of those poor tillies. When I saw the bachelor gals at the wigwam soaking themselves in the papers I got a lowdown that helped. The evening papers print what they do and get away with it because by afternoon the human mind is ruined anyhow. Everything has been cracking down on it since breakfast, it'll take anything. Or you turn on the radio and listen to the world thinking out loud, which is another way of saying not thinking at all, just muttering.

The most wonderful thing that happened, saved me from the horrors, was Wyn turning up. That year July Fourth came on Friday so there was a long week-end, the only holiday I'd get because I'd only just started work. Mac and Martha wanted me to come spend it with them, they were going to take the baby and drive up to Delaware Water Gap but I didn't think I could face it. Thursday afternoon I had the phones on my head taking some of Delphine's letters off the cylinders. I was thinking if we'd had a dictaphone in the office of *Philly* I could have saved one of the cylinders of Wyn's dictation and run it over once and a while to myself. That poor hophead Sanka we had on switchboard and reception said there was a gentleman to see Madam. Eventually we had to fire the poor kid because she couldn't get the difference between Madam and Madame. I went out to do a stall because Delphine was leaving on a trip, and it was Wyn.

Delphine shot way up in the higher brackets as soon as she saw him. If there's anything she knows at sight it's quality, and in five minutes she had him carrying her bags down to a taxi, and gave me a big French wink that meant a sort of mixture of Have Fun and Be Sensible. And she whispered it would be all right to put on some of the Olympia, which I'd never done before because she didn't want it associated with working girls. It was all kept in the safe in the laboratory and she had to tell me the combination. That was Delphine's biggest gesture, and it made me feel like a million dollars.

Delphine was very proud of her little reception lobby which was stylized like a swell powder room, with dressing table and spotlights and all the products shown off as intimate as a French personal boudoir; and of course plenty of mirrors. There was one little crystal showcase and through the back of it Delphine could get a glimpse right from her desk of who was in the reception, as they came to the window to explain themselves to the hophead.

Delphine told me afterward she knew Wyn was tops because he never even seemed to notice the mirrors all round him. My poor baby! as if those Main Line men needed looking glasses to know whether they're all right.—Imagine Mark Eisen left alone with a mirror.

Wyn said he'd wait at Giono's while I put the office to bed. As soon as we had one good look at each other we knew things weren't as bad as we'd thought. He was on his way to Rhode Island, but he didn't get there as early as he planned.

He was wonderful, instead of going reproachful and baggy-eyed on me he had a snort waiting and we started having fun at once. I hadn't had a drink since Fingercross Inn and I guess I needed it. I told him what I knew about Delphine Detaille, Inc., which wasn't much then, and he allowed it was more fun than working in a bank. "If what you're wearing is the Olympia I'd like to get to know it better." "Then you'll have to work fast, big boy, our whole campaign is that it's wistful, a parfum should evanesce."

"We've had too much of that already," he said.

"Maybe I can smuggle you a little tube of it, you can sprinkle it on some of those lovely bosoms up at Bailey's Beach."

"Listen babygirl, those aren't bosoms those are the White Mountains. Shall we have another snort?"

"May as well protect our investment."

"Tell me about that lipstick. I never saw that color."

"That's Ta Bouche. We'll have it on the market for Mediterranean cruises next winter."

"Is it kissproof?"

"No lipstick is if you let yourself go. I thought you

knew."

We helped each other round a corner by a little kidding,
and then things were so sweet we almost forgot how sharp
that corner had been. The last I let myself remember was
going to a Western Union for Wyn to wire R.I. he
wouldn't be there in time for the Fourth of July racing.
"Parry Berwyn's up there," he said, "he'll be tickled to
death to take my place. Anyhow my hands are too soft
for racing, after that damned paper-work at the bank."

"Goodness, darling, do you race on your hands?"

"Kitty, you're sweet."

There was other times, after he got back from R.I. Wyn
would wire me from Philly and I'd leave the office at
5.30 and go across to the old wopeasy. I'd sit in the corner
of the red leather bench and nurse myself an iced tea,
which was what Giono called a highball in Prohibition.
That little dim passage led out to the street. Summer days
the front door stood open though of course the iron gate
was locked to keep out snoopers. You had to ring a special
bell that looked like it was meant for some apartment upstairs, there was even a card for "Mr M. A. Kenealy" who
was imaginary. Giono made up the name, he was proud
of it; he said the M.A. stood for Marcantonio. Anyway
when you rang three times for Mr Kenealy a buzzer
sounded back of the bar and Giono knew you were O.K.

Those late sunsets people were hurrying along the sidewalk on their way home, walking in that blaze of light
that comes crosstown at quitting time. There's not any
light in the world that can hurt you so much when you
leave the office and think you haven't anywhere special to

251

go. Sitting in the corner of the bench you could see every-body go by, like paper dolls cut out in black. Maybe Wyn was a bit late, every figure that went past gave me a start. If anyone turned in toward the doorway, like in the song My Heart Stood Still.

The bars in that iron gate was black against gold air, the people outside walked in pure brightness. Like gods, I used to think. Maybe every one of them was like a god to somebody; I hope so. And K. Foyle was sitting in that dark corner looking out on flashes of things she couldn't ever know about or understand. It gave me what Wyn called in our own language the M.P., that was the Mortal Pang.

He'd get in a while after 6 o'clock maybe.

"Did you get the M.P., you blessed?"

"I've got overproduction on M.P.," I'd say. "I've got a warehouse piled up with it and no trade outlets."

"We'll take care of that by and by. I got the M.P. this time just about Metuchen."

"You should of got it sooner than that."

"I know," he says, "but I happened to get a glimpse of Princeton and that put a lot of commonplace ideas in my head. I didn't really get back to us for quite a ways."

We knew you've got to play fair with the M.P. You can't fake it, or know beforehand when it's coming, or do much about it when it hits you. Sometimes it makes you happy, sometimes it gets you down. But you can't ever imagine anyone else getting spiked with it the way you do yourselves.

The minute he came in, everything was all right. Giono

was so pleased about Wyn coming all the way from Philly to have snorts in his place he'd rush out his special stock. Wyn pretended he couldn't get a really good drink in Philly and had to come over to Snorty West Forty for the real McKay.

I'm going to think some more about this, it helps me not to think what I know has got to be thought about.

Wyn used to get the old 4 p.m. out of Broad Street until he found quite a lot of his friends took that train too when they were having an evening in the big town, and it was hard to shake them. Then he switched to the through train at West Philly, one that comes up from Washington, D.C. That's the old cruiser that sneaks through town in a tunnel. Wyn never liked it so much because you see such badly dressed people on it, statesmen wearing black spats they call Congress gaiters and some pretty terrible Labor leaders who needed a haircut. Like all Main Line people, Wyn figured a train ought to go to Broad Street Station or it might as well stay home on a siding. He never did like their turning West Philly into 30th Street; it sounds like the N.Y. Garment Center and stuff. Also that train from Washington is usually a bit late, and he couldn't make Giono's until near 6.30.

How that Yellow Cab used to shine in the sunset when it pulled up at the curb. I could just see the nose of it from where I sat. Once Wyn revised some poem, I never knew what—

From the dust of the day's long road he leaps to the P.R.R.,
And rides to Snorty West Forty in a flashing and golden car.

I found the M.P. so tough I quit getting to Giono's beforehand. Wyn liked to have me there first, but a girl needs to make her Entrance. Sometimes I'd get Nicolai to give me a hair-date at 5, that allowed Wyn just time to get interested in his first iced tea by the time I got there. Nicolai always says mine's the kind of hair that can't be hurried; I guess he tells everybody that. But the hair-dresser is a swell place to duck M.P.'s. It fills you with worldly kind of thoughts, and what's furthermore when they get to know you well they have a good slant on a woman's feelings. Nicolai has the damnedest way of know-ing if you're priming for a special appointment. Maybe they can feel right through your scalp whether it's just a business date or are you really in a tizzy.

"Don't run your head against a stone wall," he said one time.

A woman talks good sense with her hairdresser, but it don't always stick when you're in a corner with the O & O.

It's your awful need that makes you so defenceless.

Golly, if you ever admit to yourself the cockeyed way things really happen. I was thinking about that dumb rabbit Sanka we had on the switchboard. I forget her real name, Pearl Velour called her Sanka because probably she never kept anyone awake. Not even herself. But my flat tire wasn't maybe Sanka's fault, it would go beyond that. I could lay it to a pair of Indian clubs or even to a bad smell in the trenches in France.

Monsieur Detaille was the mystery man of the office. He was the chemist, never said much, spent all his time in that little laboratory. It was funny how things that

254

didn't smell so good by themselves could come out as sweet as the Olympia when he put them together. It would be cheaper to have the lab somewheres else at lower rent but Monsieur and Delphine like to confer together all the while the way French people do. Monsieur is quite deaf since the War, what we used to call at home "Ed's War." Ed used to say "It was my War and I'll stick to it." Another angle: it appears it stunk so in the trenches that Monsieur said once in French "By God, if I ever get out of this I'll go in the perfumery business." I guess he hunted round till he found someone who smelled specially good and found Delphine. They pooled the good smell and the chemistry and that started Delphine Detaille, Inc.

Monsieur was not only a chemist, Delphine told me he used to be a very swell gymnasium performer when he was a young fellow. The French were all nuts about swinging Indian clubs in those days, it got them exercise without having to go out in the open air. Monsieur Detaille had gymnasium medals up at their apartment for being champion of some French county or something. Anyhow when he got fed up with the laboratory he'd go in our little stock room, the only place we had any room to turn because we were selling stuff as fast as we could make it. There he would take a ten minute breather with a pair of Indian clubs, ebony with mother of pearl passementerie all over them. It was cuckoo but at the same time it was wonderful the way he could make those things spin. One mistake and he'd have ruined most of our stock of Elixir Plastique and Cinq-a-Sept.

That's where Sanka comes in. Once and a while Monsieur would get called to the phone. It didn't happen often, because Delphine handled the trade all the way down the line, but of course there had to be check-up with their confidence man at the factory, the only other person who knew anything about the chemistry of the stuff, and they always talked machine-gun French. Mr Detaille was doing himself a spin on the Indian clubs to ease his mind and he got a call. Poor hophead Sanka tried to attract his attention, he was facing the other way and didn't hear her, she tries to dodge in under the clubs to poke him. Just then he gives the Indian clubs double bezique and Sanka gets a terrific clout on the skull. She passes out cold. They had to send her to hospital for several days with concussion, and after that she was goofier than ever. But Delphine didn't like to fire her too quick for fear she'd sue.

Pearl used to say it was civil war, an Indian club laying out a dumb-bell. Anyhow it was poor Sanka's general dumbness made her forget to give me that message from Wyn. I didn't know he was coming and I hadn't made any preparations for it. And I'd just had my first raise and moved out of the wigwam into a room of my own the first of October. I guess I was a bit too much on top of the world.

Remember, Wyn, it was Halloween. Another of those crazy coincidences, we went over to Giono's and after you'd had a sniff of my ear-lobe something started you thinking about a wop liqueur you hadn't tasted in so long. I think it had a kind of sugar-tree inside the bottle, I'm not sure. It was the color of listerine, and Giono said "I know what you mean, The Witch, Strega." "Why do you call it The Witch," you said. Giono said "That's what it means, see there's a picture of a witch on the bottle." It was a fact, an old woman riding a broom with owls and black cats and stuff.

Jesusgod, we thought, this must be a lucky drink for Halloween. Nobody had called for it in so long the cork was sugar-crusted into the neck of the bottle. Giono was tickled to be reminded of it and he took a slug with us for luck. And we were so tickled of course we took too much of it, on top of highballs.

It makes a good alibi, maybe; Indian clubs and Hophead Sanka and Hophead Strega and Hophead K. Foyle. It fits together so good maybe it couldn't ever have been any other way. Remember how we laughed, we walked over to Times Square and you had a notion to do what we called sociology in the subway. The Upper West Side always gave you a kick because you said there couldn't ever be anything like it in Philly. In the subway we saw the signs *Times Sq* and we said it was Times Skew, that's what the times are, definitely skew.

You can't always take precautions, it wouldn't be human. Maybe I'm kind of proud we didn't.

26

Maybe education would be to learn the things you need to know while you're still young enough for it to make a difference. Delphine had a good one, I bet. I get the idea that French people are taught things that help them to be French. Maybe it's not worrying too much about things that everybody knows is so. Wyn said being French is hard on the kidneys. I bet it's no worse than all our whipped cream and tuna fish. Delphine used to laugh herself wild over colored pictures of Milady's lunch table in the magazines. "That's not salad, that's garbage." I guess in France they don't need a very big garbage pail. When the Detailles had me up to their apartment I saw how her maid could take leftovers and put Ritz on them. They even did that to me. And Pfui, she caught him so young, when I saw him again he looked like a foreigner. You'd never know he was plain Illinois dog.

That autumn Delphine first started going to town and how we worked. The winter trade began going up like the Empire State Building, West Indies cruises getting popular and we were ahead of the crowd on our Caribbean Kits. Delphine was readying me to do something else besides stenography, and I will say she needed help the worst way in her promotion. Smart as she was you had to watch her for terrible breaks once and a while, like the time she was going to run a broadside on the new lipstick. Her catchline *For Sheeny Lips* would have sunk us. I killed it at the printers just in time. That was really what got me my first raise, to 25 bucks. Sometimes an accident would help us, like the misprint *eyelush*. We used it as trade name for an eye cream and it caught on. Pearl Velour was wonderful on copy that had oomph. Long jumps in the train she would watch women make themselves up when they got bored, she figured out what they were thinking and how their eyes were fatigued with scenery and dust and not being looked at. She'd write down something that would make you feel the old orbs were just a pair of clinkers unless you could roll them in some of Delphine's lotion. It gave me dark rings to read her pieces on the nerves of youth and the network of hairlike muscles in the eye sockets. As for Delphine, about 5 p.m. she looked a thousand years old if she didn't know anyone was looking. Then she'd say "Keety, we try our own medicine," and lean back a few minutes with the Day Dream eyepads. She and I would grind over Pearl's letters, and sift out the ideas so fine you could blow them through a pair of silk scanties like that face powder. When old Miss Elliman at Manitou said I was good in prose composition I never guessed how I'd put it to work. Nor the Lady of the Lake, neither. I said something about it one time and Delphine got one of her broody spells. We had something there, she felt. "How's about it for Bath Soap," was my idea. "Lady of the Lake, the Soap of the Highlands, soft as mountain

259

water. Will lather even a Scottish face." Delphine decided this was only a joke. "No Keety, Scotteesh is not good sales appeal for beauty."

It's a laugh how we worked in that little dark office figuring how to get the sun on the income side. "Keety, we explain there is two kinds of beau soleil. There ees the bronze, we want it; ees the red, we avoid eet. How do we say these cream mollify the sunshine, split heem in two, encourage the golden tan and prevent the redness. You ask Monsieur what can we say about *les rayons actiniques*. Tell me the Caribbean lotion in ten words for these Cunard cruise."

"The Lotion for the Ocean," I said, and we would laugh and Madame forget about her broken French and get back to dictating. She almost always got good ideas under the eyepads. The Moonlight Sonata body sachet was one.

It was all definitely wacky. Delphine wanted me to get wise to actual selling so maybe in the afternoon she'd look me over, and shoot a spray of Cinq-a-Sept into the air, tell me to count ten and then walk through the vapor. The Cinq-a-Sept is too strong, she said, never apply it direct but just walk through the ghost of it. "Otherwise even Abbé Constantin go Tarzan at you. You know what make the fortune of a French resort, Royat? Some English writer print that the air there is so bracing, it make a bishop bite a barmaid in the neck. The Cinq-a-Sept is like that. Cinq-a-Sept, means what the English call Feef O'clock, l'heure du thé, but here it is the time of the illegitimate cocktail. Five to Seven in Paris, that is the time a gentleman save for hees petite amie. It ees understatement. Now Keety how do we say these cream minimize pores so they almost disappear except enough for skin breathing?"

If she thought I looked presentable, she would take me round to some of the swell stores and beauty parlors, just to see what went on and meet the buyers. And I'd have to go back to the office and catch up on my dictaphone work at night. I used to wake up in my room in the West 70's muttering some patter about handmilled soap and filtered sunlight. I couldn't do any typing up there because an old maid in the next room beat on the wall if she heard any sign of life from me later than 10 p.m. Usually there wasn't, by then I was licked.

Molly and me had a talk one time about the White Collar Woman, there's millions of them, getting maybe 15 to 30 a week, they've got to dress themselves right up to the hilt, naturally they have a yen for social pleasure, need to be a complete woman with all a woman's satisfactions and they need a chance to be creating and doing. And the men their own age can't do much for them, also the girls grow up too damn fast because they absorb the point of view of older people they work for. Their own private life gets to be a rat-race. Jesusgod, I read about the guts of the pioneer woman and the woman of the dustbowl and the gingham goddess of the covered wagon. What about the woman of the covered typewriter? What has she got, poor kid, when she leaves the office. Molly and I certainly had most of the breaks but I remember when Molly got past her first enthusiasm and said about her and Pat "Do you know what we are? we're sharecroppers. We work like nigger hands in a cotton field and give Palmer's more brainwork than they'd know what to do with and what do we get for it? Eight hours sleep, I guess, because that's about all we're fit for."

I guess nobody minds so much being a sharecropper if he's damn sure the crop's worth raising. But it must be nice to feel some of that ground you sweat on belongs to yourself.

Holiday season I had to slack off my letters to Molly, of course she understood how hard I was working. It was good I had that alibi because things happened I wouldn't feel like writing. Not so much fun thinking about neither. Your mind gets along fine not thinking about some things, except maybe in the middle of the night. I could do with nights that don't have any middle.

Of course a girl can't kid herself very long if things go wrong. Female plumbing is just one big burglar alarm. Specially if you've always watched the Quaker calendar the way I did. But I cosied myself thinking maybe I was shot by too much nerve strain at the office, or I'd got a chill, all those things. Then one night I was working late with Delphine, feeling terrible. She said let's take a breathing spell. It turned out to be a fainting spell. I didn't know it till I came to smelling cologne and she looked at me sort of queer. She probably guessed right then, even before I did; I wouldn't put it past her. She was a grand sport, rode me home in a taxi, told me to take a day off and go see a doctor. By luck Pearl was just in from the road, and I felt I could do it.

I was nervous going to the doctor, I said a phrase I hadn't thought of since Manitou. "I haven't fallen off the roof for a couple of months." I guess because so many people were jumping out of windows then, he didn't get me, maybe it's just Middlewest. He wasn't very helpful, gave me some pills and stuff. Nowadays, Mark says, they'd call in the helpful old rats, there's some business about injecting urine into a female rat and it proves something. I told Mark, it's a joke if it takes rats to put civilization back on its feet.

That doctor called me "Mrs Foyle" when I went out. That made me sore, but I knew it meant he was perfectly damn sure. So was I.

It's funny, that feeling "But things like this don't happen to *me*." I felt like one of those assy letters to the Woman's Page. Oh I know about fright and misery and despair and what makes poor kids open the window too wide. I walked round that Verdi statue near my room and wondered if the Ansonia was high enough to jump off of. It don't make sense, it's just because you feel so sick and lonely. I envied old bums sitting on benches, they had nothing to worry about but a cup of coffee. There's some sort of female figure on that statue, the muse of the hurdy-gurdy maybe, showing her respect for music by sliding her dress off. You keep your clothes on, sister, I told her, you'll get yourself in trouble.

I went and had myself a small brandy at a speak I knew over on Amsterdam Avenue, and all of a sudden I saw the right side of it. I was proud. This would solve everything. I wanted to write Wyn, I really did hold his love in my body. How pleased he would be, I'd go away somewhere and take care of that baby, it would really be Wyn Strafford the Seventh, and I couldn't ever be lonely again. I was creating something, I was part of the world. I could go down South, Wyn could afford it and he'd be proud too and come and see me sometimes. The hell with cosmetics. Jesusgod, this was what I was meant for, and anybody who was worth worrying about would understand and be proud too. If there ever was two people who could make a good-looking baby it ought to be Wyn and me. I was all set to tell him "If it has your looks and my brains, and we keep it away from the Main Line, it'll go places." I wouldn't need to wait long to tell him about it, he was coming over on Friday. I was fixing to wear that Irish lace collar he got me because he said he was proud of his White Collar Girl. I'd got the enamel off my nails too because I could see he didn't like it, what he called spar-varnish. Mark always wants me to put it back. He says I'm practically naked without it.

Wyn liked me practically naked.

Easy, Kitty, easy. I don't have to think this out in detail.

I don't think it mattered stalling Delphine with a lie, just those few days. She knew anyhow. I don't believe it's possible to lie to French people, at least not about anything below the waist. I figured as soon as Wyn and I got plans made I'd tell her. I could still work maybe till Easter. That would be a nice time to go South too. How's about Bermuda, with a Caribbean Kit. It's funny how different it happened when I *did* go to Bermuda.

I'm sitting at Giono's, waiting for Wyn to show up. As a matter of fact I'd just had my birthday but Wyn didn't know that. He never did know my birthday, I'm pleased about that because poor baby it might give him a day that would hurt. I never would give him the date and he came back by saying every time I saw him was my birthday.

He was late, I was figuring out just how to say it the best way for Us. Giono asked if I'd have a Strega on the house while I was waiting, but I didn't feel like drinking, anyhow not that. I had some ginger ale, I knew that would surprise Wyn, and I would say "I don't want it to grow up a dipso." He would say "what grow up a dipso?" Then I'd tell him.

Giono laid an evening paper on the table. It was just behind the water bottle, and after I got through thinking I noticed it. There was a few lines of type magnified by the water bottle and I noticed how the lettering was thrown up big and a bit wobbly by the light through the glass and the water. Then I saw what they said—

> of "Welshwold," near King of Prussia, an-
> nounce the engagement of Miss Veronica
> Gladwyn to Mr Wynnewood Strafford VI

Just for a second I was sorry all I had was ginger ale. Ronnie Gladwyn and the big mills at Conshohocken. Jesusgod, that was a doe's head for the trophy room at Darby Mill. My poor darling, how did they put that across him. Served him up along with baked clams at Bailey's Beach, I shouldn't wonder. No wonder he hadn't written much. He was on his way over to tell me about it. Well, she's probably a lovely girl; God knows the *Ledger* had said so often enough. "Miss Veronica Gladwyn with her doll-like beauty almost lost in masses of white tulle and a single white camellia, grown in the hothouses at Welshwold." Or was it a gold girdle and several gardenias the *Ledger* had her wearing at the Assembly? I better order a

265

snort so I can drink her luck when Wyn gets here—

But Jesusgod, he must never know. If he knows it'll churn him all up. He'd be crazy enough to break off the engagement. He'd be worried all his life. Poor boy, he'd feel guilty.

I can't sit and listen to him tell it to me. I can't, the Main Line would come out on him and he'd be so damn gentlemanly and conscientious. I don't want him that way. Quick, Kitty, think quick. I've got to get out, Christ he'll be here. Talk slow now, something you just thought of.

"Jonny, I'm sorry, I've got to go. I've got an appointment I can't duck. Don't tell Mr Strafford I was here, tell him I phoned. Tell him I had to go out of town on business, I can't see him today. Give him a big drink Jonny, so he won't worry. Give him a big one. Keep him at the bar where he'll talk to people. Tell him I'm all right, I'm fine, I've just got some important business."

I could feel my teeth trying to chatter, but I threw all my Irish into it and said it slow. Of course Giono knew something was wrong, but he thought it was just a lover's quarrel, which Italians practically invented. Anyhow I had to trust him. I put down a dollar for the ginger ale and didn't wait for change. It was a black night, I went out of there like the witch on the broomstick. I got as far as Sixth Avenue when I saw a Yellow turn from under the L. I bet that was it, the flashing and golden car.

27

I KNEW I BETTER ACT BEFORE I COULD STOP TO THINK. I wouldn't go back to my room because Wyn might follow me there. I took a cab right to Delphine's apartment. She and Monsieur were just having a glass of port wine before their dinner. I guess she knows I don't forget how kind she was. To see Delphine in that apartment, tapestry chairs and a glass mantelpiece with porcelain snuffboxes on it, a dog that smells like cologne and a husband wearing button shoes and a velvet coat, you would think she was just bric a brac. But she can take things in her stride, irregardless what's happened. She told her maid to lay another place for dinner, we had sorrel soup and artichokes. It was the first time I ever had artichokes and my hands were too shaky to make a good job of it. When Mr Detaille's home and thinks he better be sociable he gets out a battery box and wears it on his head, but she waved it away because she could see I wanted to talk private. What was best, she didn't even make me wait to go through dinner before telling her, she let me blurt it right out.

All she said at first was, "I guess it was my fault, Keety, to let you wear the Olympia. It is too subtle for the

267

young."

I said "That would make a wonderful ad, if we could use it." Then maybe I laughed a little too hard, she saw I was near the edge. I was thinking of a rhyme I picked up when I was a kid, "This is the day they give babies away with half a pound of tea." It's not fair, the things that come into your head just when they'll hurt you most. So she made me take another glass of port and we had dinner. Mercy of God they didn't have company. After dinner I guess she figured I was scared to go back to the rooming house for fear I'd run into Wyn. So she told me to phone the landlady I had to go out of town for business and sent her maid round there to pack my bag. She gave me such a hooker of brandy I went right to sleep in her guestroom, as I faded I could hear her talking French over the phone.

The maid brought me coffee in bed next morning. I was just thinking I better make a run for the office when Delphine came in, dressed for work. She handed me a card on which she had written a name and address.

"Keety, these is not ethic. I ask myself, am I corrupt by Park Avenue ideas. You must be quite sure you do not want these baby? Do not think of the business, you can have your job back after, perhaps we invent a new talcum powder for heem."

I guess I couldn't talk about it, I just shook my head. It would be too hard to explain. Oh, if Wyn knew about it and helped me and the child could have an even break, it would be different. But Wyn must never know. All of a sudden I could see, Wyn wasn't big enough to have a bastard; or the folks he had to live with wouldn't let him be. It would be making people unhappy for the sake of somebody that didn't really exist yet.

It was funny to see Delphine, all made up for business in her smart black and the little Vuitton leather briefcase, suddenly look almost soft. "I think I understand. I had a bébé once and he died. He was frightened by the War, before he was born."

That's all she ever said about that. It frightens you a bit when someone successful and sure of herself like Delphine lets you backstage. It's pretty awful if the whole cosmetic business was just a sort of compensation for something else maybe she once had in mind to live for. One time I asked her how she happened to get into it because I think it was her who got Mr Detaille started, not the other way round. She said a line she pulls once and a while when she's playing hunches. "Bichara saisit la fortune!" I think it's the motto or trade mark of some beauty-goods in Paris.

I was too dumb, or too sick, to see it then, but I guess maybe she'd have been rather happy if I did have a baby. It would have given her a kick and likely she'd have sent it to France and made a frog out of it. It would turn out to be a Frenchman with button shoes and come back with a ribbon in its lapel and be entertained on the Main Line. But I wasn't going to have a baby just to please Delphine, or because Mr Detaille was lazy. It's kind of a personal matter.

"Tout s'arrange," she said, her French way of saying O.K. "You go down and see these docteur. I have telephoned an appointment for you. I get his name from friends who say he has the high-class trade, he relieve embarrassment all the way from Fiftieth Street to York-ville. But remember Keety, these idea are not French. My dear, it is better to do your precaution before and not afterward."

I tried to say something about getting back to work. "You stay here in my apartment until you are well. You must be sick several days, poor Keety. It is undignified and I think painful, they cannot use anaesthetic. Anyhow you go and see these docteur and do what he tell you."

It was like Delphine to think of dignity. That part of it wasn't much on my mind. I guess having babies isn't dig-nified either coming or going. When I think about it now, which I don't often, I remember how skilful and decent that doctor was. He was a good egg, I liked him at sight, and the day I went down for my operation I took him a china elephant with mother-in-law plants on its back, for luck. That gave him a laugh. In that kind of practise I should think he needs it. We got to talking about things and he told me a lot of intelligent information which I reckoned I wouldn't need to use. He liked the Olympia too, and I told him we were keeping it very exclusive, it might make too much business for him.

I wouldn't have guessed I'd be able to get a smile out of that affair, which was pretty grim. It was like being boiled in oil. While I was sick at Delphine's, and feeling damn low, I tried to think things over a bit. Maybe I just haven't any moral sense. I felt sorry, and selfish maybe, and like I'd lost something beautiful and real, but I couldn't feel any kind of wrongness. I did what I had to do. What hurt was having to write a lot of nonsense to Wyn. Of course there was a long letter from him when I got back to my room, all about Ronnie and the engagement being announced sooner than he expected and sweet things he said which weren't any sweeter than the truth. I hated to write him, poor darling, a lot of crap about I'd been away on a trip and too busy to write and so forth. Things are never quite the same somehow after you have to lie to a person.

He had his own hell to go through, most likely, the way Rosey Rittenhouse said. I didn't see why I should be bitchy to him just because he'd taught me how lovely things can be. We taught each other.

It was queer to be there in Delphine's lovely little guest room and she'd come back from the office and tell me what happened. Every time I heard her or the maid coming in I had to hurry and pick up that slippery silk quilt I couldn't keep on top of the bed. I guess French people don't thrash round so much once they get to sleep. She'd make me wear the prettiest little bed jacket of her own and said I made a romantic looking invalid, like somebody that had been through the French Revolution. You wouldn't know how maternal Delphine could be when she wasn't dictating but she'd arrange me like I was something in a display window and I never can feel that bed is a place to be putting on an act. She talked so much about black circles under my eyes, I always thought that was just an Irish specialty but she said the French go for it in a big way. I said maybe it's just people who had to live alongside the English all their lives. She got a real laugh out of that and made Monsieur put on his battery to hear it too. When Monsieur had to put on his battery and get a load of Keety I knew I was getting better and not die of blood poison. Delphine always studies any situation and when she did me a make-up for a call from the doctor she got an idea about special hospital make-up boxes for invalids. She flirted with that idea a bit but we decided the psychology was bad.

I had to rouse up and play ball for Delphine when she was there, like Pfui had to earn his keep chasing a rubber bone when she felt like having him do it. All the same I don't think I was kidding myself when I had a chance to think. She pulled me through a tough spot but in a way I'd given her a sort of mortgage on Me. I wasn't going to welsh on any payments. The way they were selling apples on street corners that winter made you kind of sensitive. That little room of mine over in the 70's usually smelled of apples I'd bought and didn't want to eat.

Maybe it's good for anyone to find herself once and a while where she doesn't believe what's happening. I didn't figure out how nutty the situation was until I tried to edit it for Molly later on. Here's K. Foyle exactly not doing everything a woman ought to be good at. She's not having a baby, and she's not cooking meals, and she's not even earning a living at a business that's only a fairytale anyhow, figured on making dames look like they don't really. She's not climbing stairs, there's an elevator to do that for her, and she's not locking the front door nights, there's a big stevedore in uniform. She's lying in a cellophane boudoir with a maid handing her trays of delicatessen. Even the dog has been plucked until he has to wear an overcoat when he goes into the weather, and he slides across the polished floor like a burlesque comedian because there's nothing he can dig his nails into. That was the winter we got our first exclusive beauty service installed on one of the cruise ships and I had to laugh thinking how even sunshine had to be filtered through some chemical cream.

Delphine and me had some talks along that line, she never minds figuring things out because she won't let it interfere with what she's doing. "These is the great age for cosmetique because the world is decadent. When people are not sure of necessity they crave for luxury. What is most necessity for living? I think it is a feeling of Future. If you do not feel sure of Future you think you better make whoopsdearie for Now, is it not so? Every lipstick we sell is just to sell the customer the idea how important is Now."

"And a little hankering for Then," I said.

"That is very sage, Keety. You will know more, later on, about hankering for Then."

I thought I knew plenty, but you don't know how little you know when the parade's going by any given point.

"You have tell me about your good old Philadelphia, but it is not really your Pheelly you mean. It is something in your mind, like Les Andelys in France for me. It is happiness and evanesce. It is some place where everything was feex for you. Keety, Philadelphia is your Abbé Constantin. We might ask Monsieur to invent us a faint cologne, we call it *Philadelphie,* something quite nostalgique and hopeless."

Maybe I laughed, I don't remember. When Delphine was riding me for a laugh she usually got it. Specially when she said "Bees, you are bugs," which she caught from me but never understood. I wish I could take dictation from Delphine when she's off duty, she's certainly got her own slant on things even if it runs a bit downhill. "New York is parasite," she says. "It live by amusing other people. Now your old Pheelly sit on her own bottom and like it. It is very sheik." It took me a while to know she meant *chic*.

I thought then it was cruel the way she talked, but I guess it was good for me, like peroxide in a cut. I could feel the sting in back of my eyes. We were hashing over the N.Y and Philly idea and I told her about the hot day Wyn and I took a boatride down to Coney Island. He said he'd seen photos of it but he wanted to be sure such things really existed. He took one look at the beach and said "Thank God nobody in Philly needs a holiday as bad as that."

"Your friend, he had the beginnings of sentiment," Delphine said one time. "I am glad you had love with a Philadelphia man. They are like an Englishman who has got over the worst of it. Keety, I knew an English officer in the War, he is very happy memory. They are simple and so dear, it brings out the best of a woman because she have to think for both. French women forgive the Germans much on account of the English men they brought into France."

I was telling Molly, I have to be careful to know what I think for myself and what I just picked up from Delphine. I wouldn't give Delphine any idea, naturally, how absolutely perfect things were between Wyn and me. But I'd try out one of her theories on Molly once and a while, to see how she'd react. Delphine says "a man must

274

not have everything, Keety. Better if he does not think, or does not hear too well, or is ugly, or cannot see a joke. Then you have that good feeling how you have heem under your wing. If they have everything, how tedious. Keep for the movies."

Molly liked that, I got a notion she was checking over the men she knew to see if any of them had the right kind of deficit.

It's a good thing that peachblow silk puff would slide off the bed. It might show up some crying stains. Poor Delphine, she has all her compensations working over-time. I guess mine haven't started to function, and I don't want them to. What hurts, hurts.

28

PUT TWO DIFFERENT KIND OF PEOPLE TO LIVE TOGETHER, do they get to understand each other more and more, or less and less? I'm thinking of Uncle and Auntie. I sat in on some swell debates between those two. I used to think, the damn old fools are keeping me from doing my home work. Matter of fact I see now it was a swell demonstration in home economics. Take gardening, mostly Aunt Hattie didn't do much outdoors, it was too far away from the telephone and the sewing basket, but once and a while she'd read something about the thrift of the pioneers or Middlewest Womanhood the Breadbasket of the Nation, and she'd run out and grab a hoe and slash round for a few minutes. Likely Uncle had set out a planting of flower seeds in a new place, carrying on some idea of his own. Auntie was sure to think they were weeds and ratch them all out. When he got sore she said "I guess the sun was in my eyes," or else trying to get me into the brawl "I never know what your Uncle's going to do." He says "How would you, you don't make any effort to find out." Or she'd go good and feminine on him and swear they weren't flowers at all, only chickweed. That was an error because

276

he saved one of the seedlings she'd scratched out, he put it in a pot and practically incubated it himself and when it comes up a nice red zinnia he lays it in front of her on the breakfast table and says "Here's one of your chick-weeds." She cries, not because she's sorry but because Uncle would go to that much trouble just to prove her wrong.

This time of year I'd like to go out to Manitou if it was only to hear the lawnmower again. That's something you miss in N.Y. The whole Middlewest sounds of lawn-mowers in a summer sunset. Uncle Elmer kept his lawn-mower shined and oiled same as his golf clubs, and he used it a lot more. He had an idea we used to laugh about, that it would be fun to put a music cylinder into it, like a Swiss music box, so it would play Bye-Bye Blackbird or The Bells of St Mary's while he was mowing. Even old Pattyshells liked to hear the grass being cut, he'd come out and lay by the kitchen steps and wag gently every time Uncle came that side of the lawn. He knew Uncle needed a little admiration when he got sweating hard. But then Auntie got her big idea, one day while Uncle was at the factory a man came by with a wagonload of some trick Japanese maples. Auntie thinks that will be a nice surprise for Elmer, and she has three of them planted in a big triangle in the middle of the lawn. Of course Uncle was gentleman enough to pretend to be pleased, but it made mowing the grass that much harder. He had to keep dodging those baby trees, and belch like Henry Eighth. He attributed it to that poem by Joyce Kilmer about Only God can make a Tree which the Manitou Garden Club sent round on a card.

If a person does one kind of thing, that's likely the way they are all the way through. Pop said once "He that is nitwit in little will be nitwit also in much."

Molly says it's not fair to get a down on women, because men have so much more time for thinking. They have sort of time between times, what a woman never has. Men don't have to tuck a dress under their knees every time they sit down in a windy subway car, or figure if they'll have a fresh pair of gloves for lunch. A man has more chance to get away from being a man.

Molly says it's been specially tough on women since lately, because they're getting to be citizens, and citizens have no sex. Sometimes I think Molly's getting a little hard, I mean a little sort of angry in the back of her mind. I wish there was some man, good and sweet enough for her, she'd go off the deep end about. There I am, getting back to sex again and the hell with it.

Molly says the Delphine Detaille kind of business depends on a woman never forgetting she's a woman, and that's not fair. She says that's a European kind of an idea, or maybe French. I said nuts, that's universal.

Tell me about America, I always ask her when she comes East and we sit down together like a couple of citizens. I like to think of that train blowing whistles all the way across Illinois and Indiana and Pennsylvania, and Molly seeing things out the window. I used to get mixed up sometimes when I was travelling for Delphine; you see a lot of people who'd like to go where you're going and you see a lot of people staying where you'd like to be. Just for a minute you think it would be nice to stay put, if you knew where. That's what they learned in Philly,

I guess, good old Sankatown.

I can feel what I'm thinking but we don't get enough practise thinking underneath, or anyhow trying to say it in words. I say things to myself to find out how they sound, but I'm not passing any votes of confidence. Molly said one morning when we woke up after a milkman's matinee, or a Scotchman's matinee, "Did I talk under the ether?" Puts me in mind how Pat Kenzie had a notion when you wake up the first of the month you should always say "Rabbits, rabbits, rabbits," it's good for luck. She took three plush rabbits to bed with her so she wouldn't forget. If young men is luck she had it all right. Molly and me was more likely to think how we would pay the rent.

If you get into a habit of doing things yourself, how people lay down and let you do it. It was comical how Pat Kenzie lived on us at Tuscan Court. That's one problem about Mark Eisen, would he want me just to live off of him? He's scientific and emancipated and stuff but they always have the Queen of Sheba picture of women in the back of their mind. Crazy stuff, the Main Line idea was they would lower themselves to take me in, and the Morningside idea is Mark would be climbing a trapeze if he got me. How's about taking a citizen at par? That's the way Wyn did, if he noticed them at all.

Molly says women overstate things when they get worked up, because they have to spend ninety percent of their lives in understating. A good citizen don't dare let on how things hurt, or what joy feels like. Yes, joy; it's funny how you get ashamed even to yourself to use plain words like joy and beauty. I put on the high-class dame act once and a while, partly copied from Delphine I suppose. But when you're putting on an act how you love to be caught up on it. By the right person, that is. How about Mark; is he the one I want to be caught up by?

I say to Molly, tell me about America. She knows what I mean but we're too bashful to say it out. I want to be a good American. Mark is all hopped up about persecutions and refugees in Europe, and natural enough, but I can't go very big on Causes that's a long way away. I got enough of them on my mind right here. There's that elevator boy in this house with a kid that's got paralysis. Jesusgod America's got her own nails to polish. We'll need plenty vanishing cream for our own puss. Mark says that's cowardly. I told him it's good George Washington sense. He made two holes didn't he, one for the cat and one for the kitten. They laughed at him, said the kitten could use the big hole. But suppose they both want to go through at the same time. The little cat wants his own little doorway that fits him. Kitty wants her own way through.

I wonder if Martha Washington ever had the jitters? She can't have been always just a nice old dame in a fichu.

I'd be a better American if I married Mark than if I'd married Wyn. The more we get mixed up, I mean race-mixed-up, the better. We got no time here for that kind of prejudice. But I suppose it's all right to wish they wouldn't be so hairy? I could have made something out of Wyn, something pretty damn fine and American too, if I'd had the management of him. I'd never need to do that for Mark. He'll make something out of himself and no mistake. I guess you need to be sorry for a man sometimes. It would be hard to be sorry for Mark. He's so damned confident.

He's got the same kind of sureness, professionally, that the Main Line has socially. He's got respect for intelligence like the Main Line has for flannel pants without any crease in them. He wouldn't let a woman get the better of him any more than Rosey Rittenhouse would let a polo pony. When Mark says how he'd operate on Hitler I don't tell him it takes a woman to see how dangerous Hitler really is because Hitler is so like a woman himself. It's bad to let them get the whip hand. But they make wonderful Sidewalk Superintendents.

It's good to think of Mr Rockefeller having a sense of humor. We're likely too hard on the higher-ups. Maybe I wasn't fair to the Paper Dolls. I got a new slant on old Mr Kennett by something Wyn said one night. He was telling me about some little hunchback lady worked in Mr Kennett's office, they had a special high chair made for her, all bent crooked, so she could do book-keeping. They had to cut down on the staff during business troubles but Wyn said the little cripple was sure of her job for life. Mr Kennett told him "When I can't afford to hire her I'll cut my throat."

Just the same I'll bet she had to be good at double entry.

It's those social columns in the papers does a great deal of harm. They can make trouble even when they're not magnified through a bottle.

You wonder once and a while if the big families are scared about something. They sure stick together when it comes breeding time.

It's Molly gets me this way. She says I've got a few real

ideas, like scatter rugs on a big bare floor. Is it all right to think about things, even if you don't know the answers?

Molly darling, if you had what I've had you wouldn't be so certain, maybe. Like Wyn used to say, there's an enigma in the woodpile.

Maybe it's not the number of ideas that counts, but how fast do they circulate around.

Molly goes back to America and I can see her riding on a green plush settee; likely thinking how she'd interior decorate those new trains so they wouldn't look like a platinum whorehouse. Molly's got real architect's taste, and sense enough to keep quiet about it in front of the customers. But how swell it is to get on the road and try to make out what is America up to. I remember one Sunday night I was riding back from Philly, I was over to see Mac and Martha and went by Griscom Street and I didn't want to think. There's too much M.P. along that Pennsy road. In spite of it being Sunday night and rainy I guessed there'd be somebody wanting to sell me something, so between Trenton and Newark I watched for electric signs to see who was really on the job. I played myself a game to see if I could live on a desert island with whatever they wanted to sell me late on a Sunday. I built myself quite a comical civilization on that island, I had gasoline and linoleum and paint and crucible steel and tooth paste and P.O.N. beer. Also something I wouldn't know just what it is or what to do with it, a Lidgerwood Hoist. I'd have to get along without Princeton University and cosmetics. Well, if I didn't have one I wouldn't need the other.

What it figures down to, I want to be a good American. I'll never forget how I heard that colored girl Marian Anderson sing My Country Tis of Thee on the radio. I cried and I hope lots of other women did too. I cried partly because I was proud of her being a woman, and partly because it was Main Line kind of people that had been stupid about her, and partly because I heard she came from Philly. I guess it's the biggest thing the old town's done since 1776.

Pull yourself together, lady. One way of being a good American this minute is take a hot bath and some shut-eye. I've been kidding poor Aunt Hattie but I don't think I ever take a bath without remembering something she taught me. If you turn the hot on first it fills the bathroom with steam. Let the cold run first and then you can let in as much hot as you like and not fog everything up. Maybe it works like that in the mind too.

While I'm in the tub I'll polish the silver snake-ring.

29

THE UNION LABEL OF THE WHITE COLLAR GIRL IS THE alarm clock. We certainly worked that summer. After being sick that way naturally I didn't take any vacation except once and a while Pearl Velour and I got a Saturday-Sunday at a Catskill dude ranch. I actually rode a horse and wondered what Wyn would think. Mostly we rode bicycles up there and I had to laugh because for some reason all the bicycles had fox-tails tied on them, to raise the social standing I suppose. I had kind of fun watching myself, when I'd meet Pearl's boy friends I'd find myself figuring what if anything could be made out of them if you took them in hand as to clothes and general behaviorism. That's what the Main Line does to you. It's not so good for a girl to get that idea of wanting to recondition all the men she meets. Anyhow that line of Delphine's about a man should have some kind of a deficit; they had it.

I got several kinds of pathos in letters from Wyn but I wouldn't let it shake me up, he wasn't so good on paper anyhow except for Interoffice Memo. I could see my only chance to play fair was to act just the same as before; why

284

should I love him less because they'd got him under contract. What him and me had was always our own and we invented it. Just the same I had to know how was I going to act when I saw him. Like Pop said sometimes, nabocklish! which is Irish for let's not worry too much. What's the good getting yourself in a frenzy to figure things beforehand. Maybe it works out how you couldn't have planned. Wyn called me on his way to Rhode Island. I met him at Giono's like old times, there was the same water bottle on the corner table. What you did to me, old carafe. But I had myself in good shape with a hair-do and a new hat I liked, and just for the hell of it I put on a touch of the Olympia. Delphine was keeping it so high-class people practically had to make an affidavit of pedigree before she'd let 'em buy it. Wyn, my darling, how could you know I was just holding myself together with an act. I was afraid you'd want me, and I was afraid you wouldn't. Every time you think Wyn's dumb he surprises you, instead of the usual Scotch he called for Mint Juleps, which sort of seemed to indicate that things had changed somehow, but his fingers in between mine felt just the same, what we called interlocking directorate, made my spine feel like it wanted to sneeze. Mint Julep helps you to talk, quicker than Scotch. Wyn showed me how if you pour hot coffee in the glass after the second julep's finished, you get the brandy that's still clinging on the crushed ice, together with just a little mint and sweetness. It makes a swell iced coffee and keeps you from wabbling. Everything was so sweet I could almost think we were still really Us and I was memorizing him more than he would ever know. Then after while he told me that Parry

Berwyn was travelling up to R.I. with him and Parry would join us for a snort at Giono's. That was something different all right. I was just a little hurt, I guess, and after while I was a little grateful because it made saying good-bye easier when they went on the sleeper. I wondered was I letting him down easy or was he letting me down easy. It's better not to wonder. There isn't any easy way down that drop.

You can't help wondering things that aren't fair. Blessed Wyn, was he simple enough to figure it would be good for my morale if Parry made a pass at me? Parry had a bit of a yen that way, back in the magazine days once and a while he'd show a Racquet Club leer and I couldn't help tipping Wyn off about it because naturally I wouldn't want Parry to barge into an embarrassing situation. Wyn said "I admire his taste and deplore his ethics." Poor old Parry, his sex life was mostly knowing all the corny limericks, which seems pathetic.

It's hard though when you have to get someone in from outside to help you round corners. The right kind of corners only have two sides to them. The way I'd have to work it with Mark would be never let him know if I was at any kind of a left turn.

I could feel the lights were changing on us, I didn't just know which way. Like when you come unexpected onto a yellow light and you don't know how it's turning, from red to green or from green to red. I guess it's good dope, always make a full stop before you turn into an arterial highway. If you're alone a lot you can think up all kinds of ideas. I wouldn't be surprised you get good at being lonely if you have enough practise.

It was funny though, that was the first time Wyn and I were together when I had to hold back and remember there were things not to tell him. When there was so much he didn't know, I guess it was only right there would be things he didn't tell too.

Even if he'd wanted me he couldn't have had me. That's the crazy way calendars work.

"The kind of person things happen to," Molly said. I thought it was a compliment too. Well God help that kind of person. Worse still, maybe everybody is that kind of person. What is it, hormones? They dry up and blow away after while, don't they?

The way I always time things, or the way something times them for me, seems like I walk right onto the razor blades. There's that day this very summer when I had to run over to Philly to see what I could do to help poor old Mac. He's been on relief, I was thinking maybe I'd better take little Kitty to live with me. She's ten years old. Here's K. Foyle, going to be just another Aunt, like Aunt Hattie?

I get off at 30th Street Station and walk out for a cab, and Jesusgod comes a station wagon just pulling up under those pillars, marked DARBY MILL. Not a nice old tumble-down station wagon neither but bran shiny new, I bet Ronnie wouldn't understand how much smarter the old one was. And sitting with the shover was a little boy in a sailor suit, pretty near seven years old I guess. In back was a nursemaid and a cunning little girl in a pink floppy hat, maybe about four. On their way to Rhode Island, most likely. He had a lovely bright little face and something written on the ribbon of his hat. Maybe it said Wynnewood Strafford VII. That might have been *my* baby—if he'd been about a year older. I took one look, and thought maybe somebody's meeting them. I felt as lonely as a Jew in Germany, and got out of there the same way.

On my way to Mac's I bought a bottle of the Pope's telephone, I thought it would do him good, at least that's what I told him. Poor old Mac, think of even him having thoughts underneath. He's getting up towards forty and you don't like to have brothers that far along. Pop said once "We had bad luck with our kids, they've all grown up." Mac was telling me how when he was little he used to wrinkle up his forehead when he looked at it in the glass because he was ashamed of it being so smooth and he wanted to be grown up like Pop. Pop always had wonderful wrinkles, maybe from squinting at cricket balls in the sun. I hadn't realized, till Mac ran into hard luck, he might have thoughts of his own inside. I bet he even idealized the Torresdale Filter until he believed she was a long drink of Planters Punch. Maybe that's what being young is for. Your mind needs an uplift as well as your bust.

Mercy of God I was too busy that '31 year to think much. You really get interested in a job there's a lot of fun in it. Oh once and a while I'd wonder a bit whether they have surf at Bailey's Beach as tall as those big green breakers with petticoats down along Jersey, and whether Ronnie had a good looking bathing suit. Once and a while I'd let out a few remarks to Nicolai, which is good for the soul. "There's a beautiful dame up swimming on Rhode Island," I said, "tell me, is there a good strong undertow up there?"

He says "Maybe her bathing cap don't fit. Salt water's terrible on the hair."

What I liked about Pearl, it seems she'd had man trouble too and we would go over to Giono's together and do a double-bitch act which rated Big Time. This was partly because I was sore when Parry Berwyn tried to make a date with me when he got to Grand Central on his way home. He told me over the phone, which was as close as he got, that Wyn had been sent from Newport out to Detroit and wouldn't come back through N.Y.

"Well if he wants to borrow money from Henry Ford," I said, "he's wasting his time."

"No, they want him to see what a Depression looks like in its home town. They think it'll make a better banker out of him."

"They'll never make a good banker out of Wyn, he's too sweet."

"Say listen, Kitty, you got bankers all wrong. What about having dinner and let me advise you."

"My capital's all invested," I said.

Delphine Detaille Inc. never had an outlet in Philly up to that autumn, because Delphine couldn't get the terms she wanted and anyhow she said Philadelphia could wait; it was used to it. Promoting anything in Philly is like getting the carbon sheet wrong way round, it just prints off on the back of the same paper. But our products were going swell, and news of the Olympia specially was getting around among people who mattered. The Big Store wanted us now the worst way, and offered us a contract for the exclusive Delphine Detaille representation. When Delphine gets the turkey on the platter she serves it right, and our opening was plotted like a peace conference. Pearl Velour went over to give the Women's Page editors the background stuff on the Romantic Story of Delphine Detaille Beauty Products, dating from the trenches of France and etc., together with handout stories on Mr Detaille as a scientist and why we didn't have to keep a hutch of rabbits in the laboratory like some of them, to try out our chemicals on a rabbit's tender skin. Pearl always makes a hit with the Beauty Editors because she's so damn homely herself, and she's too smart ever to say anything specific about age in her copy. Everybody knows the middle age group is the real butter and eggs of the cosmetic business, but as far as we would let on in print middle age is something we never heard about. With the advertising big shot from the store doing a little crooning in the background Pearl would plant the publicity dope, and on the opening Madame Herself would come over from N.Y. to give her lecture and consultation. It had to be good too, because every competitor had somebody there taking it all in and ready to get out the knife any way he could. There wasn't any Robinson-Patman Act those days about treating all dealers alike, and the whole discount situation was simply who-all would spoon out the richest gravy.

Delphine liked to give actual demonstration on a model together with her lecture. But for some reason, I think she thought she was doing me a favor, she decided to take me along with her for the Philly opening and work on me. Then I was to stay there as demonstrator in the store, till we got one of the regular staff broken in so she could do justice to our line. The last thing in the world I wanted to do just then was be around the old home town, but after all Delphine had done for me how could I duck it.

They had the auditorium crowded, I remember how pleased the cosmetics buyer was because even old Mrs. Foxcroft was down front with her ear trumpet, which set the tone of the occasion. Actually I think the old lady was just wandering round the store and came upstairs thinking it was something about literature. Those dowager charge accounts get most of their education in the department stores anyway, it's more fun than going out to the university or the art museum because you can buy something.

That was the first time I heard Delphine do her stuff in public. It's a wonderful act because she never tries to do any selling. Of course as a matter of fact our whole technique is to prevent people from buying anything unless they've had a personal analysis and been told what to use. Every once and a while she'd say something in French as if she'd just thought of it for the first time, and give them a kick by not translating it, sort of assuming they got it. But she always takes care to put over the same idea in English a few sentences after. I bet it's the only beauty talk in the world that never mentions Youth, which is a fighting word for lots of dames. She says the poet is all wrong who said beauty is only skin deep; beauty begins in the mind. That's good dope, because everybody figures she has one. It's not hooey either, there's a famous doctor in N.Y. who sends his melancholias to see Delphine as a part of his treatment, he says no woman can be really healthy unless she feels she's looking her best. Delphine says "Beauty is not luxury but self-respect, le joli c'est le necessaire," and they give her a hand.

Then she has me come out, looking plain and mousy and with no make-up of any kind. She explains that I'm one of her own assistants, she won't do anything showy by calling for a stranger from the audience because she wouldn't want to embarrass her. She illustrates how we work out our questionnaire chart, skin reaction and acide sébacique and what modern civilization does to dry up the face, and please be careful about soap because soaps are alkaline and il faut vendre cher la peau. She puts different colored lights on me to show how some people's eyes change with the scenery and how different tones of lip rouge bring out different ideas. She says how Virgil put it that woman is mutable and this is our mutabolism test, that slays anybody who happens to be there from Bryn Mawr.

She puts the cream right into my hand, makes me do the whole octave of finger motions and you can see ladies unconsciously trying to memorize them by waving their fat hands as they sit there. We go through the questions on the chart and she fills it in for my own Personal Requirements. The cleansing cream and the astringent oxidizing cream—try a facial cocktail instead of hootch. It'll make you feel just as good and don't damage your insides. And the powder base and the rouge and the lip rouge and then the powder after the rouge and how the powder on the lipstick helps to set it. And how to vary your different parfums for different days and different times of the day. You wouldn't want to use the same fragrance on a Thursday afternoon, when the maid goes out, as on a Friday evening when you have your box at the Orchestra. That combines the homely touch and the shi-shi and they're all pleased.

I sit there while this is going on, and she explains that I have natural wistful purple in my eyelids so I don't need much eye-shadow, and that woman's beauty must be co-ordinated to the occasion, the simple discretion of the Killarney would be all right for me in church or on a Thursday, but for the competitive hours of evening maybe I might soar as high as the Olympia. One final caution, she says: If you think you're going to do any crying, better use the waterproof mascara. But clients of the Delphine Detaille treatment should have no occasion for weeping.

Oh yeah?

I'm wondering if anybody's there from Darby Mill, but at least by the time Delphine gets through with me they wouldn't recognize me.

Delphine went back to N.Y. after her lecture and left me to do demonstrating at the store for a couple weeks. It's good I was busy, of course I had to train the girl who was going to take over the work. Delphine said I should take a room at a hotel, I guess she was right, I was too tired to commute out to Mac's in Tioga. But it's a funny feeling living in a hotel in your own home town, it's not good for you. That's probably what's wrong with a lot of us, living sort of hotel hideaway with no front door onto fresh air. Jesusgod, the whole world ought to have home-town feeling. There's thousands of people right here on Riverside I bet never even saw a back yard and think

Pekinese are real dogs.

It's more than your skin that gets dried up.

I had to send a report to Delphine every night on the day's business, but there was one thing I didn't mention by name. Mrs. Pingry, the cosmetics buyer, tells me she's made a special appointment for a very important customer. I must please shoot the works on this dame because she's readying herself to make a killing at the Assembly, and if we sell her the line and get her chattering about the Personalized Service then we're right inside the Holy City. Naturally most of our contented cows had been in the middle-age bracket; the kids are too sure of themselves to worry about crepy cheekbones, and I supposed this would be another Main Line veteran. Then Mrs Pingry happens to say if we take this customer into camp we have the whole Younger Set in the bag. Just to be polite, I ask "Who is this Blessed Damozel?" Of course it's Ronnie Gladwyn.

Waterproof mascara for her, is my first thought.

Of all the damnedest things. That certainly put me on a two-way stretch, going over Ronnie to brighten her up for what I couldn't have. Maybe I was a bit hard on her in my mind, but in a way she was a nice kid. Oh she's no ball of fire and I wouldn't be surprised she has trouble with her skin if she hunts the fox too much. She might get that wholesome tweed-skirt Wayne-Devon-and-Paoli look. You can't use your face as a windshield the way a horse can. She's got a nice natural wave to her hair but not much sparkle to it, that off-color between mud-blonde and brunette. The geranium lipstick she was using made her mouth look even bigger than it needed to. What she didn't know about make-up would fill Saks-Fifth Avenue. Her manners were so pleasant it would be hard to know was she really dumb or not; of course all those vintage Main Liners pride themselves to be just lovely with the lower classes as long as they don't go beyond their proper station, which would be probably Overbrook. I could have sold her anything, Jesusgod what a chance to load her up with the wrong tones and an overnight cream that would cockle up that puss like a nutmeg grater. Just once and a while, with my hands on her neck, I could have snatched out a tonsil or two. Matter of fact I gave her the best I knew how, and if she follows instruction those pores round her nose won't show up till it won't matter anyway. But it's not what I'd call a really good skin and I guess Bailey's Beach hasn't helped it.

She'd heard about the Olympia, like everybody, and of course she wanted some. She said she was going to wear a very swish job for the Assembly, gold net over white satin and insertions of green lace on the skirt. I wasn't so sure about that green lace; sounded to me like it would pick up the color of her eyes which had more than enough green in them already. Still and all that wasn't my department. Nobody in her senses offers too much advice about a woman's dress after she's already picked it out. I toned down her lipstick department, it was killing whatever she had in the way of eyes. A touch more orange would bring up the gold in them; I imagine they'd be really good by candlelight. But I wouldn't sell her any Olympia. I'm still kind of proud about that. She begged hard, the kid had a notion it was just what she needed, but I argued her out of it. In the first place it was certainly too subtle for a wallpaper effect like gold net and white satin, and it wouldn't have the authority she would need after the cloakroom Clover Clubs had worn off. But the important thing was, why should I want to hurt Wyn? The minute he got a whiff of Olympia he'd think of nothing but Kitty. I knew what it meant to him. It meant twilight high up in that hotel and bell chimes floating outside, and it meant the smell of my hair when we were dancing, and maybe just nibbling his tooth on the lobe of my ear while Giono was turned the other way behind the bar. He said it made him think with his nostrils, and I said that was as good thinking as he was likely to do, and he would whisper let's be carnal. Poor blessed baby, men like to think they're so amorous and if they knew the half of it, they're really so helpless.

I guess Ronnie wanted to be smart by quantity production, but it don't come that way. That's just shi-shi, things that would be smart if there weren't so many of them. To let her have the Olympia would be selling what's not for sale, memories of our own. I gave her the Killarney. It's got a delicate naive quality that a girl ought to need after going through the debutante market and it might be a novelty at the Bellevue. As Delphine says, it's discreet enough to wear in a cathedral. The girl was going to church, wasn't she?

I took a lot of trouble and she was grateful. She asked if she might have my name so she could come and consult me again. I said we weren't allowed to give our names.

I told Polly, the girl I was training, never to let Miss Gladwyn use the Olympia, it had just the wrong wavelength for her type. Polly made a note of it on the Customers' Histories file and said it's wonderful Miss Foyle, how do you get to know these things by intuition? I said it's a kind of instinct, you've got to develop it.

Of course it's no use to think you won't meet people in Philly. All the shopping that amounts to anything socially is along those few blocks on Chestnut and Walnut, and sure enough one day when I went out for lunch I ran into Wyn. There had to be comedy about it, he was standing by the curb scraping one of those beautiful brown shoes on the edge. He said "Kitty this is very embarrassing, I walked on some chewing gum, I can't imagine where."

"What were you doing on Market Street?" I asked, and he said "Kitty, you're adorable."

"Talking to me is good for you," I told him. "It's a pity we can't have about fifty years of it."

It was just before I was going back to N.Y. and I had my work pretty well under control. Of course I didn't tell him I'd met Ronnie, and I was glad I played so square in the cosmetic crisis because even while we were kidding I could see the black centers of his eyes get bigger and I knew we were going to have one more time to ourselves. I had built up so many things I couldn't tell him, it was good to be able to come clean about one thing, that was that I loved him. It's sweet to remember how the last time I saw him we were all by ourselves and no tallyho from the sidelines by Parry Berwyn. That night he took me up to the Rising Sun dance hall and got them to play our favorite tunes. "But we don't have to stay till the sun rises," he said. I was happy though that he didn't seem very certain where we could go after that. It's sweet to

297

remember and yet with Wyn and me everything always was so natural that the details vanish away. It's queer, when there's so many ways of loving a person you seem to lay so much stress on just one.

Last thing he ever said, "Goodbye darling, take care of yourself."

Take care of *your*self, Wyn, I can't do it any more.

30

Wyn used to say Is it all right to do so and so, like "Is it all right to think about Us just for a few minutes?" or "Is it all right for me to admire that little hollow back of your knees?" I loved him terribly when he said, "Is it all right." But it's no use telling yourself what you're not going to think about. You think about it that much more. Probably Delphine knew that. She could see how I was empty inside, like one of those crabs you find on the beach. She celebrated my 21st birthday by giving me a raise and sending me to do demonstration in Chicago.

I guess there weren't many people getting raises in January '32. That was about the time they said grass would be growing in the streets; it wasn't likely, too many people were pounding them looking for work. But there won't never be a slump in a business that makes people feel pleased about themselves. I notice how you'll take medical advice from the hairdresser quicker than from most doctors, because he knows a woman who looks attractive feels healthy right away. Nicolai says I can do with less salt on account of I've got some blood pressure.

That two years in Chicago was a Comedy Period. A

little comedy was good for me just then, though there was plenty of heartburn underneath, and I don't mean just what we got from the antipasto at Enrico's place. Like when we started calling the apartment the School for Brides, or when Molly pulled the gold lamé dress out of a cedar bag. She'd saved it all that time, the Assembly Dress. We covered some cushions with it, I wasn't going to let anyone else wear it.

Molly said of course I must live with her and Pat Kenzie in their new place at Tuscan Court, furnished studios off Michigan Avenue with a yard full of stone sculptuary and Enrico's spaghetti joint on the premises. It was a good chance for me to help them out, I was getting 28 a week and my push money extra, I felt badly to be paid so much more than those kids. All three of us were at Palmer's, me in the Beauty Salon and Molly in Decorating and Pat had been switched to Stockings. We had the alarm clock in common, but besides that was the team play a troupe of girls learn when they live together. We called Molly "The Madam" because she sort of took charge. She said she was never sure which one was the real Comedy Relief, Pat or me, but of course it was Pat. You don't get fed so many laughs unless there are men in the picture somewhere and Pat had a whole rodeo of them roped for beef. Looking after her was good training in what you might call strategy, though once and a while it would get tiresome sitting through a movie becaue Pat wanted to entertain a boy friend at the homestead. Naturally we developed the usual forms of female tact; if Pat had a special Date on hand, Molly and I would come into the living room wearing wrappers or hair curlers or cold cream, anything at all so as to look homely. If any one of us was out in the evening she had sense enough to phone before coming home, just in case. We took turns on cooking and marketing and the ironing board and in the bed department. We slept in rotation, two in the big Double Murphy and one on the davenport. Molly said that her boss Mr Krebs would realize the advantages of her Two-and-One Bedroom Suite idea if he'd come and spend a night with us. There wasn't much allure about that, but she sold the idea later to Modernage Interiors and they got it into the Chicago Fair, what we used to call the Century of Progress. The way things were around Palmer's in '32-'33 I guess Mr Krebs was content if he could sleep on the floor.

Pat might wake up with her morning announcement of Rabbits, Rabbits, but when she crawled in at night she was usually more practical. The last thing she muttered when she hit the hay sort of summed up what had happened, like when she said "Oh, I forgot to tell Jeff I'm not going to see him any more."

I couldn't see Molly wink at me because the light was out, but I could hear it in her voice. She says "Don't be silly, he's part of your training."

Pat says "I don't understand how a man that's so happily married can make such a pass."

Before they got that one solved I guess I was asleep.

I scarcely got moved in at Tuscan Court when we had the big blizzard. I was on the davenport so I wasn't near the windows, but on their side of the room snow had blown in 8 inches deep. First thing I saw when I woke was Molly running around in galoshes and bathrobe trying to mop things up, and Pat half asleep scooping snow in a big mixing-spoon forgetting we had a good shovel in the fireplace. We started out to try to get to the store but the wind was too strong. It knocked me flat as soon as I got out on the boulevard and blew Pat right into a drift. We struggled along a couple of blocks hanging onto the buildings and then gave it up. When we phoned the store I couldn't raise anyone in the Beauty Salon until after ten o'clock. There was one sales girl there then, she said she was behind the counter in her bare feet waiting for her shoes and stockings to dry. That was one day Complexion took a holiday. I hadn't ever seen Chi in a real blizzard so I went out again later in some ski-pants of Pat's, just for curiosity. They had ropes along the sidewalk for safety and I waded as far as the Tribune Tower and the bridge. When I got back Molly had phoned Enrico's for a bucket of hot spaghetti, and some of the neighbors brought in chianti and logs of wood for the fire and it was a good frolic. That was what put me in mind to buy us a load of wood, which the girls had been economizing without. Also a carton of cigarettes if Pat would learn to cut a hole in the pack with nail scissors, not just tear it wide open. Some of the best evenings that winter were when Molly and I would sit by the fire and get on with our knitting while Pat was most likely out dancing at the Ivanhoe, her favorite place to give swains a workout. I liked the Ivanhoe too on account of the Sir Walter Scott decorations which made me think of the Lady of the Lake, but Molly and I were in a homekeeping spell. It was good to be able to talk to somebody about Wyn, but I wouldn't tell even

Molly very far under the surface.

I caught myself the grippe that was prelavent then, and remembered Pop's remedy, hot whiskey and water with sugar and a lump of butter. He always said "What butter and whiskey won't cure, there's no cure for." Molly lived up to the high school motto about pain and anguish wring the brow, it didn't take her long to mix up the ingredients. She gave me a red hot tumbler and wrapped me in a blanket and brought me up to date on Manitou doings.

It was funny to think the class of '32 was still in college down at Prairie while so much had happened to us. Spring vacation quite a number of the kids came around to see if we had any ideas how would they land jobs. Peg Ramsauer reminded us we were bound by the old Gammagam oath to help if we could. Matter of fact the oath was cancelled if you had connived anything to lower moral tone, so I figured in private that my obligation was cured. But later Molly noticed an ad in the paper offering a job in a mail order jewelry house. Peg landed it but she only lasted a week. It was one of those jobs where you are stenographer and switchboard and receptionist all at the same desk, and probably have to teach the billing clerk to take No for an answer. Anybody might get rattled. Peg's first day she was doing several things at once, thinking she was switching a phone call onto another extension she pushed a button nobody had told her about, she just happened to notice it. She hears gongs going off and stairway doors bumping shut, then a sirene and pretty soon in come the cops. Everybody is scared stiff, and the whole building which is all full of jewelers is under guard while they search top

303

from bottom. Nobody knows where the robbery was or who stole what, and poor Peg didn't even connect the excitement with that button she pushed. It was the Jewelers' Protective burglary alarm. "Anyhow," Peg said, "it saved me 25 cents for my lunch. Nobody was allowed out of the building for an hour, and Mr Gorsuch had to phone for sandwiches."

Maybe sour grapes, but Molly and Pat and I figured that three white collar girls living together learn as much as college. One thing that happened at Palmer's was when Dean-of-Women Bascom came in to look over the Delphine Detaille line. Naturally she didn't recognize me, and I didn't let on too quick, it would have killed the sale. She was going to some conference of college deans—what a riot that must be—and fixing herself fit to be ravished. She inquired around about the Olympia, which was much too Charles-of-the-Ritz for her short wave broadcasting. We were being very cagy about it, never let it be named in advertising but kept on a word-of-mouth basis, word-of-nose rather. The idea we got over was, something too subtle to be mentioned to the gross public; we don't want to be embarrassed by the wrong kind of people asking for it. Then we would pretend to be upset when the glossy books like *Vogue* would mention it for Milady in the Know. I had to persuade Bascom that the Killarney was more spirituelle and wouldn't stampede a crowd of deans. What's furthermore she was worried that academic life dries out the skin and do I recommend the vegetable cream? That puts me in mind and after the sale is rung up I ask "Did they ever get those vegetables cleaned off

Selfridge Hall?" She was surprised and we had a good talk. She's really an old sweetheart. You never get to know how humane folks can be until you meet them away from their job. But how's about having a job that lets you be human at the same time?

Molly and Pat and me had so much fun together evenings, going over the day's roughage, we wouldn't even mind we couldn't afford to go out often. Sometimes we had dinner at that wopjoint in the yard, though it raised a terrible heartburn after a load of deep-sea antipasto and spiced meatballs. I have an argument gives Mark Eisen a bounce, that the way Italians behave in politics is really indigestion. A good dose of bicarb would let the wind out of Fascism. The Nazi business is more dangerous because it's a kind of cockeyed religion, you can't cure that with drugs. Mark likes the idea. Everybody does when they think it already.

Anyhow we found that the one who ate meatballs better sleep on the davenport. Then if she wakes about 2 a.m. with a prairie fire in her liver she can sit on the edge of the bed and smoke a cigarette without disturbing the others. Sleeping arrangements were Domestic Science 1 at the School for Brides. Pat held off getting engaged for quite a while, because her family certainly couldn't give her Eight of Everything, which makes a bride feel she's got at least one leg on reality. By the time she weakened we had hammered a lot of discipline into her, and cured her trick of lying diagonal across the bed which you certainly can't do all your life. That's Nazi, it's what the Germans want to do in Europe.

Mac sent me a clipping from the *Ledger* when Wyn got married that spring. I could of got along without knowing the exact date. I guess Ronnie got the Eight of Everything, and not plated either. It was kind of a comfort to think that she and Dean Bascom must smell pretty much the same. But I was thinking, after I saw those lovely kids in the station wagon, I wonder if a nice girl like Ronnie hasn't slowed up the Strafford family for quite a few generations; just because she's a nice well-bred girl and nothing else. Mark tells me something about the cross-pattern of the genes. It sounds eeny-meeny-miny-mo like counting stitches when you turn the heel of a sock. Still and all, if I was a Family I'd like to knit some genes into it that wants to get somewhere. Wyn's genes had a little hankering that way, they could have been taken places. Now I wouldn't be surprised the family will have to wait for Wynnewood Strafford XII. They'll get along in the meantime with pink coats and jodhpurs.

If you ever really loved somebody all the way through, I mean loved them the way everything seems part of everything else so there's nothing to be shocked or troubled about, then you understand everybody else a bit better. You know how people feel and how it hurts to be keeping a little dark emptiness inside. There was something so sweet about Pat. Nights when Molly and me were alone we'd clean up after her, straighten the bureau drawers and almost weep because there was something dear and childish in her odds and ends left every which way. There was her working bra on the chair looking flatter than usual, and white gloves fallen into the tub, and the glass necklace that broke crackling round the floor, and face powder over the handkerchiefs. All that was sort of physical symptoms of a state of glory, she probably had a date at the Ivanhoe and hellbent to get there. Molly's the opposite, orderly, likes to take time to think. Nicolai says he wouldn't be surprised she's short on thyroid. How I envied that girl the way she would sleep. She always counted up the hours she'd had; no matter how good she felt, if she figured she had less than eight hours sleep she began to think she was pooped. Those days there wasn't any benzedrine neither, to keep you in there fighting. Lots of career girls have got raises for their ambition that was really benzedrine sulphate.

That would have been a good time for benzedrine, business the way it was. Of course I never had to take the Depression so seriously because the DD line was moving fast. Matter of fact bad times made good sales talk. You've got to be more beautiful and subtle than ever to cheer up the anxious bullshooter when he comes home from a bear market. That's what Pearl Velour and I always told them and it mowed them down. "Beauty in its entirety" was a motto Palmer's used in cosmetic advertising, and there wasn't a corner table at the Drake or a conservatory on the Gold Coast where you wouldn't get a whiff of Olympia if you knew where to follow your nose. Chez Pierre and the Tavern Club and the Saddle and Cycle went in more for the Cinq-a-Sept. Chicago's always dizzy about anything French if you don't insist on their pronouncing it. Delphine was tickled pink and kept telling me not to work too hard. I mustn't get black rings because I had to look like Sheba's bath salts when I turned up at the Salon. Molly had a tougher time because people weren't buying much furniture. The North Side wisecrack those days was that Wine, Women and Song had turned into Beer, Momma and the Radio. Molly was smart enough to figure out novelties for home barrooms because she saw Prohibition coming to an end. There wouldn't be any fun drinking in speakeasies when they became legal. Pat was doing fine because people always have to have stockings, and she said legs could do as much as complexions to keep men cheered up. One time who should Pat wait on but Jess Cornish. Pat handed her the salestalk about the new airedale shade being very leg-flattering. Jess says: "Maybe it's better if I don't flatter them too much, they've got me into a plenty of trouble."

What was important, Molly and me got a day off to go down to Manitou to see the class graduate at college. They were a solemn looking crowd, it was a funeral compared to the high school show in '28. I was in a mixed mood, partly showing off because I was a Career Woman and a Skin You Love to Touch, partly I had an inferiority because I figured those kids had something I would never get. I wanted to hear the Baccalaureate which I thought would sum up the whole of the college education and I could make out where I'd been sold short. I guess the kids in the class had been too stupefied by Commencement hoopla to worry much, but Molly and I were all fresh from a long restful ride on the train and our minds were wide open. The college hired some State Governor to make the spiel, likely he was full of Agrarian Unrest or else had an eye on the elections coming. Anyhow he dragged Almighty God into it more than was cricket. The kids looked so young and clean and decent, and so like they didn't know what was going to happen, it was a shame to threaten them that way. Definitely I don't believe Almighty God even knows the exact date of Prairie College Commencement. Oh it was all true in a way but it just wasn't so, if I know what I mean. It sounded like it had been said before and was getting ready to be said again, probably at Wheaton or Rockford. Molly said that made it good Preparation for Life, but I don't think the Governor intended it that way. Anyhow two swell things happened; Fedor Vassilly graduated head of the class, summa cum lousy as the kids call it; and Dean Bascom looked very smart the way I'd taught her to do makeup. Some of the men profs looked so frightened in their colored gowns I'd like to give them a touch of rouge too. What is it makes a man with brains so milquetoast when he gets away from the blackboard?

Mark says, how's about that bunch of Columbia profs that took over the government for a while? They certainly rolled pretty high dice.

That's all right with me. Even their mistakes were interesting kind of mistakes. At least they kept the Union League clubs awake in the daytime.

What I would need in a graduation speech, where does it check with life the way I know I'm going to need to live it. Never mind about God Almighty sharpen the swords of these young crusaders. They're not young crusaders

309

most of them, and they're not going to have sharp swords but most likely broken flyswatters. I always wonder in a speech what was he thinking about that he didn't say. I guess it's a bad habit.

Uncle and Auntie had some of the old gang up to Thanksgiving Avenue for a porch supper. It was too bad not to see polite old Pattyshells, he always thumped his tail when people laughed. Uncle was in fine spirits because he had the lawn shaved down to the quick and all the hangnails pared off of it. Even when somebody, most likely Trudy Weissenkorn, spilled mayonnaise on his ice cream suit, he didn't get to burping. Lena's fried chicken never tasted so good, and we had the old gag about giving Fedor an extra leg because he was one shy. Even Bernie Janssen was there, I had to laugh how I used to imagine he was my Swedish Cavalier. He'd given up his idea of being General in command of the army and was working in the State Dairy School. He was full of some new idea that would spin the milk round in a churn until it was all homeopathic or homogeneous or something. That would make it the same all the way through and no Top of the Bottle. What for would they want to do away with the Top of the Bottle, I asked, it's the only part that's any fun. He hadn't thought of that. Good old Bernie, I bet by this time he's accumulated an awful lot of things he hasn't thought of. Socially there'll always be Top of the Bottle, and poor Bernie won't be among those present.

The one who will be is Fedor. I don't make cracks at college educating when I see what it did for him. It was grand to find one of the kids you could really talk to. He told me he'd made a switch in his studies, been doing premedical and was going to study doctoring in Chicago. Account of his aluminum leg he wouldn't be so good for regular practise but he had a chance to research in infant paralysis. He told me a lot of interesting dope about relative mortalities and what could be done by radio wave and massage and so on. He said one thing that came right in and hung up its hat in my mind. "Kitty, you've got wonderful hands for massage." I hadn't thought about it before, but I guess the demonstrating work had educated my hands quite a lot.

Of course Fedor wouldn't know why some of what he said was so special to me. He'd had a bad break as a kid which was what started him interested in children and so on. He's a Catholic and has some of their scruples about birth control, though honestly I can't see what that has to do with religion. But anyhow he was telling me about the Cardinal in Chicago who instead of bawling in the pulpit about contraceptions and abortions went ahead and got an inexpensive maternity hospital started. Of course you've got to be legally wedlocked before you can use their delivery room, that's a disadvantage, but the point is they sell you the whole doings for $50 and people that couldn't afford it otherwise can throw a baby there and like it.

That's what I call citizenship. Naturally I think a good deal sometimes about making up for the baby I didn't have. I told Fedor "I'd pretty nearly turn Pape myself to have a good fifty dollar baby. The trouble with wedlock is, there's not enough wed and too much lock." He thought

311

I was just razzing.

Molly and I talked it all over in the train going back to Chi. She has a habit, it's annoying sometimes, of turning a ham saying backwards to see if it makes better sense. Once and a while it does. I said something about bring a child into the world. Molly says there's something else just as important and that's to bring the world into a child.

When Fedor came to town later, he took me down to see the paralysis clinic, and that's how I started going there Sundays to help with the children.

Mac told me one time, in his hard luck spell, he couldn't afford to go to the dentist for a long while. There was one tooth he should have lost by rights, the nerve was almost exposed, but when he had it looked at the dentist said it had been saved by "secondary dentine." Some sort of ivory that grows up and takes care of the nerve. It was maybe like that with me thinking about Wyn. I mean the nerve was alive and close to the surface, but I guess I was so busy that secondary Me covered it over and kept it from hurting too much.

Even before I started work with the crippled children there was always plenty on hand. Summer's a grand time to scare women to death about their complexions, and the Middle West climate is a godsend for the cosmetic business. It was really wonderful the way Delphine and Pearl Velour would plant semi-confidential publicity dope on the Beauty Editors about what sun and wind and dust and soot was doing to the noble womanhood of Illinois, and they'd rush it into print just to torture themselves. The

Store backed it up strong with advertising until our customers would come in almost apologizing for still being in town at all. It was comical to see the dames hustle in worrying about windburn and sunsquint and brittle nails and what all. We loaded them down with oiled cotton nail-mitts for gardening and pedicure unguent so the chlorinated Chicago water wouldn't bleach their sturdy feet, and the Nepenthe depilatory that wipes away leg-fuzz. We even got the Store to spell glamorous with an extra u in advertising, saying Delphine had to have it that way. Then Molly and I would go out to the Dunes for a week-end. You take the Illinois Central rattler down through Tin Can Gardens, and past all the wop cabins each one with a goat, which we called Italian police dogs. All we'd take was castile soap and eau de cologne and a nail buffer and I'd tell her about the dames who couldn't have a vacation unless they were burdened with tweezers and masques and pastel nail enamel and a special can of portable mudpack. Otherwise, take it from Palmer's, their complexion would turn into horsehide.

That was the year I got the idea for the swish beauty kit shaped like a little hatbox, the kind the dress models always carry. I used to see them trotting into the photograph studio at Tuscan Court carrying their dunnage in hatboxes. If the box was marked Lily Daché or some other swank name they took good care you'd see it. If it was only a Chicago hatbox they pasted a New York label onto it. Molly, who was so smart with her fingers, worked up a sample box for me and Delphine was nuts about it. They were all over Park Avenue next season.

I guess I'm not the natural female, because when I see a shop window I don't think what can I buy out of it, but what can I put into it for someone else to buy.

When Pat Kenzie got married, Peg Ramsauer joined the School for Brides. She was working in a bank, but we weren't sure if she was a legitimate pupil for she was on the toboggan about an advanced young cashier who didn't believe in marriage. "I bet his parents didn't either," said Molly. She didn't like him because he had to keep tossing his head to throw the hair off his eyes. In private life he was a musician. But we could see poor Peg had to work this financial bohemian through her system and I guess we'd learned not to do other people's moralizing for them. Sheepdog, we called him, invited Peg down to the Dunes for a week-end, but some of the old Manitou inhibitions must have kicked up and she wanted Molly and I to go along as chaperones. She had a funny idea of chaperoning, because the cottage only had two bedrooms, Molly and I took one and I suppose Peg and Sheepdog used the other. Anyway Molly and I had a nice quiet week-end. The Dunes is the only place except Griscom Street where I ever had what you might call my own back yard to sit in, even if it's the side of a sand hill. It's funny to see that surf and then find it's fresh water. When it got to be meal times Sheepdog would sit down and play piano and Peg listen to him in a fever, so it turned out that most of our chaperoning was cooking the meals for them. Peg washed up because she said musicians have to be careful of their hands. Molly got sore after while and told Peg

314

"It's a pity he don't believe in marriage because you'd certainly make a good oldfashioned frau."

At night Molly and I laid out on the sand at the top of the hill and lost our tempers telling each other how beautiful the stars were. What was funny, Peg and the Sheepdog on one of their walks or whatever got into some poison ivy. It came out on them all over, more than if they just walked on it. When they both turned up at the bank spotted like identical twins it must have spilled the beans. Bankers had too much grief just then to be thinking about frolic, and Sheepdog lost his job. After that he didn't believe in banking either.

When liquor came back they put a revolving bar in the Pompeian Room down at the old Congress, like a little merrygoround. I always loved that place, partly because that perfume in the lobby had memories for me. Molly and I would go there sometimes and ride round and round slowly, just one Scotch taken in a circle gives you as much kick as three sitting solid in a corner. Maybe that's why they took the bar out later. It seems everything was like that those years, all of us riding round on a carrousel and the government grabbing for brass rings and blue eagles. Molly says we didn't know what was going on, we wouldn't know what to think about it if we did.

I wouldn't be surprised that's one way to keep happy. There was summer nights at Ravinia to hear music, and once and a while we'd take in a lecture at Northwestern. Peg went back to Manitou where she belonged, but there was usually a Bride on the waiting list. Fedor came up to see us, I could hear his artificial leg bumping on the stairs, and we'd drink beer and I'd wish Molly would fall for him. He got me interested in the hospital work and that cured my feeling cynical. Then Delphine sent me on the road, to check up our demonstrations all the way out to the Coast and back. That was Pearl Velour's work, but Pearl was going to be married. There seemed to be plenty of people who believed in it even if Sheepdog didn't.

31

I HADN'T HAD A REAL HOLIDAY FOR ABOUT TWO YEARS when Delphine made me take that trip to Bermuda. I didn't really know where the place was except that we named a skin lotion after it and the Main Line used to go there for Easter. This was August however so everything was pretty folksy, Bermuda had just been discovered as the stenographer's vacation. Delphine bought my ticket and saw me off, when she looked the crowd over she said "Keety, what you better drink this trip is Bronx cocktail." Delphine's always a bit snobbish, but if a woman isn't a snob of some kind she's probably short on a gland. Anyway she had me fixed up in a deck cabin and private bath and a chaise lounge reserved for me. I was feeling rotten, one of those heavy summer colds, and it was hot humid weather.

It wasn't Bronx cocktail, it was Planters Punch. That was new to me then like lots of other things. I didn't even know Bermuda was British, I supposed in a sort of way it was part of Florida. As a matter of fact if you scummed off the tourists it acted a good deal like the cricket club wing of Philadelphia. I recognized the tourist bunch all

317

right because I'd seen them stripped for action in the Cat-skills. The girls wore shorts up to the timber line and by the time they hit Hamilton they were as burned as grilled chickenskin. Not even our Caribbean Cream could take care of exposure like that. It was a shock to them when they landed, they found they had to get the shorts down to the knee or else really wear something. Bermuda didn't seem the least bit curious about the Upper West Side pelvis. They consoled themselves buying sun helmets.

Delphine knows all the ropes aboard shipping, she must have given the deck steward some big sweetening because while I was flopped out in my chair he came round to know what he could do for me. "I can hear all the lunch bells ringing," I said, "I guess I ought to go down and eat." The steward explained those weren't lunch gongs just the bellboys. I didn't know what they would be doing out in the water, unless warning people away from Staten Island, but I was too limp to argue. He said I could take my lunch right there in the chair. I said I would be more conscientious for my first sea voyage, I better go downstairs and eat a square meal, "feed a cold and starve a fever." Then the man in the next chair pipes up. I'd sort of half way noticed him because he was watching things as if he was amused. He was Jewish so I figured he'd probably been cruising before. "You misunderstand that," he says. "It means *if* you feed a cold you'll have to starve a fever later. Subsequently. With a cold like you got it I'm pre-scribing Planters Punch, maybe some jelly consommé and toast Melba."

The last thing I felt like it was starting conversations,

318

but the steward thinks that's a good idea and brings it to me on a tray. And Dr Marcus Eisen, that being who it was in person, didn't make any attempt to carry through. He went off downstairs and got his own lunch and when he came up again I was asleep. By evening I felt better and even got into the diner. I found him at the same table with me. I just supposed maybe the seating was arranged according as the chairs were on deck. Well of course when my wits got sorted out I realized he had fixed it with the maitre d'hotel.

It was fun to be talking to a man again, just socially. It's like a good highball after a long spell of soda fountain. He was smart enough to see I wasn't in a mood for any forward passes to be thrown at me. I guess he used me for his intellect stimulus and when he wanted chicken gumbo he'd go after some of the deck tennis gals in shorts. I figured I must be a pretty sour old spinster to accept the situation like that, but Gulf Stream air just makes you let things slide. It was hot as my old bedroom under the roof in Frankford, and everything was new to me, the funny smell of a ship and that sort of anxiety in your stomach and such blue water with big yellow sponges floating. I guess the sail was only two days but it certainly seems like longer.

Of course Wyn got me so conditioned about men's clothes that I hate to see them overdressed. Mark's striped pants, creased like a knife-edge, would blackball him at any cricket club, and those black and white yachting shoes with perforated breathing holes were definitely Hollywood. What put Big Casino on the outfit was a polo shirt wide open to the fur and a blue tweed coat with a hand-kerchief made of the same stuff as the shirt. That's pretty terrible, because a man ought to look like he's put together by accident, not added up on purpose. Poor old Mark, you could just see he'd been spending his Saturday afternoons figuring out this cruising kit. It looked like all that bear-skin robe on his chest was sapping the energy from his scalp, which was getting a bit scarce already. Then you'd notice his hands and forget about the other foolishness. Massage and chiropractic I studied out in Chicago made me observant about hands. When I learned he was work-ing in the Children's Hospital we had lots to talk about. He was curious what kind of line was I in and I wouldn't tell him. After a couple of Planters Punches some of his stories were a bit corny, but I'm not too easily frightened that way and a few of Parry Berwyn's old Racquet Club favorites were even-Steven with his. There was a good many ways Mark would look like the answer to a maiden's prayer, if you were that kind of a maiden. What inter-ested me was how he knew his stuff about kids. On the voyage back, two weeks later, he was on the same ship again, it was end of August and we ran into one of those hurricanes. A little boy fell downstairs and broke his collarbone and Mark and I happened to be standing right there. The ship's doctor was busy with trouble, and Mark had the child bandaged up and comfortable before you'd know it. That made a big hit with me.

We were staying different places when we got to Ber-muda, and I was having fun with another crowd so I didn't see much of him. I ran into him one day over at Elbow

Beach, tanned as brown as coffee, with a bunch of the G-string girls. He took me dancing on the hotel terrace one night, he's a good dancer too though he was crowding a bit more than is comfortable in Bermuda August. There's a terrace right alongside the water and the colored boatmen drift their little sailing boats up to the edge like butterflies in the moonlight. We went for a sail in the harbor, but I had to explain to him that I starved one fever successfully and I had no intention to start up another. He was so good humored about it I was a bit piqued. Of course Mark, successful and bright the way he is, can always get as many of his own kind as he'd care to whistle at. I was someone outside his routine and I had him puzzled. They certainly do like to know all about everything, and he'd lead up questions to try to get me placed. The most I would tell him was I came from Philly, and he'd say Well, it's only two hours away. I think he believed I was some kind of a trained nurse that hadn't had the advantages of a New York or John Hopkins training. If he'd known I was getting ready to move into my own apartment on Riverside he'd have had the number out of me after two Aquarium cocktails. I had to smile when he told me how he'd moved his Mother down to West End Avenue, which is their idea of Seventh Heaven. I liked the way he talked about her. That Jewish feeling about old people is all to the good. They're wonderful to children and old folks, they can be pretty tough with everybody in between.

He told me a lot about infantile paralysis, how it usually moves from South to North and comes in a kind of annual epidemic, mostly late summer and early autumn. Matter of fact he said he was taking this vacation to get good and tough for an extra number of cases when he got back. That was why he always stopped after the third snort, and I liked that in him. With a crowd he could get to be a pain in the neck, he was so damn full of high spirits, but get him by himself talking about the children and you forget that alligator belt with his initials M.E. on a gold buckle. He had an inferiority hidden away inside him that must have took a hundred generations to build up, but there wasn't any inferiority when he picked up a microscope or a sick kid. We took a picnic to one of those islands where there's an old prison and the cockroaches spring at you as big as mice. Mark was so excited about them he couldn't believe it, he caught one in an olive bottle and took it back to his hotel and dissected it up with a razor blade to see what it was all about.

I knew in a way that I was going to see him again because he could teach me a lot, but I thought it was good for his soul to stall a while and I wouldn't give him any address. What's furthermore I thought likely I'd run into him somewhere along the kosher belt on upper Broadway. He gave me his card. "Any time you get paralyzed," he said, "call me up."

What I liked, he had something to work for that was worth it. I think of that when I go down to visit Mac and Martha and see little Kitty sprawled out asleep in bed. What's wonderful is to have something besides yourself. Maybe these white collar girls, business sharecroppers Molly calls us, who've been through it and learned what to do without, wouldn't make such bad wives after all. Learning to do without things is the only weapon we got.

It was a long time till I saw Mark again. To be honest I guess I forgot his existence except for a snapshot someone took on that boat, his shoes showed up strong. I had plenty to think about. After Pearl Velour left, and Delphine not in such good health, I found myself practically running the office. It began to look as though anyone in the cosmetic business had no private life at all. With the Government thinking up new kinds of regulation all the while, and distribution costs shooting uphill, it was a good idea to have your nails enamelled so you wouldn't bite them in your sleep. Delphine said "Keety, by what it appears, the Government does not wish its ladies to be beautiful. What do the wives of the Treasury Department look like? Are they all homely? You better call Soap and Glycerine Producers, see if they make progress on that excise tax repeal." As a matter of fact all that federal regulation was maybe a good thing, it will help to crack down on some of the competitors that don't pay what we do for pure chemistry and use all sorts of synthetic allergies. What hurts Delphine is when they want us to label quantities in fractions of pints instead of ounces or drams.

She says *pints* is a word that's got no glamour, it suggests only milk or hootch or house paint. To anyone that was brought up with Pop, drams suggests hootch too, but on our billing we always spelled it *drachms*.

Mr Detaille didn't have so much time for swinging Indian clubs, he was busy reckoning figures. It was certainly a wallop when he worked it out that our distribution costs were 72% of factory value and nearly 50% of retail value. Cost of production was about 66% of factory value, not even reckoning Mr Detaille's breakage with clubswinging. There's not much margin there. Delphine went to Washington once and a while to talk things over with some official at the Treasury, she always wore the Olympia for those visits, but that man must have had hay fever, it didn't seem to do any good. She came back very depressed. "Keety, I have it straight from the mouth of the horse. If there is a new Food and Drugs Act we will be under the control of the department of Agriculture. Believe that! We better apply for Farm Relief, it's all the government worries about."

I didn't take much time for lunch, and sometimes to get away from perfumery I'd stop in at a quick eats on Sixth Avenue and read the paper while I had a sandwich. Everybody there looked so hard-run it cheered me up. I didn't figure out at first what made the place look queer, then I noticed it was because all the men ate with their hats on. The chewing made their hats ride up and down, you would almost feel seasick if you watched it too long. One day I see a brown plush fedora that demands attention and sure enough it's Mark Eisen. He was so pleased and respectful, and I was feeling solitary, I couldn't very well avoid him walking back as far as the office with me. It seemed to give him a great kick when he learned what line I was in. "And I thought all the time you were taking people's temperatures in Philadelphia." After that my phone bell began to ring on Riverside. Reminds me of the call I got from his nice old mother. She rang up, said Mark talked so much of me and wouldn't I come to their apartment Saturday afternoon, they were going to have bar mitzvah for Mark's kid brother. I said sure; I supposed that was something to eat. Then I found it was a confirmation ceremony and made me practically a member of the family. They'd been at the synagogue all morning making a man out of Hillel because he was thirteen or something. We had schnapps and sponge cake and I guess what the kid had been through brought out the family excitement, anyway he got sort of fresh before long and wanted to keep on making a speech about his Maturity and Mark got peeved.

They certainly take their religion seriously, I like that, though Mark gets comical about it once and a while, he has a line he pulls when he's had a good snort. "Wherefore on this night rather than all other nights do we lean back in our chairs and relax." It's a quotation from Passover.

It seems funny I pick up so many little bits of other people's religions and don't get hold of one of my own.

When I go over to Amsterdam to do my marketing there's a little tobacco and newsdealer, they've got a youngster about three years old, a cunning boy in a sunsuit plays out on the pavement. He's got that lovely golden skin and United Cigarstore eyes, the Jewish hasn't come out on his features yet but you can see it there ready for when it'll be needed. It's fun to think about things without taking sides and I always say to myself That kid's my

325

candidate for the year 2000. If he keeps away from Hitler, that is. But it starts me thinking. I won't never see the year 2000; I'd be 89, which is too much of a strain on imagination; but that kid will most likely, and there's lots of them being born right along who'll write January 1, 2000 on an Account Rendered. That date will be a Saturday too, I noticed on one of those Perpetual Calendars. Trust a white collar girl to make note of that. It'll be a week-end I'd like to take part in.

So it gives me a bounce when I see that kid, little Manny Silberman. He has brown curly toes and fists and sort of copper lights in the fuzz on the back of his neck. I like to know if he gets a good nap and a trip to Rockaway once and a while, I gave Mrs Silberman a clipping about what beaches are substandard on bacteria. He's my secret candidate for the Future. That's a thing a woman thinks about. My baby could have been going strong in 2000; at least he wouldn't be 70 yet, and with all those wonderful genes—Jesusgod every woman has a right to have some candidates for the Future. With all the physiology nuisance she goes through she's bound to guess what she's here for. She gets tired being told Birth Control is the solution for everything. She's got a right to a baby if she needs one, same as a man's got a right to pay income tax.

Of course you've got to be careful how you talk about these things to men, they're easily shocked. Everybody thinks it's fine for her or him to know facts but he better protect someone else from knowing them.

Mark, being as he's Jewish intellectual, takes things different from me. He's crazy about books, even got me started reading after some of his favorites but I watch myself not to get carried away. I can find out about things without having it in print. Poetry though, that's something else again. There's something there if I had time to figure out the language. It says things the way you feel them. If I could have maybe a week at Pocono, sunshine and swimming and a blanket in front of the fire and Wyn to read some to me I'd know what it was about even if he didn't, poor darling. I could even tell him some of it. He was so adorably simple, like when he thought girdles always had to be pink.

It's no use asking Mark to read to you, he's too eager to get to the end.

Is it all right to be thinking these things to myself, maybe the last time? There's a moon over the river as big and shiny as a gold watch. It's so beautiful maybe it would teach me to quit thinking about Me. Does everybody torment themselves that way? I guess you never get happy except by thinking more about other people. I think I was nearest what's true for me when Wyn and I were loving each other, but naturally that sort of thing is too sweet to last. It's not a regular part of life but just something that lights onto it once and a while. Where danced the moon on Monan's rill. Maybe there's some way I can get closer to what's true for everybody.

It's kind of exciting to be learning things the way you know every other person in the world always had to.

Nobody knows what she really believes. You've got to guess at it by how you find yourself acting.

32

I GOT A NEW SLANT ON MARK THE WARM AFTERNOON HE
and I took a walk up Riverside. I invited him up to the
apartment for a drink, and of course I offered him to go
in the bathroom to wash while I was breaking out ice
cubes. I went in there myself afterward to prink up a little
and I saw he hadn't used the embroidered guest towels I
put out. Naturally I wouldn't mention it, but after we had
a highball he said, "I guess I made a faux pas, I meant to
rumple up one of those guest towels, just for good manners."

"It was a kindly thought," I said, "but what's the idea?"

"I couldn't help taking one you'd used yourself, it
smelled so sweet of *you*."

It was rather dear, the way he said it. I was almost embarrassed. Kind of ashamed too because somehow I didn't
like the idea of those big blue cheeks in my face towel.
Some skins are just different, and what are you going to do
about it? Delphine says, c'est une question de peau. She's
got me so I can almost talk French when there aren't any
French people listening.

It made me think though, I guess it really is good for a

328

woman to be loved, or anyway admired, even if only for smell. It started a little spark shining down inside me, somewhere that hadn't had a glimmer in ever so long. Poor Mark, he admires me in such a mixed-up way, partly because I'm so Aryan he calls it and it would give him a kick to fascinate a Gentile, and partly because he's proud of me being in the Beauty Business.

But can you marry a man just because you're so interested in the work he's doing? I guess that's the something more than Four Legs in a Bed old Pop talked about. But maybe you'd marry because you do enjoy using the same towel. I didn't know which one it was Mark might be talking about so I dropped them all in the wash.

He's so proud of me having a glamor job he'd most likely be tickled to have me keep on with it. A while, anyway. I'm proud of it too, I hammered it right out of a hall bedroom and a School for Brides. And sometimes I wouldn't care if all the complexion on Park Avenue turned into leather. The skin I like to see keep fresh and get color onto it is the kids down at the hospital. Sure, I know I'm obligated to Delphine and she's moved me along wonderfully. With bonuses I make $3000 a year and she wants to let me buy stock in the company. But I reckon I've given her full value too. Nine years of it, nine whole Quaker calendars.

Naturally I know why Mark's crack about the towels bothered me. It was Pocono, Wyn wouldn't dry himself till he could use the one I wiped with. He said it made him feel closer. I wonder if he still has the scar on his shoulder where I bit him.

So much of yourself is locked up inside and you can't get it out when you want it. Molly was East lately, she comes to N.Y. every once and a while to get advance dope on furniture trends. That was the first chance I had to show her the new apartment, I looked forward so to taking her round the neighborhood and explain everything that makes me feel like home. You work yourself into a place until you have your own special picture of it, and I thought how swell it would be to have her know about things. Like the chain store where the harelip Scotchman takes my marketing order, you have to go there yourself because over the phone you can't tell is he saying broccoli or chocolate. And the French Home Laundry that calls for wash, the drug store on Broadway where I get hot coffee after I'm frostbitten in a movie, and my nominee for A.D. 2000 though Mark says Manny won't know what A.D. means. There's this view from my window, the new parkway on Riverside and Hudson River sunset and people on open bus-tops the way they sit so straight outlined on the evening light. I wanted Molly to get a load of all that, she could take it back to Michigan Avenue with her the way I still see the Wrigley Building white like wedding cake at night and smell the Congress Hotel. I guess I was tired after the office, or both of us were tired, I could feel I wasn't getting anything across. Likely it's no use trying. So often one or the other is tired, or worried about something, or checking off how much time have we, the worst feeling in the world.

Then we came up to the apartment and flopped ourselves down and perked some coffee, and when we quit trying to say things they began to come. Molly said how nice to see the old snowstorm again, the glass ball with the child on a sled.

"Little Girl on a Sleighride," I said. "She's had some bad spills, but still coasting."

Molly twirled it so the snow flew round inside. "Looks just the same, doesn't she. *Things* don't play fair."

"How do you mean?"

"They don't change, the way we do. What a memory they have, keep pulling you back. That's why I like the modern interiors, all bare and stripped and no sentimental bric-a-brac. They're not always reminding you of bygones."

"Maybe I like to be reminded."

I honestly do, if it isn't too soon afterward. I took Molly to lunch in that outdoor place on Rockefeller Plaza, the fountain makes a splash just like a waterfall, that and the birch trees in tubs made me think of Pocono, but it didn't hurt. Molly was the one who complained, the sound of running water always makes her uneasy. In the School for Brides you couldn't even take a shower without her needing to get in the bathroom. Molly is almost as good as Wyn for funny things happening to you. We were getting in the subway to go out to the World's Fair and a whole crowd of boys in soldier cadet uniform came in, each one had a doughboy cap that said on it *Harrisburg Patriot*. A man in the car shouted out "What is it, a conquest?" I knew, having been to Harrisburg, the *Patriot* is a newspaper. It was probably all their subscribers, the paper was taking a day off.

I told Molly how Harrisburg was the first place Wyn and I ever went together. It's kind of sad when things don't hurt any more. I certainly hang onto old Molly, because while there's things I don't tell her I can tell her enough. She gets the idea.—She speaks of Fedor once and a while, how he's proceeding on his short-wave radio treatments. It would be funny if we both married a doctor. Mark says I should because the snake on my ring is the symbol of medicine but I told him if so it's only a coincidence. Of course he's curious about it, the way he is about everything. As a matter of fact Wyn told me a snake eating its own tail is a sign of eternity.

Oh my sweet was I unworthy of you? Maybe I should have told you, waited for you that day at Snorty West Forty. Should I have kept you and taken you away from the Paper Dolls? How does a person learn to be worthy of love, big and patient enough for it? She gets too full of nerves. We could have learned, worked it out together. But I guess you're doing what you were meant to. Wyn, are you all right?

I wanted you to have beauty, not just be comfortable and amused and such a charming host.

Don't be hard on the Paper Dolls. Wyn, my poor dear, have you forgotten about everything else? I hope so. It's a good kind of life, it's clean and healthy and solid too. Even come the Revolution it'll take some licking. There'll always be a Main Line everywhere, like our little snake it's a sign of Eternity. I bet Eternity is just not to be thinking.

I was telling Molly about the goofy dream I had, I suppose account of reading so much in the papers about press conferences at the White House. Or maybe it was tied up with my having to make a speech at that convention of Cosmetologists, and also all the talks Molly and I had about the idea of a W.C.T.U. as we call it, a White Collar Trade Union. I dreamed I was at a meeting of newspaper correspondents at the White House, but not being a regular there wasn't really room for me, the place was crowded and I found myself sitting on the floor under a piano but right close to President Roosevelt himself. I was proud of him on account of what he's done for paralysis, and look where he is in spite of his handicaps, having to go to schools like Groton and Harvard. In the middle of all the dialogue he interrupts himself and bends over to look under the piano and says "Kitty, are you all right down there?" Naturally that raised a laugh among all the newspaper boys, they laugh pretty easy. It isn't everybody among the big shots will take trouble to dust under the furniture and find out if people are all right down there. So that horse laugh by the boys, which is all the I.Q. they are, most of them, made me sore. I was wearing my new lip rouge, Delphine's Azalea that makes me feel like a million dollars, and I didn't have any hesitation to crawl out from under the piano and start making a speech telling them where to head in. I forgot about the President of the United States and everything else, I just figured this was my everlasting chance to tell some of them how the White Collar Girl feels about things and what a bloody mess and etcetra. I was definitely on top of the world,

333

things came into my mind the way I like them, so they sound comical and at the same time they're true and they sting. The big grand piano right behind me acted like an amplifier, I could hear my voice tingle an echo among the strings and I thought Jesusgod I'm knocking them cold, they'll never forget this, and then the way it always does in a dream some kind of frustration has to work into it. It's so terribly urgent what you want to do and at the same time something gripes you so you can't accomplish. A regular palzy came in my speech and my voice got muzzy so the one thing I wanted to say, which was White Collar Girl, I couldn't pronounce it. I struggled and couldn't get my tongue onto it, I sounded to myself like I was drunk and the newspaper boys started razzing me. I woke up in a horror. I think I was crying.

You see, I told Molly, I really did want to say something for them, the W.C.G's that is, your poor damn sharecroppers in the Dust Bowl of business. I see them in subways and on busses, putting up a good fight in their pretty clothes and keeping their heebyjeebies to themselves. There's something so courageous about it, it hurts me inside.

Yes, Molly says, a Pooh-bear on the bedspread isn't enough. If they try to escape by marrying a good provider maybe he's got no brains or he don't talk her language. If they marry a man who's smart he may be more interested in his work than he is in her. How are you going to find a man that's both dumb enough and sweet enough?

It's asking too much, I said.

"I've got an idea," Molly says.

334

"Dibbies on it first."

"There's lots of things worse than being lonely."

"We work like sharecroppers to keep body and soul together, and is that all the answer we get to?"

"Maybe it's a mistake keeping them so close together," is Molly's suggestion. "They're different and they need different kind of things. Maybe we could keep body and soul a little bit separate."

The session pretty nearly broke up then because I thought for a moment we'd have to get dressed and go out for some cigarettes, but I found a spare pack I had hid away for emergency. A man can always fall back on his pipe if the cigarettes run short, but what can a woman fall back on?

We'll skip that one, Molly says.

"At least," I suggest, "you couldn't feel such expert loneliness unless there had been a time when you weren't. Let's skip that too. I'm talking the way I do when I'm all by myself. Most likely it doesn't make sense. That's the best of being lonely, things don't have to."

"If I ever marry," Molly says, "I think it better be some good stupid bozo, so stupid he'd always be kind to me. Fedor's not stupid, that's the only trouble with him."

"Well, that's what's wrong with *my* gentleman friend."

"The clever guys can't take it."

"It's because they know what they're being made to take."

"It's interesting about Fedor, you know what I used to be morbid about, I mean the aluminum leg, I really rather

335

love him for it now. He's so damn plucky and doesn't ask any favors on account of it."

I didn't quite like to put it in words, but that made me wonder, maybe Mark's being so racial is like Fedor's leg, something that just happened and you've got to put up with. But how much of Me could I really give him? That feeling I had about the face towel frightened me.

I was so pleased by what Molly said about Fedor I wouldn't make much of it for fear of scaring her. I'd like to have told her what he said about her cowlick long ago. As for him being short a leg, hers are lovely enough to do for both.

It was a good Milkman's Matinee, and ended like they should with scrambled eggs and toast and marmalade. Though Molly wouldn't take any of the marmalade, she says those Seville oranges come from Fascist Spain and the only kind of bitter oranges that are politically honorable are the Jewish ones from Palestine. Of course that takes me right back to my own problem, but damn it I don't bring my politics or my religion either onto the supper table. So we turn in with a big noggin of milk.

"Let's drink a nightcap to the Milkman's Wife," Molly says.

"I wonder what she does while he's out on his rounds," I ask.

"Here's luck to her. Maybe all her problems aren't solved either."

"Tomorrow's Sunday. We can stay home and read the ads."

"Did you notice that little pillbox trick of Suzy's?"

336

"I didn't mean that kind of advertising. I meant the marriage publicity, a wedding has been arranged and will shortly take place. Mr and Mrs F. X. Turfman of West Burial, L.I."

"I never thought of it that way," says Molly. "Of course every one of those social announcements is really an advertisement for the Status Quo. Well, why not? They got a right to push their goods."

When Molly visits naturally I give her my bed and I shake down on the living room couch. But we have the door open between because you can't tell what you may want to say before you drop off.

"I guess I'm as much of a snob my own way as any of 'em, God help me." I call that out to Molly. A while she doesn't answer, her voice is pretty drowsy.

"You're Mehitabel the cat," she says. "Remember? It's being abducted so many times has spoiled you for a wife."

"Molly, you're bitchy."

It's good to have a person call your attention to something you're so used to you almost forgot thinking about it. I mean the glass snowstorm-ball. Molly's back in Chicago and I take the glass ball and give it a whirl. In spite of all the baby blizzards that's been round her, Little Girl on a Sleighride settles down clear and quiet. It's kind of intelligible to start up a storm and say to myself while it blows white I just won't think, I'll wait till it clears and then see what I find myself thinking.

What a swell time it's been for being alive. Jesusgod, Molly, all of us kids has lived through a whole revolution already and even if it's been tough at least we knew something was happening. Some people didn't even guess, they don't tumble to it yet. I bet I was wrong when I told myself it had been ugly. Well sure, I bet history always was tempermental when it was happening. But they lived through it, didn't they? Some of them always did. So will we, some of us, even if they tear the world in pieces. If the whole dollar system goes buttsprung we can still barter, or we'll dig and spin and raise vegetables. Matter of fact the Main Line could be good at that. I bet a horse that could ride to hounds could ride to potatoes, or however potatoes are made. I wouldn't be surprised I'm getting a little sense, Molly's right, I'm phonier than *they* ever were, my damn Cinq-a-Sept and stuff. I bet all that smell of horse was their way of reaching for what's real. Now I'm grown up I'd like to talk to Rosey Rittenhouse.

Everybody has his own way of reaching for it, it's a big error to think you're the only one that's doing the thinking. I bet everybody has that same feeling, Now I'm alive, how grand it is and it's passing every moment.

You don't mind thinking these things to yourself. Nobody is ashamed when she's alone. How would you get in the world more of the kind of people that you can feel alone with? I wonder if I could teach Mark not to tell me more than I can listen to.

Mark says I'm so cautious. Wary, I guess was the word he used. Me! It's not the way I want to be. Which day's child is it that's Loving and Giving. What I mean, a woman loves most where she gives most. She loves you for

338

letting her give. A person wants to give everything. It would be awful if Mark acted grateful, sort of "I certainly do appreciate this."

I wouldn't want anybody to feel there was a kind of Social Significance in my loving them, or be too earnest about it.

I can't go on giving him the runaround. It's not right.

I always wanted so for things to be beautiful. One person by herself, there's so little you can do, except for the kids.

Mark said he'd call me today, he wants to hear what I think about his article on Socialized Medicine. He knows damn well, what some of them don't yet, doctors and everything else that's important will get to be socialized sooner or later. But that's only an excuse for phoning. What he really wants to know is something else, something that can't be socialized, something that's just K. Foyle herself and the way she feels about it.

I had a terrible idea, it would be good if a person would grow old a bit faster? It seems a long time to wait for that Change of Life I hear about. That's no way for a woman to feel. That shows what it does to you, being by yourself. Listen, snowstorm, you can't do that to me.

I might go over and visit with Delphine, she and Mr Detaille are always home Sundays. There's that memo to the Toilet Goods Association to check over. Besides it's always fun to watch Pfui try to dig his nails into the slippery floor.

Mark said he'd call, but if I got out before the bell rings? He's always hurt if I don't say darling. He says "You don't greet me darling? Is it an argument?"

They must have possibilities or they couldn't be so sensitive.

Well I can say darling without committing myself to nothing. Darling is only politeness nowadays. Dearest is what I couldn't say unless by accident?

I bet that's him now. Jesusgod, what will I tell him.

Hello darling.

DA

HIGHSMITH 45-220